THE
STARS
AND THE
BLACKNESS
BETWEEN
THEM

THE
STARS
AND THE
BLACKNESS
BETWEEN
THEM

Junauda Petrus

DUTTON BOOKS

DUTTON BOOKS

An imprint of Penguin Random House LLC, New York

Visit us online at penguinrandomhouse.com

Library of Congress Cataloging-in-Publication Data
Names: Petrus, Junauda, author.
Title: The stars and the blackness between them / by Junauda Petrus.
Description: New York : Dutton Books for Young Readers, 2019. | Summary: Told
in two voices, sixteen-year-old Audre and Mabel, both young women of color
from different backgrounds, fall in love and figure out how to care for
each other as one of them faces a fatal illness.
Identifiers: LCCN 2019003294 (print) | LCCN 2019006934 (ebook) | ISBN
9780525555506 (ebook) | ISBN 9780525555483 (hardback)
Subjects: | CYAC: African Americans—Fiction. | Blacks—Trinidad—Fiction. |
Trinidad—Fiction. | Lesbians—Fiction.
Classification: LCC PZ7.1.P474 (ebook) | LCC PZ7.1.P474 St 2019 (print) | DDC
[E]—dc23
LC record available at https://lccn.loc.gov/2019003294

Printed in the United States of America
ISBN 9780525555483

1   3   5   7   9   10   8   6   4   2

Design by Anna Booth
Text set in Dante MT Std

*I dedicate this book to the constellation of queer ancestors
who have loved and healed through space and eternity, regardless.
And to Pearl and Kelvin. I love you sweet dreamers so much.*

*And to Ngopti for being the mountain to my hurricane.
You really love me for my wild, sweet self, and your love is king!*

*And lastly, to Mom for pinning the balloons on my tight winter coat
when I was seven, when I needed to fly to space. I will always love you
for your sweetness and your limitless belief in my magic.*

THE
STARS
AND THE
BLACKNESS
BETWEEN
THEM

PROLOGUE

We outsmarted oblivion seven times in a row
and made it look like jazz with no chains,
like shaking our butt with no shame.
We moonwalked past the ghosts of this living world.
We decided.
To free ourselves out of the estranged,
strangling of this reality.
We swan-dived and centered in our magic.
We found an eternal life that couldn't understand
        prisons or any other enslavement.
We was not at the frequency that could catch or contort
        our souls.
It wasn't easy, but destiny is destiny.
Our bodies
levitated by the stardust of the ancestors in our bones.
Our ecstasy
got divined in limitless existence.
This is how we figured it out.

*—Heard on an echo of a breeze, in a playground somewhere
in the future, where kids is feeling free and they are double-
dutching, singing, gardening, and twerking in the radiance of
their ancestors' laughter.*

CANCER SEASON

season of Yemeya
our bottomless dark
deep wet healer
warrior of our waters
and conductor of our tides

the moon shines on you
you are floating on her waters
she is pleasure immersive and she soaks you to heal
and rocks you to sleep

she is the constellation
of the armored warrior
of water and sand
she protects softness
she a shelled thing that scamper away
and hide and protect

protecting the pearl of sacred sensuality
a mango seed, an intuitive lover
the heavy and healing waters
of your motherlands
and eternal shades of the moon

AUDRE

"YUH FAS' AND ARROW AND SENSUAL AND MANGO," Queenie tells me, "so, Audre, please put some molasses in yuh feet for dis walk, it ain't supposed to go fas'," she says, as we walk through the woods. I is crying so hard, my body is shudder and breath and wet with tears. My glasses fog up and I wipe them with my shirt so I can see through them and see the back of my grandma, my guide. My heart feeling like it get bus' up for calling somebody mother a jagabat.

Queenie is pure light and sweetness and obsidian skin. She smell like spicy earth things, like sandalwood and cinnamon and dirt itself. She is strong and warrior, moving through the trees like a river, carving her way through mud, elegant, dark and slow like the molasses she say we should invoke for this journey. She have on a long white dress, with a white scarf wrap around she short white hair and shoulders like a woman in prayer. The woods are a green and quiet bush between her house and ocean that I know very well. Too well. I have cover every part of them bush, with the bottom of my feet and the eyes of my soul since I young.

Queenie got silver bangles 'round she wrist like broken Saturn rings, jingling each of her movements through the forest. She moves with her walking stick made of bamboo and mahogany and wrapped tight in thin copper, rose quartz, and citrine, so it could be strong and light and absorb power. She takes the lead on our journey and let me cry in her wake.

Queenie stops quick and backs me up with her forearm. She looks up and reads the air. She smiles. She points and I see leaves whisper at us, shimmying with breeze and speaking Spirit. She looks at me to see if I am reading the signs. I barely able to lift my head, so soaked am I in my own river and ocean, my eyes cloudy. And to be real, I ain't want to see the full story yet.

I'm already feeling a change. I've been soaked in the feeling of Spirit's song since we started walking into the bush and up through the hills by Queenie's house. When Spirit speak to Queenie, she says she sees it first, and it feel like life become a dream and has a whisper of iridescence, "like the world get soft before I get revelation." For me, it is different. The only way I can say it feels is like a tingle, a feeling, from the earth through water, and I is surrounded in a power that's bigger than me. Queenie can shape her magic like she feels, but I feel like mine shapes me, controls me. I can sometimes feel what anyone else feel, but I never know when or why I have to feel it.

I look at her, and my body still trembles. She pulls me up in her arm, while she holds us steady. She ain't afraid of my bawling, and she kisses me on both my cheeks and forehead, blessing me with my own tears and her Queenie love. She turns forward and keeps walking. My sob follows us and is whisper, then wail. We move into the curve of the hill like we're walking into heaven, then the path bends down and we are walking easier and I is feeling it, the pull of Our Water Mother, in my skin. I keep crying, following Queenie to the sea.

Queenie swing an orange blanket onto the ground. She grab dried cocos, big rocks, and shells to secure the blanket into the sand. I is numb and just looking at the ocean and feeling like I is going to fall over. Queenie sit me down and pull out her machete and start busting fresh cocos she bring.

"Drink dis, nuh. I sure you did dry yourself out, with all of that crying and grieving of love, my dahlin'," she say, handing me a coco. "Your first tabanca is a heartbreak that feel like a bit of death, yes. It hurt me to see you going through all of this hurt for love and your mother is totally out of place—" She stop talking before she finish that thought and she look like she is hurting too.

"I know how it does feel, yes." She sucks she teeth, and I find it hard to believe Queenie ever was hurt for love like I is now.

We is on sand between edge of water and forest, and she asks for me to pull out my pouch. I hesitate, hoping that I can deny what I already feeling is true by not doing a reading. Still, I pull up my skirt and untie the pouch from my thick and dark-brown thigh. This is where I hide it from my mother and the world when I is traveling. Queenie asks me to drop my shells. I take them from the pouch and hold them in my hand. I feel the smooth indigo shards until I hear their song in my marrow. When their pitch is ripe, I throw them on the mat of lavender silk, raffia, and leather we use for reading our castings. The shells tumble around and reveal their message. Queenie nods and then looks up at me with her blue-rimmed brown eyes. She smiles, showing her ivory teeth with a gap twice the size of mine, but her eyes are sad. We can both read the confirmation.

The pathway is open, and this journey across the ocean is anointed for me to take. She says that tonight we will prepare a new pouch for me for the States; my child one has dried up its purpose. I touch the soft, faded, light-blue leather pouch. The one my mother don't know of. I sleep with it under my pillow at night, and it has held every dream I have had since I was nine.

Queenie pulls up her skirt to bring out her own pouch, deep-green-and-silver leather with a cowrie design. Whenever she does this, I feel like I looking up God's skirt. She have the prettiest legs to me. She starts rolling a spliff of lavender, damiana, marshmal-low, and fresh ganja and does a quiet prayer to the spirits of the herbs, asking that they honor her temple. Queenie is beautiful and still look like she did in the pictures in her house from when she was a professional dancer. On our walks in the hills and the country, she moves like a gray-haired teenager, her legs are muscular and smooth with scars and dents that I have memorized and made her tell me each of their origin stories. My favorite scar, though, is the one she got on her cheek when she was being initiated as a young woman. That is all I know about it, but I love it 'cause it make she look real gangsta.

My grandma does only sometimes let me smoke with her after ritual. She says don't smoke with my Rasta cousins, Episode and them. "Just us old ladies know how to do everything right with ritual and sweetness," she say with a wink and smile, revealing her back four teeth, which are dipped in gold. Queenie can roll a spliff faster than it take to light the flame. When we first started to take our walks together, I was nine and I used to love to just watch the smoke push wild from her mouth and circle her head into a cloud. Now I is sixteen, and she passes the fire my way and lets the news of my imminent trip sink in.

"I always barefoot and I ain't wan' lose my roots. I know I go miss the ancestors. I Aquarian and Oya." I crying all of these things, and Queenie corrects me.

"Audre, you are a wild nurturing. You are a complicated specialness. You are ancestral perseverance and sacred erotic," she says, like she praying, holding me close to her. I cry louder.

"Gyal, you been in constant communication with Spirit your whole life and you been taught that Spirit speak loudest when we deep in the water, drowning in trouble and fear." Queenie suddenly closes her eyes and is quiet and breathing, which I know means she is receiving messages. "And that is when you must let yourself get quiet and still. You must let yourself float above it until you are safe and levitating on the water and beneath the sky and just listen, Audre." She opens her eyes and looks at me. "And, dahlin', let me tell you something for truth: America have dey spirits too, believe me," she say, and she puts out her spliff, rubs my back, and starts humming a song into my spine. It a quiet and low song, and I feel my heart inhale the love of it.

"Audre, I was at a ceremony in Brooklyn in '84. The brothas and sistas in there, from everywhere—Cuba, Nigeria, Mississippi, Peru, and India—and they beatin' them drums good, gyal." I look from the ocean and up at my grandmother and her storytelling. "And I is with Auntie Mahal, who bring she cavaquinho and play it good right with them drums and she almost in a trance. You woulda think we was back in the motherland. But every land is a mother's land, I discover." She laughs at this thought. "And I is in there, winin' and spinnin' and slicin' my arms in the air, gyal, 'cause the rhythm find me and hold me. They is in their singing. I swear I was going to disappear, but I can't stop." Queenie stands up and starts twirling and twisting she arms in the air with her barefoot drumming on the sand.

I can never cry when Queenie dances.

"And, Audre, somethin' take over." She starts to kneel down low, her movements flowing and soft. With each cypher she is lifting and ascending into the air. The sound of drums seems to be coming from my heartbeat. Her feet are flying sand all around her, until I see my grandma rising above me. She is in the rapture of her memory. I lie back and watch her flowy, all-white attire, a cloud of origami, fold and contain and blossom her from movement to movement as she hovers above me several feet in the air. I watch her embrace the sky and the sky lift she up like a child of feather. She whipping in the wind, living in the rhythm of the breeze she create. After she finishes her celestial windup, she starts to descend, stair-stepping on air. Once her feet touch the ground, she crouches down next to me. She is laughing hard, and it rumble the ground beneath me. She fall back and lie on the sand, heart toward the sky.

"Crazy, nuh? I feel I is not in my body no more; I feel I is of some next world. I ain't know I could do dat until dis day in the States of all places, I tellin' ya. But, Audre, that is when I begin the journey to figure out my spirit, who I is, for real." She gets up and moves to sit next to me, and we look on the water together.

I lie into she shoulder, wanting to feel the wind and sky she pull down cool my chest and lift up the space my heart is crumpled in.

"Life is strange, and it will break you to help you heal ancient wounds, me dahlin'." She rubs my back and my head fall into her lap.

My tears fall across her thighs. I really don't want to leave. I don't know if I ever going to see Neri again. I feel like I don't exist if Neri don't look at me. I miss the pulse of holding Neri's hand and I caved in with suffering, missing Neri's body next to mine.

MABEL

I'M TRYING TO SLEEP AND I CAN'T SLEEP. My belly hurts and my hips too. All I can do is lie in bed and think of young Whitney Houston from the eighties. I have her album *Whitney* next to my bed. I found it at the thrift store last week when I was there with my mama, and I been sleeping next to Whitney every night ever since. My mom thinks it's cute since Whitney was her idol growing up, and she was inspired by her singing and style and stuff. But I feel like Whitney and I are connected in a special way for some reason. I have loved her since I was a kid, when my mom and I would play her greatest hits and dance to "I Wanna Dance with Somebody." At the part when Whitney says, "Don't you wanna dance? Say you wanna dance! Don't you wanna dance?!" Mama would pull my dad in. He would do his reliable and raggedy two-step, thinking he is killing the game and she would be in her intricate Afro-modern-hip-hop choreography—which is a lot of shoulder-shimmying, lyric dancing, and old-lady twerking. My mom can dance though, for real, and she could always get my dad to just let go and be goofy.

Anyway, I'm up staring at my ceiling, in my memories and my feels as usual, listening to my "quiet storm" mix (as my dad calls it). It's all emo and soft music. Soon, I'm thinking of Whitney and her fine self from back in the day again. She just had a lot of layers to her, which is a thing I think I like in people, like Ursa and Jazzy. Even Terrell has layers. I like that sometimes Whitney was graceful and poised like a church lady, but she was really kind of wild and cray, and straight hood, too.

I'm like that, I got a lot of layers too, but I think other kids think I'm just this whatever tomboy Black girl, who always reading and playing ball or working out or something. I basically fit in, which is okay, but sometimes, I wish I felt comfortable to put my layers out there more.

If I'm honest, part of my renewed curiosity is because recently I found out Whitney Houston fell in love with this other girl, Robyn, when they was teens and working a summer job in New Jersey. I was just looking stuff up online and found some things about her "rumored romance" with her basketball-player best friend, Robyn. I don't know, but it just seems cool to know that she had this connection with this other girl. And that the other girl was a beautiful *basketball* star, and Whitney fell for her butt, called her the "sister she never had." *Mmm-hmmm*. I feel that. I think I've felt that way before. With Ursa, my bestie, I felt that somewhat and in another kind of weird way with Jada, this girl from math.

I read that when Whitney hit it big, Robyn was her for-real, ride or die. That she became Whitney's assistant and her confidante *and* always had her back. For real, for real. They shared a huge apartment together that was bad and beautiful and was living that good life together.

When I listen to "I Wanna Dance with Somebody" after reading more about their connection, I imagine Whitney and Robyn slow-dancing in an icy and lit penthouse in the eighties and it's all back-in-the-day fresh. A world of windows, looking over the city lights and skyscrapers, black and white everything, with leather couches, a big sound system with mad tapes and CDs, glass tables and a neon chandelier. Old-school and tasteful. They are two Black girls, slow-dancing, teen twin flames who loved each other. Inseparable.

I feel it.

Anyway, some people deny it, but when I look at pictures of young Robyn and Whitney and how they are smiling and close, a part of me thinks it's true. I just do. I can totally see why Whitney loved her. She is cool and smooth, more swag than any of those cheesy, Jheri-curled dudes probably trying to push up on her. I also read that one time, Robyn also maybe whooped Bobby Brown's butt. I wanna be like that—smooth like Robyn. Just a tender thug who Whitney would love.

Maybe Robyn was her true love. I wish she coulda stayed with her if that's what she wanted, and they'd be in love forever. Maybe the world would've loved her if she was queer. I would've, no doubt. Whitney was an angel and what if Robyn could've been her bodyguard? Why did that basic-white-boy Kevin Costner, with no swag, have to save her? It should've been Robyn's cool self. Ain't Black women always saving everything anyway? Why can't we save Whitney?

When I listen to Whitney sing, I'm feeling every feel there is to feel. Lighthearted. Melancholy. Joyous. Romantic. Her voice can do anything, and I get chills hearing her riff and vocalize. I put my head under my blankets, bring my knees to my chest and cocoon myself with Whitney and the darkness and softness surrounds me.

The next song on my list is by my favorite band, BLK LVRS. All of the musicians in the band are weird Black kids. Like me, I guess. I really like the lead singer, QWN Asantewaa. I like them 'cause they is just beautiful and different. They wear simple clothes and a fade haircut and sneakers. Their voice is really soft and deep and emotional, and they write most of the songs and play guitar.

I think if I'm honest, I'm pretty sure I like girls. But I'm not really sure either because a part of me also likes guys, like Terrell. The first time I thought about this in a real way was when I went to see BLK LVRS—my first real, grown concert—and I had this serendipitous, moment-long micro-situationship with this girl.

My mom and dad had surprised me with seeing BLK LVRS for my fifteenth birthday. It was an eighteen-plus show, but apparently the venue allows kids to come with their parents. It made my whole Black life that year, because this was, like, one of the few times they had gotten me something that really felt like me. Not some dumb light-purple frilly blouse or skinny jeans with floral embroidery on the butt or dangly earrings with pink shells or a bougie manicure and pedicure (side note: I did low-key like that ish, though. It actually felt good. Soaking my hands and feet in water and all of this concentrated attention to my fingers and toes made me tingle. I found a dope iridescent-emerald color called Octopussy, which was a weird name, but it made my nails look like the back of a beetle).

So, I'm at the show, I have on my BLK LVRS shirt, black skinny jeans, and a silver chain with Saturn on it that my mom got me for my birthday. My hair was in a braid and I had a big X on my hand to show I wasn't drinking, which I thought was cool anyway. My parents was back in the cut, where some of their friends was chillin' and they got appetizers and drinks and was just being bougie adults in the way my mom loves and my dad is awkward about. My mom says it's good for him to talk to beings besides his plants and his seeds (seeds—as in his children, Sahir and me, but also his actual seeds for Black Eden, the seeds he collects and germinates, and the seeds he raps to once they're in the dirt. The Fugees, mainly). Mom says if she ever dies, he going to need some friends, maybe even a new wifey. He hates when she be talking so reckless about things like her dying. I think maybe 'cause his parents died when he was young, and the idea makes him feel scared, like a world without my mom would feel.

The energy of the show was very intense for me. All I could do was take in all of the fly people, their different looks and colors. They were beautiful. I had never experienced that ever before. My parents let me wander into the ocean of audience and be free of them, as long as I stayed close to the stage or their bougie district and kept my phone handy. I walked around and tried to be low-key and blend in, but in that space, part of me wished I had let myself let loose and pick an edgier outfit.

I said "excuse me" about ninety-nine-eleven times, and twisted my body through the crowd until I was standing real close to the front, right on the edge of the stage. I wanted to see QWN as close as I could. The wait seemed forever to come out, but there was a DJ playing some bops to keep the crowd ready. When the band got to the stage I was only a couple feet away from QWN.

They was smaller than I thought they would be, but they was also more everything else. More beautiful and dope, and I couldn't stop looking at them. The whole audience seemed to love and want QWN. I mean, my whole body was vibrating. They was all in the zone. QWN didn't seem to notice us at all, except for between songs when they would talk and tell little stories in they deep speaking voice, otherwise, they would let their guitar talk and harmonize their singing alongside it. Their voice made me feel like they cared about me. I know that's weird, but that is the only way I can explain the way it feels when I listen to them.

> *I memorize your skin*
> *and you tattoo your love*
> *and your poetry on me*
>
> *You love like rain*
> *You beautiful sweet*
> *You saturate me*
> *my ancestral wifey*
>
> *give me touches that*
> *sweeten up*
> *complexities*

with all of the tenderness
with all of the permission
You are temptation
and goddess perfection.

Moaning their lyrics, behind the bass line, the whole band was going hard and hitting that beat. I felt every note in my gut, really underground in me. And the whole crowd was feeling it too, and I was swept into our collective energy.

I'm not gonna lie, I was also feeling super awkward, because I ain't even know if I knew how to dance at first. But then this girl next to me out of nowhere starts to groove with me. I still remember what she got on, she was so magically pretty. She was looking all witchy, with a lavender-colored Afro and white boots and a necklace of mandarin-colored flowers. I started dancing back before I could think about it. She was real smooth with her movements, twirling around me and dropping it low, like bow! I was like, damn . . . I did a helpless version of my dad's two-step, and to my surprise, she seemed impressed. She soul clapped at me even—like I was killing it. She smiled and I just kept doing my thang, grinning back at her. And I don't know why I still re-member this, but she smelled good too, like cocoa butter, jasmine flowers, and a little alcohol on her breath, even though there was an X on her hand like mine. All of a sudden, a crew of her friends came back with drinks, and she smiled at me and then floated away among them and I got pushed farther back. It made me feel a little disappointed, but I get it: Those were homies. But for some silly reason, I had wished we coulda danced all night together to

BLK LVRS and I coulda maybe even known something about her. Next thing I know I hear a familiar voice.

"Mabel, they is so fresh! I had to get on this dance floor and do my thang, baby!" and there was my mama behind me, shimmying and old-lady twerking her heart out to the music.

We played BLK LVRS on the ride home and I was still buzzing from their weirdness and freeness and Blackness. I tried to relive all I saw on the stage that night: the bass player, BLK Rose, who is tall and dark with a pretty smile and a pink fade, and his jumping up and dancing all over the stage. And BLK Dahlia, their drummer from Senegal, who was raised in New Orleans. She moved between every style of rhythm from congas, wind chimes, to her drum kit to a djembe drum that she played on some of the slower songs. The keys player, BLK Iris and her glittery periwinkle dreadlocks past her fat, fine butt, wearing a mint-green wedding dress, her eyes closed as she did rhythms on her beat machine. And of course, my favorite, QWN Asantewaa, and their emotional voice.

"She's a butch, right?" my dad said from the front seat, promptly killing my vibe. "She could sang her ass off. That falsetto was a young Prince in his hey. Ooooh and she play real good, like Jimi all day on that guitar. I'm glad we went, ladies."

The way he said "she" and "her" really annoyed me. Like he knew them or understood something about them because of how they rocked they hair or clothes. "Why can't you just enjoy the music, Dad? Why the first thing you wonder about them is if they butch? And *they* don't go by *she*," I blurted out, feeling heat in my face. Then both me and my dad got quiet.

"Sequan, the singer—QWN Asantewaa—goes by 'they,' baby," my mama said. But she didn't stop there. "And *oooh,* that little cutie, QWN is a fine, little tender-roni. I can see why all y'all kids be acting wild behind them," she said, revealing cougar feelings about QWN Asantewaa that nobody was wondering about.

"Right, *they,* not *she.* My bad." He looked at me in the rearview mirror, but I don't think he noticed me rolling my eyes. "They used to call 'em butch or stud back in the day. I wasn't trying to be mean, I ain't know. I did enjoy the show, though, I said that. I liked it." I just kept rolling my eyes at his fumbling. Whatever.

"There are still butches or studs, but there are they and thems and more too." Mom put her hand on Dad's. "This indigo generation is next level. It took me a while to pick up on it, but I get it better now. I know you wasn't trying to be insensitive, 'Quan, but just be mindful okay, honey? They go by 'them' and 'they.'" After my mom broke it down in her own way, my dad and I both stayed quiet the rest of the drive. I felt like I wanted to cry for some reason and a couple tears came down and I wiped them slow, so no one would notice and I felt even more dumb, since I was grateful I got to go. My mom turned up the volume, and as QWN's voice filled up the car, I looked at our city glitter by.

Even though we still close, my dad gets weird around me in certain ways that makes me awkward. I don't know how he would feel if he knew I liked girls, because he was kinda too geeked when I got a "little boyfriend," as my mom put it when I first started chilling with Terrell. I'm pretty sure my mom wouldn't care, since she's always had lesbian and gay friends. I think my dad would feel some type of way about it, like a little disappointed or confused, to be honest. I don't feel in a rush to talk to them all about my feelings, because . . . nah.

Listening to QWN tonight on the mix reminds me of that night a little. Low-key, a little bit 'cause I always wondered what happened to that lavender-'fro girl, to be real. I just wonder if she thought about me again, which was a long shot, but what if? What if there was a Whitney-and-Robyn connection? Either way, that BLK LVRS show was the dopest night of my life—even with my dad being basic. It's weird that even listening to QWN, with myself alone now in the middle of the night, two years later, I feel like I'm still in that room and a part of them in a way that gives me a good feeling.

AUDRE

WHY I HAVE TO LOVE SOMEONE I CAN'T LOVE? My mother beat me and shame me for being "nasty" and I start to wish myself dead. But if it nasty, I find that nastiness in the church I try and avoid my whole life.

My mama and I was always different but the older I get, the harder it is to live with she. She never seem quite at peace with life. She certainly never seem to feel peace with me. When I was young, she would be in she bedroom for hours, sleeping or watching detective shows. Queenie would come by and cook and lime by us and sometimes comb my hair. When my mama was happy, though, that was my favorite world to live in. We going to the beach, she buying new clothes for sheself and me, she would get new lipstick, perfume, and things that make she feel pretty. We cooking and liming together. But if she in she shadow place, nothing is okay, and I staying out of her way and in my own world. When I was eleven, in addition to going to Queenie's on Saturdays, I started going down the road by Auntie Pearl and Episode's house, watching TV and exploring the hills with our other cousins and neighborhood kids. Episode is Auntie Pearl's youngest son and my favorite cousin.

My mother's dad died from drugs and madness when I was twelve; that is when she started getting really into church. I remember my grandfather Ivan was funny and kind to a point, but it was only on the surface. I ain't know if it was because drugs or he had a hard life, but he would promise my mama something and then he wouldn't do it, or he'd do something else stchupid she ain't ask for, like bring me a bike with two flat tires when I asked for them shoes with the wheels in the heels of them. Then he get mad when I was disappointed, like he brought me what I ask for. He was always doing things like that. He blame it on when Queenie left him in the eighties—just like his mother did his father when he was a boy, which he seem to blame Queenie for too. Either way, after he dead from overdose, my mama decided to start going to church on Sundays, and then church was all of the time. The next thing I know a corny, clear-skin man always hanging around and that seem to be the official thing that separate me and my mother: a husband named Rupert.

After a while, it was either I go to church or we always arguing about it, because she feel I is "acting like I is a woman" since all I do now is hang out with my cousin and his Rasta friends, plus I stopped eating meat and ain't straightening my hair. She sentence me to weekly services to "put me in my place." I beg Queenie to ask Mama to let me choose. But Mama got her husband now—a husband that she find in God's house—and she and Rupert insist, since I is in they house, I must go to they church.

And that is where I find Neri.

I saw her right away on my first visit to church. I liked how she opened the doors for all the grandmas. After some weeks, I saw she was always wearing something yellow—whether it was a yellow suit or a yellow scarf or yellow blouse. I noticed that and brought her some yellow flowers from Queenie's yard one Sunday, and she hugged me and I was fluttering inside my body. Every Sunday, she sang real pure and close her eyes. Her voice sweet and perfect and angelic from Goddess. And she noticed me too. After we saw each other a couple of Sundays, she would find me and sit next to me.

Neri was my mother's pastor's granddaughter, and I loved her on sight.

One day during service, Neri held my hand where no one could see. I was feeling something when she did that, like it a special moment. I thought maybe it a church thing people do, I ain't know about, and I loved it. The energy in our hands was singing a gospel the whole time, and I felt the sermon through her palm. My mother's God's grace in Neri's hands. I get real religious after that. I ain't never kissed nobody before. I ain't even feel I wanted to kiss anyone before. But Neri made me wonder: What would it feel like to kiss her right on her mouth? I ain't know what to do with the feeling so I pushed the thought back out of my head.

Church became actual *church* to me. In my head, I renamed it C.H.U.R.C.H., which stood for "Come Here U Rebel, Come Here." I knew I was a conjurer and feeling weird for being there and finding Spirit. But Queenie had always told me Spirit is everywhere, and that since I was going to church, be open and see what is there to learn about the Spirit of Jesus and the way the Christians try to understand the divine. So when my heart start tingling, I ain't surprised that I found Spirit in church with Neri.

One day I decided to take Neri to the ocean, by where Queenie live. It is a private spot that emerges from a walk through a thick grove and a narrow path. We convinced all the adults—and ourselves—we was studying the Bible. I was in a Sunday dress, pink and ugly and making me look like a tall five-year-old. My glasses are old-school frames that used to be Queenie's, but I like them better than the new styles. My mama hates them, but she never get my style anyhow. I thought I looked funky and original. Neri looked more sophisticated in a navy skirt, with a cream blouse and a yellow scarf, and in her braids she'd tucked yellow flowers that we found on our walk to the water. I laid a scarf for us in the sand. I kicked off my shoes and took off Neri's shoes too. *Pretty feet*, I thought. I held she foot and sang a song. She giggled and swung herself closer to me. Hip to hip, she leaned her head on my shoulder but then caught herself and sat back up.

The ocean witnessed us, and as I sat there with Neri, I felt shy. The water blue was loud and welcoming, like a long-lost tantie. She came close to touch us, then receded back into herself, almost as if to get a good look at us, and then she lunged for us again. I laid my head in Neri's lap and I was surprised when she glided her hand up my back and played in my little Afro. Inside of me started dancing and I felt alive and I faded into her a little.

The water came for our toes, and I told Neri, "This is my real church." I wondered what she thought. She was quiet but nodded.

Being by Neri felt sweet, and I started to shake a little, as if I scared. I didn't want to leave her for any reason. "Audre, you lookin' sad. Just watch at the ocean. Listen to these seawater hymns, nuh?" said Neri, smiling at me and then looking at the water all the while she was making an instrument of me. Stroking my earlobes with she fingertips, twisting little twists in my 'fro and loosening it, sweeping she hand on my face and neck.

When the moment opened up, we both fell into each other. She grabbed my hand and I felt the ocean talking to us real deep inside. Church. My spirit found rhythm with the water and Neri's breath. I overwhelmed my good sense and kissed Neri's hand, then tucked myself back into her lap. She lifted my head up and looked into my eyes. Then she leaned down and kissed my mouth. This the first time anybody kiss me. I was trembling. (I am trembling remembering it.) I stopped breathing for a little moment. The ocean kissed our toes. Her lips on mine were a warmth, and my body started to bloom within her arms and melt in her skin. And from then on, love was all we knew how to do.

We "study the Bible" by the ocean for three months. My mama was happy thinking I finally accepted Jesus and finally have a church friend—any friend at all since I ain't really close to anyone in school either. (I is cool with people at school, but I always feel like I is a different type of person and no one there really get me. I have Epi, who is my cousin, but more like my big brother, and Queenie, who is my grandma but also feel like she is my sister-best-friend and even a mom to me.) Neri was different though, she was a girl my age and I felt a closeness with her that was new and special.

And every Sunday, we went to the ocean, explaining to everyone that we wanted to study the sermons deeper. "Apply the gospel to our hearts." And we did, in our own way—talking about life and our families and our secrets. We worshipped in each other's arms with our own devotion, sand in her braids and my Afro, our Sunday dresses wrinkled. We peeled down to our underwear and swam in the water and floated on eternity, together. We lay out under the sun and dried, together. She held me in her arms and smiled at me and her eyes made me feel like she really, really saw me. We packed up everything, smoothed our dresses, and headed back to our different worlds. Until that next Sunday.

Between Sundays, I was my usual self but different. I enjoyed everything about life because I was thinking of Neri. As usual, I got good grades in school and was helping around the house, but now I avoided talking back to Rupert even though he ass still a idiot. Now I smile at he and do what I asked to do.

Between Sundays, I hung out at Epi and he girlfriend Sarya's place only occasionally and not every chance I got. Mainly I went to see what Epi was cooking up new and to hear gossip from he and Sarya.

And even though I was going to church on Sundays, every Saturday don't change. Since I was nine, after chores at my house, I was doing my lessons by Queenie and learning about herbs and baths and rubs and songs, of the spirituality my grandma created for she self and share with me. One Saturday, my grandma felt a feeling and begin to investigate me.

"So you find Jesus or you fall in love?" Queenie asked me, while we in the backyard bottling her homemade bush-plum wine, doing we usual thing of making and studying and just being together. She caught me off guard, as I was thinking of Neri and singing a song from church.

I was changing the album on her portable record player. Her question was a thing I ain't know what to do with. It stayed in the air for a second and I acted like I focusing on the Ma Rainey LP in my hand. Queenie felt like hearing some blues that morning, and she was in a Ma Rainey mood. She said, "Dis wine we is making is for drinking slowly, for contemplation and healing emotional weight that is and ain't yours, like the blues women."

I decided to play it cool with the question and slowly looked up at her. When I see she face smiling her big gap, I couldn't help but smile a little, 'cause in my heart I was thinking of Neri and I is so happy.

"I find Jesus," I said, and look back down in the crate of records.

"Eh-heh, I bet you find he all right." Queenie stop short and bus' out a wild laugh while holding she belly at the thought of me being a church girl. She let out a big, loud sigh when she recover from my comedy. She was wearing a maroon-and-turquoise African-print dress with skinny straps and buttons down the front. Her lipstick was glittery purple, and her gray hair was clipped low. Her body was perspiring and strong, and she dabbed her chest and neck with a handkerchief the color of a piece of sky. She topped off the last bottle, corked it, put it in the carton on the ground with eleven others and took it into the house. I put on an Anita Baker record and put the Ma Rainey one back in its sleeve.

"Anita is a good pick for new love," she said when she come back out. She snuggled me while she giggled.

"Ugh, Queenie, wha' new love? I tellin' you I is save. Jesus and me real cool now." And I started smiling, even though I was trying hard to stay serious. We was looking out at her Queenieland, with its zaboca, mango, guava, plum, plantain, and cherry trees, dasheen bush, bhaji, cassava, sweet potato, and several chickens who she let me name. And out beyond Queenieland was Yemeya, the ocean, the goddess of me and Neri's C.H.U.R.C.H.

"Mmm-hmm, you used to tell me more ting, but lips tight

today. But that is what it feel like to be in love for the first time I guess. You wan' feel like you did discover a ting, no one else know," she said pretending she was trying to figure me out, but I knew she already at her conclusion. I could tell.

"Hmmm, I wonder if is someone I know . . . ," she asked, bumping she bum bum into mine.

"It no one you know," I bust out, and leaned on to her shoulder, wanting to tell her every little thing about Neri, but not feeling like I could either.

"Oh, so there *is* a someone. Hmm. Someone from church it seem, then. Well, your mother will like that, maybe . . . I never know with she," she said, holding back she mouth. Then she find a next thought to share with me. "Good for you, my dahlin'." She smiled. "You is smart and strong. I ain't worry about you, but always be safe, yuh understand? You must protect yourself."

"Queenie, it ain't even like that, if you think I is going to get pregnant," I started to say.

"I ain't just talking pregnancy. Protect your heart and spirit. You is open and that is powerful but also vulnerable. I had to say something 'cause anything can happen in the world of love," she said. I remember I nodded, but I ain't really know what she was talking about. I looked around not wanting to look in her eyes and tell her too much. I felt a furry slither around my ankles and looked down to see Bastet, her cat, wound around my ankles. I picked her up and cuddled her, and then as usual, she escaped after a couple moments to hunt lizards in the garden. Queenie came close to me, more soft and less preachy.

"And listen, Audre. I want you to give attention to every second of this moment, this feeling. Enjoy love." She stroked my head as she said this. "You will lose yourself in it and then find yourself in a new way. That is just how it work and maybe supposed to work. So be strong in who you are, eh? Don't be a bobo-lee for nobody, you understand?" she said. She turned to me and looked me in the eye. "Remember you is the granddaughter of Queenie. You is my royalty, okay? You can always talk to me, eh? I was young once, and I know things. All kind a things." She smiled, looking mischievous and a little sly. From that smile I knew I ain't telling she nuttin'. She wise and is good with secrets. But what if she decided to talk to she sisters and then everyone from Laven-tille to Chaguaramas would know by the evening, including my mother, and that would put shame in she eye. But even though I feel I wanted to keep it for me, I appreciated that she even noticed I'm different. Because I feel I was too.

That last Sunday, I woke up early and was ready for church before everyone. I opened my eyes, looking forward to seeing Neri and getting to be with her all by myself. But first, I was sitting with her in the pew all morning amongst her granddaddy's sermons on the deeds and stories of the Bible and the Lord and Jesus and Mary and the disciples and the wife of this one and the son of this one. I listened and applied his stories to my life in whichever way I could, which is what Queenie said I should do. But I also mostly daydreamed about Neri, who was next to me in a chapel of per-spiring aunties with baby powder on they chests, their perfume warm and lingering; a chapel of pious uncles of the church who are hard-backed and in white and pastel colored button-up shirts with their eyes wet and their souls weary for the Lord. Children was there too, memorizing the instructions for their holiness and to become obedient to the Bible and the Lord. No matter how I felt about some of the beliefs of Christianity I ain't agree with, how I didn't—and don't—understand all of the things about church, I loved (and still love) the village feeling when I was there and the music always touched me until I would cry. I was feeling love and current in the space between me and Neri's shoulders as we prayed and stood and sang and praised in her grandfather's house of God.

Afterwards, Neri and me went to our private church, where the sky was thick with clouds moving towards us, levitating above our bodies like Goddess herself. The water crawled up and saturated the sand as though she was paying attention to me and Neri's worship. The sky wasn't too much expanse for the water and the water wasn't too much deep for the sky. They were reflections. I slid through the sand closer to Neri. I sat behind her and just held her, smelling her neck before I kissed it right on the place where her thick hair was lifted from her neck.

I waited all week for Sunday, for this sweetness. For when I could be by Neri and feel like myself. Neri was wearing a beige blouse with tiny yellow daisies and a yellow skirt. And I was feeling proud, 'cause she smell like Ocean Love, the perfume I got her last week, when I went by Episode and Sarya's apartment for a scent for she. They was all in my business trying to understand, why all of a sudden this ragamuffin want to smell sweet.

"For what stchupid, dirty-pantie-boy you wan' impress? He know I is ya cousin?"

"Epi, no one studying you. And ya tink anyone scare of a skinny-ass Rasta? Yuh wan' meh business or no?" I asked, able to block his nosiness better than Queenie's. I was sitting on the couch in the living room connected to their kitchen.

Episode laughed and said he is happy that the church ain't cure my mouth and continued to cut up chadon beni for the pigeon peas he was making. Sarya floated out of the room, long dreads swinging near she ankles. She got skin that is dark like melongene and just as smooth and shiny; she look like she could be a model from Nigeria or Senegal, but she is Trini 2 the bone, like we is. She returned and laid out oils before me. I read the names as I picked them up and smelled individually, trying to find something just right. Cool Water smell like a man who want to be cool; Kush smell sweet but not the same sweet of Neri; Frankincense remind me of Catholic church, which isn't quite what I was going for. I sniff Opium, J-Lo, Beyoncé, and they all smell beautiful but still not right for Neri.

I picked up one of the oils, turned it around, and read, "Hot Pum-Pum." Sarya smiled with pride at me. "That is a good selection! I see ya cousin got taste, Epi! That is a Sarya original, special and limited-edition fine oil! You ain't gone find that one nowhere, but watch out," she said, then leaned in to whisper, "it drives all these stchupid men out here crazy." I put it down quick. I saw one that said Ocean Love. I smelled it and felt something in my heart.

When I gave it to Neri the next Sunday, she gave me a real nice, long kiss.

And that last Sunday on the beach, I should have realized that the clouds was talking. Neri and I feeling sweet and full of love, yet I was feeling something in my spirit. Neri was laughing loud at the sky.

"And, gyal, I get up in de tree and I ain't realize how high I reach." Her head was thrown back as if she were looking at herself up in a tree. I couldn't take my eyes off her beautiful neck. "Yuh see, I scaaared! I looking down and imagine me foot slip, me head bus', and me granddaddy have to give a sermon for he granddaughter, who dead over mangoes, trying to get this one real up high for you." Neri leaned in close to me and our eyes almost crossed we focused on each other so tight. "But I ain't care. I know it was sweet and of course you deserve the sweetest." She had brought it in one of her yellow scarves. Once Neri and I was out of church, she was herself too—funny and weird and more free and willing to say anything she want.

"Before I kiss anyone," she told me once, "I used to practice on mangoes. Especially the sweet juicy ones. I would sneak them in my room and pretend it was someone I was liking. If you see the mess I did make," she told me, and we giggled about it. I asked her if she ever love a girl before, and she looked at me and smiled and nodded and we ain't say nothing more.

I thought of her kissing practice as I peeled the mango skin with my teeth and lips leaning over the sand to not spill on me self—it was juice, soon as you bite. I took another taste, she took a bite, and then we drinking from the fruit, from our own fingers, and then from each other's lips. Everything slow with tenderness. If I close my eyes now, I can see it.

Our garments open up. Arms slide out of sleeves and around each other. Neri lays me down, and I look up at her and see the sky beyond her head. She takes off my glasses and places them to the side of us, carefully in my bag, like she always does. She kisses my eyelids and I touch her face. She starts humming a song from church and I start humming with her. Neri get me to feel the beauty in them gospels. My breath catches in anticipation of her movements, how she will touch me and where. I love how her body feels, rocking into mine, blooming into mine.

She starts to kiss me, her lips and mouth warm and tasting of mango, and I exhale out like I was drowning in air until then. She lets her kisses travel to my cheek, linger at my chin and neck. My body is trembling and moaning, by the time I feel her lips on my collarbone, my underarms, licking my nipples, she delighting all places of me soft and cover up to everyone else. I roll into her sweetness, her touch relaxes me into the sound below us and she becomes ocean, kissing my skin, like she always know how to love me. I roll on top of she and I return love to her by gliding my lips along every part of she skin. She feels so soft and I longing to taste she. I move my lips down she neck, shoulders, she chest, waist, and belly button. She places her hand on top of my head, and my lips move slowly across her navel and her hip bones, which make she giggle.

Suddenly, my hair is being pulled and I is being dragged backwards.

"JESUS! GET THE DEVIL OUT! YUH DISGUSTING! YUH IS so SICK, Audre! Why you bring this shame to God? God, why you give me this SICK GIRL?!!!"

With each lash of she hand, I tried to cover myself, my mama like a hurricane around me, pushing me down into the sand. She ain't care. My face, back, shoulders, breasts, ass. She lashed all the places that Neri just kissed. I was crying and shaking, I ain't know how I even got moving. In remembering it, I still feel this shame, this torrid feeling.

Neri was crying and screaming, grabbing for my mama, begging her to stop cuffing me down, please, that it was she. My mama screamed for her to put on she clothes and go into the car and stop lying. She yelled she knew I influence this. Neri protected me from my mom's lashes by standing in front me and me mother hit her chest once, before she grabbed me from behind. We were all scuffling in the sand. I was thinking if we should run to Queenie's, but my spirit, my body, everything was paralyzed. My mother screamed and took us both by our arms and command us back down the path, back to she car, commanding Neri to get in. I got in the back seat, crying and feeling her licks on my body and the one on my heart. Neri and I in the back seat, and I couldn't even look at her.

When we got to the pastor's house, Neri quick squeezed my hand, like we were in church, but now the gospel is screams and sharp and afraid. My mother seemed to be in the pastor's house for all of time and no time at all.

When we get home, the yelling and lashes start back, and when she get fed up with me, I was sent to my room. I hear her and Rupert talking in the other room when he get home late from work. He barely seem like he around but you feel his influence nonetheless in this house. I felt alone in my house. I felt like I was her enemy and not she only child.

The next week, after she and Rupert return from church, she told me her decision: That I is to live by my father.

Queenie was already waiting outside the house in her vintage white-and-chrome Mercedes-Benz convertible. With the top down. I don't know if my mama called her or if she just know. I slid myself in the front seat and we roll off. I was numb and felt like myself was all poured out. We drove in silence for a while. Finally, she asked the verdict. I whispered. "She sending me to the States by my Yankee father who I barely know," I say and my throat thickens with each word. "My mother don't want me anywhere on the island to shame she with my nasty ways," I say, sinking further into the red leather of she car.

We pulled up to the wood's entrance that leads to the beach. Queenie put the car in park and before I knew, she swung to the passenger side, pulled me out of the car into her body. "Stop calling it nasty, dahlin'," Queenie said. I was in she arms, and I instantly collapsed into tears. I felt like I did as a little girl, when I would be hurt and she would swoop me up and hold and rock me.

She said she always knew who I was and it makes me special. She apologized for my mother. I cried harder when she said that. She started crying too, which made me scared. Fight come out of Queenie, before tears, but she was crying for me. I asked she if I can stay with her forever instead of going to the States. She was quiet, considering. "Dahlin', I wish, I wish I could, me dahlin', but I can't cross me daughter. I love she, but I know me daughter. She will never forgive me and she will make your life hard. I ain't know, gyal. Maybe it would be easier for you wit' ya fadda.

"But," she said, "before I take you to me home, let's go to the water and see what Spirit say." And then she asked me if I had my pouch. I closed my eyes to collect myself and prepare for ceremony.

AUDRE

AFTER WE GO TO THE OCEAN FOR CEREMONY, we came to she house to make my next pouch, and then Queenie slip off to do something. When she come back, I's in she big chair, curled up like a sick kitten, looking out the window, my new pouch tied to my thigh. She swoop down on the ottoman next to me and slap me ass in the silly way she do, even though I'm a mess and been crying. I sit up and look at her and she smiling big with her gap and she satisfied with sheself. She says she went by the pastor's house and got a message from Neri.

"How you get dis?" I ask, my hand is shaking holding the letter.

My grandma steupse at me and rolls her eyes. Then, she leans closer to me and look me in my eyes in that way she do when she want me to understand she real good. "Ya think I 'fraid he?" she says simply, and steupses again, her eyes squinting and incredulous at the thought of fear. "Listen, gyal, there are those of us who have more persuasion than Jesus, especially to those in he flock, ya understand? And no pastor was always a pastor, dahlin'. I tellin' ya," she says, smiling. And then she winks. My grandma is magic. I start reading:

Dear Audre,

Your grandma is magic. I look out the window and I see she convertible park up. I hear my grandfather open the door and hear he giggling, and next I know she knocking on my door and tell me to write you something. She tell me you going to go live by your father in the States and she taking my grandfather on a ride in she new car and I is to be done before she get back. Jesus, I is shock at she powers.

I love you and I love you forever. Audre, I ain't know what to do and I feelin' so sorry I pull you into this way. I have prayed for you and that your mother show mercy on you. I can't bear thinking of how she vex and fighting she own child so. I can't . . . I begged for Jesus to forgive me for my sins and help cleanse me of desire for you. I can't explain how I love Jesus and you at the same time, but somehow it is true. I ain't understand how God finally make sense in your arms and in your church. I think this is why this punishment, because I even at times loved our way more than the way of Jesus.

They sending me away to family in Tobago and I begging them to let me stay and work in the church and show them I done sinning, but my grandfather say the decision is final. I is off tomorrow. I can't believe your mother is sending you so far away. I thought Tobago was far, but the States? This break me heart to the core, Audre. I ain't know if I will ever see you again and this hurt me heart even deeper.

But if to love you means this punishment—this hurtin'
on my heart—I ain't know why I still ain't regret it. I love you
still. I don't know what to do, besides devote my life to Jesus
and pray that I can purify my soul to feel the way I feel for you
for him. I will pray for you to be safe. I will pray for us. Every
time I look at water, I will be at church with you. I love you.

Forever yuh rebel,

Neri

I look up at Queenie. My face soak up with tears and I shaking and all I can do is moan. Queenie wrap her arms around me and pulls me close to her and wipes my face. I shuddering in she arms and a breeze encircles us and I breathe the smell of my grandma, mixed with my island and the ocean and know I will miss that smell.

LEO SEASON

you that cool cat
who bought the three-piece suit off layaway
and wore the alligator
Stacy Adams
to the club so we could bask in you
a yearning to be in the care of your arms
the protection of your pride

deep warm Bastet
sun queen of kings.
lover of lovers. generously ours
bounding in power and flourishing
in your softness

you make the dapper divine
and the royal real
and you roar heavenly laughter
all sweet
a lioness sunflower
full of seeds and heat

you are an immediate feeling
adored for your sensuality

and fierceness and for the luxury
of your smile

Leo sun, wild for us hot for us
to surround ourselves in your glow
and sultry and burning

MABEL

"IMMA MAKE MYSELF GET THROUGH THIS." That's what I tell myself, even though I feel like I can barely lift today. I made one of my dad's protein smoothies that taste like cocoa-dirt-flavored chalk. I needed to put something in my stomach so I could get through the workout, and that nasty shake was all I could figure out.

In our basement, my dad has a bench press, some dumbbells, a big heavy punching bag, and a small punching bag that looks like a teardrop. We used it to practice fast jabbing like you see Muhammad Ali doing in one of the posters on the wall. We've also got a trampoline, jump ropes, and some kettlebells too. I used to chill down here and watch my dad work out, and eventually, he showed me some jabs and hooks. I was a natural at boxing, like he was at my age. Boxing is fun because you got to be smart and fast and powerful. I loved how my muscles felt after me and my dad would be punching and ducking and jumping and lifting and sweating, and then we would go eat a Popsicle together as a cooldown treat. Our little ritual.

Lately, I work out on my own or come down when I want to be by myself and let off steam in a certain kind of way. Mainly, when I'm frustrated or mad. I just push my body really hard, and when I can't go no more, I collapse on the futon and stare at the ceiling and feel my body buzzing from the effort. But I've been having a harder time getting through my workouts, and in the last couple of days, I haven't been able to finish them at all, which has me worried since I need to get really strong if I'm going to get on varsity.

Today, after just a couple of reps with the weights, I was tired. I decided to just stretch since I was feeling weird in my stomach, kinda like I was about to get my period, but then also like I ate something weird. For some reason, this whole summer, I ain't been my usual self on the workout tip.

I head up to my room to get ready for bed. I wash my face, put on my du-rag and pajamas. I get under my covers and start to scroll through videos posted by homies.

Ahmed, my homie from poetry class, had discreetly taken a video of a drunk dude behind him on the bus who was singin' loud as hell, and beatboxing between verses. He added a filter that emits smog out of the dude's mouth. The caption read, "Sanging Poison and your breaf smell like it too . . . #gotdamn #listerine-works."

Jada posted a video of her on the beach looking cute and twerking all silly with Nevaeh and blowing a kiss to the camera. She looks pretty and like she is enjoying her summer. Whatever.

Next, I see a vid with my best friend, Ursa, doing push-ups while the new homie Jazzy is gloating about how she beat Ursa in basketball.

I think about posting something, but I don't have much to show for my day besides my unsuccessful workout session, me arguing with my daddy for the gazillionth time about what clothes I got on for my summer job at the community center, or Sahir crying because Mama told him (again) he can't put André 3000—that's our cat—in his backpack for a bike ride. Ever. I decide to post a little video of a chrysalis that I found in our garden in the patch of milkweed, black-eyed Susans, and purple coneflower. My dad and I planted these to attract butterflies. I sat in the patch and chilled with the chrysalis for an hour and played it some Whitney while I read *Wild Seed* again. The almost-butterfly was just there, chilling and getting fatter, slimy and metallic and almost like it was ready to burst open. My dad calls this phase butterfly puberty, because they eat like cray and then they are in this cocoon that is awkward and internal. Yet they will bust out of it one day, grown and free. Besides the chrysalis, there ain't really much in my life to post, so I put my phone down and put on some music.

The house is quiet like I like it. I love my family, but to be honest, they all get on my nerves in one way or another most of the time. For real, for real. And it ain't until it's late when everyone is in their own room and not sweatin' me that I can even feel like I'm myself. I listen to my music and snuggle up under my blanket in my own cocoon. My reading lamp is glowing through my covers and I look at my body under the tent I've made around myself. I got on my white tank top, my faded light-blue boxers with glow-in-the-dark dragons on 'em, and some black socks. It's weird but I can't sleep unless I got socks on, even though I wake up with them kicked off.

Looking at my body, I watch my stomach grow and float up

when I breathe in and then disappear behind my titties when I let my air out. I mean, not that I got much titties. Mine are medium-small bumps, and I hope they stay little 'cause Ursa got double-D boobs and she has to wear three sports bras when she plays ball and she hates it. Terrell used to like touching my titties and that was actually nice. He would just gently massage them, which was kinda calming. Neither of us had really done anything before, so we took things slow. I remember when we first kissed it was a hot mess. His mouth smelled like cherry Jolly Ranchers (his favorite "breath mint") and his tongue was wet and big and all up in my mouth. I was trying to not gag. After a while, I asked him if we could hold off on all that tongue. He ain't seem embarrassed. He laughed and agreed to back up on salamandering my mouth. Kissing him wasn't bad, 'cause we was homies and he was real cool. It just didn't feel big or exciting, which was weird to me, since we was boyfriend and girlfriend.

Around the same time earlier this summer, Jada and I was kicking it and hanging out. She would come to the crib, and we would ride bikes and hang on my porch. We would just be talking, and I would feel something special whenever she came through, like a hot feeling. One evening, me and Jada was hanging out on my porch and the sky was getting dark with rumbling, which is my favorite way for the sky to be, that feeling right before it rains. I offered to walk Jada home before it started to storm so we could chill some more and feel the sky and air together.

"You and Terrell are a cute couple," she said when we was walking. Which I guess was true, but it seemed random for her to bring up, but maybe not random 'cause he was my boyfriend, I guess.

"Terrell is a cutie," I agreed, and thought to myself that he got cute qualities. He got a sweet smile and his butt sits high, which my mama said was why she could see why I liked him. It wasn't why, but his butt makes it so that he walks with a little bob to his step, which I guess is cute.

"But YOU cute too, thoooough," she said, bumping me playfully, and I feel that feeling in my chest—that flip that ripples down my thighs to my feet when she is around.

"Uh, um. Thank you, I try," I said, wanting to sound chill, but I did actually try when it came to us kicking it for some reason. Maybe 'cause she is dope and fun and be flawless. I was in the bathroom for an hour getting my hair and clothes right. I'd even put on some of my dad's bougie cologne before she got to the crib that day. She said I smelled good. She was always looking good and smelling pretty too. I didn't bother being all extra with Terrell, since we always played ball and was gonna get sweaty anyway. And apparently, he likes my funk, 'cause once when we was snuggled up in his room, he put his face in my armpit, which was ticklish, and then he breathed really deep and said it smelled really good, which had me rolling, dying, 'cause I ain't understand how he like my mustiness, but he really did.

The sky was getting darker with clouds as we walked, which made it feel later than it was. I could smell the storm in the breeze, and it was making me feel tingly all over. And being next to Jada was making me even more tingly. Then she comes out the blue and says, "When I first met you, I wasn't sure if you liked girls or boys. Especially 'cause I would see you in school with Ursa," she said, glancing over at me while she strolled forward with her sexy swag I wish I had.

I didn't know what to say, so I just said, "Oh." I guess me and Ursa hung out a lot. I wondered what about us hanging out made her wonder, though. We kept walking for a little bit and I was quiet.

"Did that offend you?" she asked. I thought for a second and realized I was more surprised by it, but I couldn't think of why I should be offended. Then I remember the raindrops started coming down slow, and one by one. A drop on my eyebrow, then my shoulder, then I see one on the sidewalk drop and then more polka-dotting the gray. And then another, was a cool wetness on my cheek.

"I'm not offended. You was just saying what you thought," I said. "Terrell is my first boyfriend. Most people had they first boyfriend or girlfriend in junior high, but I just wasn't into that then. I guess I just be doing me," I said, and feeling a tingle run through me every time her arm brushed mine.

Jada was quiet, just listening.

"We used to play ball all the time last year and I ain't even know he was liking me until a couple of months ago," I said.

Which was for real. We was playing ball, a lot. A lot, a lot I guess. We would ball real good together actually. He is competitive like me but I be more focused and aggressive. Terrell, though, he play ball in a pretty way, like he is dancing and flying with a ball attached to his fingertips. He told me that he likes strong women, not girly girls and I was like, cool, whatever. And then one day he asked if he could hold my hand when we walked home, and it was actually kind of nice to hold his hand, although a bit of a shock too. After that we kinda just started going together. That's when we started fooling around and making out and stuff.

"When y'all started dating, I thought that was cute," Jada said as we cut through the woods and along the creek right by her house. The trees and their leaves above us were being tapped by the rain as it came down. Then out of nowhere, Jada stopped by the creek and closed her eyes. Just all of a sudden. It was just us down there and she looked so beautiful in the woods. Her extension braids looked like the vines and branches all around us. I lowered my lids to match her, to see if I could figure what she was feeling.

Next thing I felt was her arms around me and they pulled me close, which startled me, and I peeked at her a little. She was just there, eyes closed and looking sweet and pretty. And smiling a little, while my heart was beating so fast feeling her that close to me. Her chest was tied to my chest, her stomach against mine, our thighs become one tree holding us together. I slowly let myself relax into her and circle my arms down by her waist. I felt her heartbeat, and my heart was beating even faster. I started to shake a little. I closed my eyes again. Then the sky rumbled so loud I could feel it in the ground, rise up, and vibrate in us. The rain started to come down full—real sweet and fat, juicy drops. Even though we was getting saturated, we just stayed there holding each other.

"I love the rain," she said, and we were breathing and being with each other, letting the warm water from the sky surround us as we were wrapped up in each other.

As sudden as it started, Jada unraveled slowly from our hug, and I was unraveled too. She checked her phone and then kept walking to her house, and the rain kept raining. The spell broke all of a sudden.

We never mentioned anything about that day. It was kinda

like it never happened. And we didn't really hang out after that either. We texted every once in a while, but something wasn't the same. I wondered if she thought I was too into that hug in the woods or something. Maybe I was. I ended up breaking up with Terrell too.

And now, like a loser, I'm remembering the rain and our bodies being close like that. My body wants to feel her. Under all of my blankets, I touch myself, thinking of her and that walk in the woods. My fingertips graze over my tank top, making circles on my nipples, thinking of how good it felt to have her chest on mine and her face leaned on my cheek, how good she smelled. I slide my hands down under into my boxers and feel myself. I touch my little button softly, pulsing my hips into my hand, and breathe hard. My whole body gets warm and I start to moan, until it feels so good, my whole body overflows. Then everything feels quiet and gentle.

I lift the blankets off my head and feel the air in my room cool down my face. When my eyes focus, Whitney is on the wall smiling at me. Her eyeshadow is bright and all majestic. Her eyes holding no judgment.

I pull up my boxers, pull down my tank top, and get up and walk to my window. I open it up and slide down to sit on the roof of the kitchen. I look at the sky over Black Eden, and the stars are poppin' and the moon is looking like an almost-closed eye, an almost-eaten slice of honeydew. It makes me remember one time my mama telling my daddy the name Black Eden is redundant since the first Eden was Black already. I remember my daddy giggled and nodded at the truth of it, but then took a moment to think like he usually do before he talk. "Of course, you right, Coco. It's just that most people don't know or—better yet—they try to forget that the first Eden was Black." Then he thought some more. "And don't you think Black Eden got a nice rang to it, baby?"

To me, I agree with him; it's true, it do sound nice. And at night it do look like the original garden. Magical and innocent.

MABEL

"HERE WE GO, yo, here we go, yo, so wuz, so wuz, so wuz the scenario?" is bumping loud as hell through the house, vibrating through the floors and shaking me out of sleep. My dad uses classic hip-hop as curriculum, proverb, reflection, and a practical tool in his fatherhood. Sometimes, I hate classic hip-hop.

It's his Saturday morning ritual to bump some wake-yo-ass-up music first thing in the a.m. to inspire his children to get started on their chores, ensuring that we will never ever grow up "trifling as hell." And his ass loves to clean and work, so he ain't trying to hear shit about our feelings. The only person allowed to ever sleep in late is my mother. She is an artist who can sing, dance, and act—or as she likes to say—"I'm a hustler, baby." She told me that early in her and my dad's relationship, she let him know that she don't play none of this crack-of-dawn ish and affirms her right to sleep in *errrrday*. We kids have no such sovereignty.

I'm still feeling sick and drained. Last night my belly was hurting and it still is, not as much though. I do feel like I can use some more sleep. I'm supposed to be helping my dad weed Black

Eden right now, but I just ain't feeling it, which matters none to him. It's his pride and joy, that garden, but I could think of better things to do on a Saturday morning. Or a Wednesday night. Or a Sunday afternoon.

My mama's Saturday morning contribution is making a bomb brunch when she finally wakes up. Brunch is my mama's only religion. And she *will* testify. "Listen, brunch is the best meal, straight up, hands down. No. Other. Contenders. Let me tell you sumthin'." (She will often start a sermon mid-meal.) "You just got so much to choose from. You got pancakes AND waffles AND French toast. And if you feeling bougie, a fluffy and moist frittata or quiche. AND of course you got real grown-folks drank—mimosas, Bellinis. Something to sip to get you riiiiiight!" She's feelin' herself, so she keeps right on going with her menu. "Then you got tofu scrambles and veggie bacon, turkey bacon, vegan sausage patties, ya heard? AND fruit salads and hash browns. I don't think you heard me. I said HASH BROWNS. And if that ain't for you, come get you some home fries, homie!" And then she takes it on home. "But it ain't just the food. It's the luxuriation of eating it! You can just kick back and eat it all day. Like I said, brunch is the best, I don't care what no one say."

She usually invites us in to her feast after we been in Black Eden for hours sweating and picking in the fields, some days family and friends will come by to eat and hang out as well.

"Mabel, you up, sweet pea? Let's knock it out before it get too hot, girl. Then you can chill all day." I hear my dad directly outside my door.

"Give me a second, Dad!" Sigh. I ain't feel like it today. Like, for real, for real. But whatever, I know after a couple of minutes out there with him I'll be into it. That's always how it is. Also, I was able to negotiate a recent increase in allowance, so thinking 'bout my money is motivating a playa too. I find some energy from somewhere, and I slowly get up and throw on a T-shirt, cut-off jeans, and my raggedy, duct-taped gardening sneakers. The only time he don't fuss at what I got on is when we gardening. Otherwise, he always got feelings about my clothes. He told me once, I need to stop wearing his hand-me-downs and wear stuff for a "young woman my age." Like he even know. My mom told him to shut it up, that it's my body. She don't be caring how I dress; even if she don't get my style she finally has stopped trying to give me her old floral hippie dresses.

Honestly, I have always wanted to be like my dad and it used to be cool, but now that he got Sahir and I got titties, he is switchin' up on me. I still wanna be like him, though. He is a smart dude, who always reading or gardening at the crib. He works hard for the gas company, fixing boilers and stuff. He loves us like crazy. My mom will go off on rants about something little, and he will listen and respond gently, even if she is the one kinda trippin'. *And* his sneaker game is *soooo* tight. He got sneakers in every color for every occasion. My mom calls it his one real addiction. Either way, I don't need to be in lip gloss and tight jeans so he can feel like they raising me right.

I head to Black Eden. His garden oasis is an empty lot next door that he transformed when we first moved to this house when I was five. He had a vision for it, and him and my mom have made it happen, although gardening is certainly more his passion.

"They was thinkin' Obama was gonna magical Negro the end to racism. Shiiiit. As Mos said, 'Same shit, just remixed, different arrangement, put you on a yacht, but they won't call it a slave ship,' that's what should be taught in school, hunh, sweet pea?" He's workin' the earth loose with his hoe, while he's workin' his stream of thought. "That our conditions in this nation have been oriented toward our demise and disenfranchisement? It depresses me when I think about it. For real. Folks way smarter than me, still locked up over a little bit of weed or a bad decision. And be gone a minute too just robbed of life . . . Why you got me talking about this shit, again?"

"For my paper, Dad. I got a lot, so talk about something else, since you getting all in your feelings," I tease him, as I loosen the soil with my trowel around deep-rooted dandelions.

We been talking about the school-to-prison pipeline for my college-application writing sample the other day, and that's had him reflecting to his core ever since.

"Hmm. I know me and your mama got some books on that," he says, which I knew he was going to say, since they always got a book on everything. I roll my eyes on the inside and listen to him.

"Actually there is this one book written by a brother who was locked up. It's about prison life and is kind of almost a spiritual book. Something like 'Your melanin is from Black space.'" He twists his beard as he tries to remember. "It ain't that, but it's like that. He was really deep, all into ancient cultures and astrology too. That was a book that everyone was reading back in the nineties. Dang, what was the name of that brother? Amun? No . . . Afua, or something like that. He breaks things down real deep. He got death row for allegedly killing his best friend and a cop, but he's always maintained his innocence. I think it would be good for you to read for this project," he concludes, and I make a note of it, although I probably won't read it. I feel bad because I almost never read any of my dad's book recommendations. They just always seem like more education then recreation. I'd rather read my mom's science fiction—or her Zane romance novels, low-key.

Dad's harvesting the collards and kale, and I'm pulling dandelions from the same patch. He got a big straw hat and overalls with a tank top and some old Timbs. He dark like me and got dimples like me. Otherwise, he has a shaved head and a big beard, and he's real built too. Like a swole Rick Ross. I drop the dandelion roots in a basket. After I weed the dandelions, I'm going to pick strawberries for the shortcake my mom is making tonight for his friend, Uncle Sunny, and his long-lost Caribbean daughter, Audre.

"Apparently, Sunny's girl was really all into 'the Lordt' for a while, which I knew had Sunny tripping, since he meditating now." Dad told us last night after he first heard from his friend. "But I remember, before he find Buddha and got saved, he dabbled with the Five-Percenters in the nineties for a good little hot second. Oh, yep, and even a stint with them Twelve Tribes cats in them Earth, Wind and Fire costumes. I'll never let him forget that." He just shook his head at the memory. "He always was seeking, though, and maybe she get that interest in the spiritual life from him."

Dad giggles again, thinking about his best friend, who I have known most my life. "Me and your mama be telling him, raising y'all generation is some new stuff—a journey. I don't know, maybe there is a reason they gonna live together now and I know he'll do his thing, even if it's out the blue. And either way, me and your mama got his back," he says, taking a moment to drink a sip of water, with sprigs of mint from a big mason jar near him. He passes it to me. The sweat is flowing down his face and he wipes it with his handkerchief. He look like he from the country for real and not the North Side hood.

"What's up with Terrell? You ain't had him over in forever. He working this summer?" my dad asks, trying to be casual and yet still managing to be extra obvious. I realize I ain't really explain the breakup. Or even mention it. I liked Terrell for the most part, especially playing ball with him, talking with him, and chilling with him. And I love his mama, who was really nice to me. I even liked snuggling on his bed with him, but kissing on him just felt like too much, and then touching his junk . . . it made him happy but wasn't really my thing. He wanted me to and I tried it out, but just was more into snuggling with him instead. He is still a homie, but I ain't want to be his girlfriend. And since we broke up he done already booed up with this girl, LaTanza, so Terrell gon' be aight.

"Terrell is cool. He looking at colleges. We broke up," I say, hoping he will just leave it at that. But he don't. He was quiet for a second.

"Oh, that's too bad. I thought y'all was cute." And this is where I roll my eyes into my head, hard as hell, and my dad chuckles, thinking I'm playing. I ignore him and get back to the dirt.

My body still isn't feeling much better, but the fresh morning air is soothing, I ain't gonna lie. It's early but getting hotter. August is my favorite time of summer, when everything is alive and ready to eat. The garden is peaceful. My trowel slides down the spine of the dandelion root, and I know how to do it just right to get the whole root out, like a femur in that game Operation. (My mom dries the roots for tea. She always doing weird things like keeping and drying weeds. She says they are medicine, that they heal the blood or whatever. I don't care; as long as she puts mad maple syrup in it, I'll drink it with some ice.)

Harvesting and weeding is the one chore I actually don't mind. Feeling the dirt in my fingers feels natural to me. I like when it is sunny and the earth is dark like this. It's weird but sometimes, when the heat is on my skin and my hand is in the dirt, it makes me feel all fluttery and sexy, like when me and Jada was kicking it. I know, that shit is weird.

All of a sudden the ickiness I was feeling before turns into a big wave of I'm-finna-throw-up. I realize my dad is talking to me, but I can barely hear him over the noise of my body.

"Hunh, Dad?"

"You think you can hang with Sunny's girl today after dinner?"

"Fah sho, I'll kick it." I don't know why I feel so wack. "Hey, Dad, I really don't feel well. I can come back out later, but Imma go lie down," I say, getting up and feeling even more sick. He starts to look worried.

"Girl, I hope you ain't got the flu. Head up to bed and I'll ask your mama to make you some of her special tea," he says, picking up the baskets and following me into the house. My dad think my mama's teas fix everything. And they mostly do.

I feel weak as hell, but I manage to make it upstairs. I'm not sure if it's my period. I feel like I'm always starting or getting done with that thing. I sit on my bed for a second, wondering if I should be near the toilet in case I actually do throw up. I look down at my feet and focus on the words I have scribbled on the white rubber part of my Chucks. One says, "It's not right," and the other one says, "But it's okay." Whitney's words always soothe me. After a moment, the icky feeling inside subsides. In a little bit, my mama and dad bring me up some water and tea.

My mom is in her silk robe and silk headscarf, and her eyes still sleepy, but concerned. "Your daddy said you ain't feeling good, baby?" she asks, sitting on my bed, feeling my neck and forehead.

"Just my stomach and feeling a little weak. I'll be aight though," I tell her. She look all in my eye to see if she believe me.

"You look like you in pain," says my dad. He's sounding worried, even though I'm saying I feel okay. My mom's one eyebrow is still up high, not convinced.

"Mm-hmm. Okay, get some rest, girl. Imma head back to sleep, but just call me if you need me though. Okay? I'll check in with you when I wake up for real. Love you, baby," she says and they leave the room.

As I lay down in my bed, I close my eyes. I hum a song and feel my body relax.

"It's not right, but it's okay. I'm gonna make it anyway." Whitney's lyrics become a chant that I use to distract myself from the pain I'm feeling.

I lie in the darkness behind my eyelids. All of a sudden I think of my mom. I start remembering once when I was seven and got sick. She took off from work, and made me chicken soup with carrots, herbs, and dumplings. Afterward, she lay with me in my bed and we watched cartoons and we sipped hot fresh lemon-and-honey tea. It's one of my favorite memories. I start thinking about Whitney and wonder who she was thinking about when she was singing that song.

AUDRE

TWO WEEKS AGO, Queenie, my mom, and Episode dropped me to the airport to leave for Minneapolis. I was trying my best not to cry and to act strong. But Epi was crying hard, like someone thief he puppy. And I kinda is he puppy, following him around since we little. We always been close. He more like my big brother than cousin, and even though he six years older, he never talk down to me. He felt sad I ain't feel I could tell him I love someone. He was pissed when he hear how my mom act about Neri and ain't understand why I was being sent off for "dis lesbian ting," that it was my business. He even tried to change my mama's mind, for I to stay with he and Sarya, even though I begged him not to, in case she do anything worse. But she ain't cared about anything he said since she think he one of the reasons I "fall astray."

I hugged my mama goodbye first. To get it over with, to be true. She did a prayer with me, which I ain't want and gave me the book of psalms, that I also really ain't want. I thank she. Next, I hugged Epi. His dreads was wrapped up high in a light-blue fabric, his skin gingery and gold. And when he hugged me and picked me up, his face was hot and wet me up with tears. He gave me a book on vegan cooking and another one on color therapy. "Sarya and I find dat for you, for da States, since we know you like all a dem healing type a ting. I love you, cuzzo. Whatever you need, eh? Respect."

Queenie was bawling too. "I ain't even saying bye. I love you, and I is in every breeze you feel and you is right here," she say, squeezing me to she chest.

On the plane, I was a mess on the inside, holding back tears so hard, my chest and stomach began to hurt. Finally, I erupted in sobbing. I looked out the window and I saw that I was rising up above the edges of trees and beyond the ocean of home. Next, we broke above the clouds and we was above the sky itself, flying away from Trinidad. *How am I going to make the trip, I feeling so busted up?* I was crying so hard that the business-looking man with a Grenadian accent in my aisle got concerned and called the flight attendant. She was pretty and had kindness in she eyes and asked me if I was okay. "Yes, I fine," I lied, and pulled my pain in.

The plane's bathroom was sterile and tight solitude. I sat on the steel and beige commode. I looked at my face in the mirror, the light burning white and cold. I waterfalled my sobs into the yellow handkerchief Queenie gave me. My face was puffed up and sad and red, and I felt stchupid and ugly and alone. Hopeless. I think of Neri and how even though she only knew me a little while, she always knew how to make me feel okay. I thought of her singing to me and how it sound with the ocean waves and the leaves shakin' in breeze. I thought of her and Queenie, and I grounded myself in her and Queenie's distant love. I breathed deep and deep and deep. I placed my hand at my chest to feel the lump of my new divine pouch. In the mirror, I looked into my own eyes again and I saw a piece of lightning and hurricane look back into me.

I returned to my seat by the window, still crying quietly, but it a gentle drip now. Most people are asleep. I pushed up the window shade and I saw the majesty of the night. The moon was real fat and luscious in its light. Full and shining on the clouds that looked like an ocean of slow-moving silvery and milky waves. I remembered what Queenie taught me and thought of Obatala for ancient wisdom and soulful peace and something in me started to feel tenderized and calm. I thought of Yemanja and being rocked and held in her depths. I thought of Queenie's words, "Spirit is everywhere," and I saw it in the ocean and beach made from night and moon and sky and stars.

By the time I reached Minneapolis to reunite with my father, something in me was feeling a little less break up. I smiled and tried to look like I ain't too bad a mess inside of me.

Since I been here two weeks, I still ain't feel comfortable at all and don't think I ever will or even want to. One thing that is real good about my father, though, is that he leave me be, unlike my mother, who was always findin' a reason to mess and fuss with me. I'm in my new American bedroom that used to be my father's roommate's room and then he "stuff" room (which must be an American thing) and now it's my room. The walls are a light shade of blue-green—for the ocean he say—which he painted right before I came. The walls are bare, except for one painting of a pretty, brown-skinned girl on a black-velvet canvas in a carved wooden frame. He got it at the thrift store, and he said he thought I might like it. I wondered to myself how he figure what I like, since he and I ain't know each other that good. Yet, even so, I do kinda love the picture. It remind of something Queenie would paint. The oil paint on the blackness. It look like the girl is emerging wet from night, her expression is looking past and beyond and still not seeing. She the closest thing to a friend I have in America.

I hear my dad outside the door before I hear him knock, and I is a lil' bit dreading talking to him. He ain't know me and I ain't really know him, and every time we talk, I ain't know what he want to hear from me. Most adults I know want you to say just the right thing to them, in just the right way, so they can love you. Everyone, except Queenie. I answer the door, pretending like I was sleeping to shorten the discussion. He is there in a brown-and-blue dashiki with a necklace of wooden beads he uses for meditation. His dreads are down and hanging at his shoulders. His glasses look like the kind Malcolm X used to wear, and I bet that is why he wear them too. He is smiling.

"Yes?" I say, trying to look and sound tired, so he get the hint.

"Audre, I made you a vegan sandwich."

Steupse, I think inside myself.

"I tried a recipe I found online." He shifts his weight like he's uncomfortable too. "It's like a tofu, spinach, avocado thing? I added some of my own additional seasonings and barbecue sauce to give it that soul-food kick and round out the flavor."

Round out the flavor of disgusting? I think to myself. He always insist on adding his "own additional seasonings" on everything and I ain't know who tell he to do that.

"Thank you. I ain't hungry now, but I appreciate it," I say, trying to sound grateful and conceal attitude, which is not one of my strengths. I ain't know how many times I tell him I ain't hungry, and if I is, I know how to cook for myself. But he insists on making food for me like I ain't survive the last sixteen years without his confused cooking.

"You sure you ain't a little hungry? I know my cooking been hit and miss, but I feel like this sandwich will redeem me."

I trying to think of a polite way to slink out of this one.

"Yes, it sound real good, but I is sleepy. I'll eat it later." Which is Audre-speak for I will wait until late at night when he sleep and throw it away in the trash. So far he ain't catch on.

"Audre, we gonna get out the house today, okay, baby?" he says. "Remember my friends, Sequan and Coco, who have the girl your age, Mabel? And a little boy too, Sahir? You and Mabel got along last time you was up here. They invited us over for dinner, and they can cook way better than me. All stuff from his garden. I told them you eat vegan like a rasta," he says. "I think it may be nice for you to talk and hang out with Mabel. She go to the same school you gonna be at," he said, looking me in the eye and pleading ever so slightly.

This was the closest thing to a parental demand he has given since I reach the States. (I refuse all the other outings so I could cry alone in my room.) Besides the natural food store, I been in this room with the velvet girl and he been avoiding disrupting my solitude, except to occasionally attempt to poison me with his culinary experiments.

"Sure," I say, not having a good reason prepared for any other response.

His face lights up a little and he seems satisfied. "Glad to hear this, yes! I think it'll be nice."

"Sure, mm-hmm," pulling the tiredness in my voice in order to wrap things up and he starts to stare at me and giggle a little. "What's funny?" I ask him, curious in spite of my desire to be back into my bed.

"Oh, nothing. Well, I mean . . . I can't believe you are here sometimes. It felt out of the blue, but also like an answer to prayer." I see his eyes start to well up, and he pulls out a handkerchief and dabs his eyes beneath his glasses, and he starts to really cry. "You're almost an adult and I've always wished that I could know you—have you live with me. I'd even written it down and meditated on it. And then your mother called. It is like something in me knew you would be here . . ." He takes a deep breath. "Don't mind your father and his tears. Always been an emotional cat. Just happy that you're here. I know I say this a lot, but I mean it: Let me know whatever you need." He finishes his little speech, and I can't help but feel a little something in my chest. I ain't know if it's sadness or anger, I just feeling my chest doing something.

My whole life he been "my American father." A lot of visits when I was younger, Christmas and birthday gifts in the mail, and phone calls, cards, and letters. My mom would send him a picture of me from school and I would write him little kiddy letters. He was like a personal tooth fairy or a Yankee Santa. I used to come and visit for two weeks every other year, and he would come down for a couple of weeks on the years in between, and we would hang at the beach and go to the zoo by the Savannah, but that arrangement started to shift when my mom started with Rupert and the church.

I know my father somewhat, but I ain't know him too. And for sure he ain't really know me, even if he happy I is here with him.

"Thank you," I say, not knowing what to say, because in truth, I ain't want to be here in his home, in his country, no matter how he feeling. But I don't want to hurt he feelings either.

"It's aight. Thank you, Audre. I know you adjusting. Your mom and I would talk over the years of you coming up here and getting to know your Black American side more, but I don't know . . . It never seemed to be a good time to take you from what you knew and the culture you was being raised in with your mother and grandmother. Then I got the call"—he smiles at me and fiddles with the long loop of beads around his neck—"I guess she decided sixteen was finally old enough."

I know better, I think to myself. I know my mother and I know she ain't tell him the whole story as to why she change her mind about me living with him, and for that, I'm grateful. I ain't need he in my business since he ain't really been so most of my life. One thing about my mama is she got pride. She believe she do good without him in our lives. Maybe that idea was change by the fact that I shame she in church and to she friends. He think she all of a sudden want me to know him and for that he is either stchupid or he ain't really know she. It's actually hard to imagine my parents as a couple. I feel like I'm the only proof of their union.

I decide to give a good yawn to officially send him on his way.

He tells me he'll come wake me up at three and then walks away. I close the door. I stand and look at the velvet girl, who looks beyond me. I sit on my bed. Then, I get up and look out the window. It's actually beautiful out: The trees are big next to my window, and the sky is blue and with clouds moving by. I see a squirrel squeeze around the tree, pause for a second, and then another squirrel come up and they chase each other away up into the branches. I sit down on my bed again. I lean over and grab under my pillow for my new pouch. This one is dark-purple leather, like a melongene, on the outside and on the inside, a bright fuchsia like hibiscus. It has cowries sewn onto it carefully with dark green thread. I feel the weight of it in my hand and think of Queenie. And then Neri. I put it around my neck and under my dress.

I fold myself on the bed and I feeling empty and weightless. Like I not even there. I don't know where I am, but I do. I'm in my father's house in the United States of America. Yet, I still feeling like I was just pluck up from the ground and thrown in the wind.

MABEL

"YOU EVER SEE SOMEONE FACE SO STCHUPID, you want to smack the stchupid off, but then you 'fraid they gone get they stchupidness on you? Dat's me stepdad, no doubt. Me mudda definitely got he stchupidness on she self. . . . I don't want to talk about dem," says Audre.

I'm in the prettiest garden in the North Side with a girl who talk so pretty she has me feeling like I can hear melodies in her voice. She seems hella intense but a little chill or maybe shy? I don't know. I am still a little groggy from sleeping most of the day.

Against all this green, Audre is cocoa wrapped in a light-purple dress with skinny straps that keep sliding down her shoulders, her booty a pillow on the earth in the midst of it all. She also has these superthick glasses with brown rims that had to be circa 1988 but still made her seem like she saw into your soul. And was unimpressed.

She just moved up from Trinidad due to some drama with her

mama. She don't want to talk about it, I do know that. And apparently from what my dad knows, she is also deep in the church too, so I watch my mouth.

Well, mostly I watch her mouth.

And I don't know why, but I was really excited to see her. We met once when she was visiting from Trinidad when we was both eleven. I took her to the raspberry patch then too. She had never tasted any in her life. She had eaten soursop, chenette, sugar apple, pommecythere, guava, breadfruit, and all of these other Caribbean fruit I ain't never heard of and wrote down to memorize. But never a raspberry, which are basically my main ish.

That day, she ate so many raspberries that she got sick and had the runs. She even had to go home, the diarrhea got so real for her. But she wasn't even embarrassed. I remember her sitting in her father's back seat, like a fallen soldier with a spattering of raspberry wounds all over her dress, and a smile on her face. She was muttering she would do it all again as the car drove off. I think I liked her since then. She was the perfect reckless.

For this evening's occasion, I'm in my dad's Notorious B.I.G. shirt from the nineties that I made him give to me (he got like fifteen of them anyway). It's faded with a couple of holes worn through but you can still see Biggie in a suit and hat and it says, "It was all a dream." I've got my favorite (and lucky) light-pink sports bra, as always in a tomboy mood.

"Mm-mmm . . . I ain't eat these in so long." Audre is now on her knees, leaning into the patch of raspberries (low-key greedy but high-key cute), picking them, and placing one on each of her fingertips. Once a berry crowned every single tip, she methodically ate each one off a digit. It's the most tedious way to eat raspberries, and yet I'm mesmerized. As she eats the berries, I see tears behind her frames, sliding down her cheeks. Audre is crying. Tight and deep to herself. I feel a stillness and an echo within me, like I am feeling her thoughts in my body. "And I ain't sayin' nuttin', 'cause I know if I say somethin', I is gon' say somethin' get me in rell big trouble and everything I manage to say is punishment." Her little Afro glistened in the summer light and greenery. And I ain't hearing it; I'm actually feeling it and I have no idea who she is talking to or about.

I see the gap in her teeth through her lips and suddenly I feel like I'm lost through the space of it, feeling her intensely. Her voice feels almost like trance, and life and earth closed tight around us. We are within our own force, like a heavy dusk holding us. Everything she says lands in me, hot and tingling.

"She always saying tings like dat, like I ain't have me own mind, like when I go natural. She telling me I following a trend, when I say I ain't wan' kill my hair wit' white man chemicals. You see we hair like going to de cosmos?" I feel her tears flowing, her face contorted in pain, justifying herself to what I assume is her invisible mother. And I was feeling sensations all over me in relation to her breath.

"Wha' happen wit' ya, girl? You ain't saying nuttin'," she ask, and wiping her face as though nothing even happened.

I was shook. I don't know how to understand the vortex her tears took me into. I felt like I was being pulled into her, sitting within her. Sorrow. I'm stunned and low-key feeling thrown off about what I just experienced. I don't know what to do, so I brush it off.

"I'm just chillin' . . . ," I say, scratching a mosquito bite on the back of my thigh.

Taking a break from her raspberry ritual, she props herself up on her hands and extends her head back with her neck toward the sky. She looks like she was replenishing her throat with words to sing. Her legs look more womanly then my skinny-ass calves. She fans them out beyond her skirt, exposing her knees. Her feet look rough but in a way that made them look strong, like they never learned the need for shoes.

"You wanna go for a walk to the park before it gets dark?" I ask her. With a mouth full of berries, she mumbles that she is down. She grabs her books and we bounce.

Audre is sitting up looking at my favorite lake on the planet, and I'm wondering if she is thinking of the ocean.

"You like being here so far?" I ask.

"I hate America," she deadpans, then collapses completely on her back, staring at the sky.

"Why?" Not that a Black girl ever needs to give a reason as to why America don't get no respect.

"Why ya tink? 'Cause it's pure Babylon, full of lies and run by devils. And it cold. No good mangoes. No ocean, no vibes. I miss the *food*. And meh dad can't cook at all. No, excuse me. At *fucking* all," she musters from on her back, irritation and sadness croaking in her throat.

I gasp, shocked to hear this church girl curse—and curse like a mutha-fuckin' champ. She kicks off her sandals and the right one flings high and lands near some ducks at the edge of the water. They squawk and waddle away all stank.

"The last thing I need to do is come to America and get skinny like Taylor and Becky, dem." Audre lifts her arms up over her head and I see that she has the full baby Afro growing from her armpit. That must be some Rasta ish, 'cause most girls here don't let their pit hair grow like that, but still, weirdly, something in me feels something. Something bottomless, like a good feeling. Sigh. Her underarm is sweet-smelling funk and got me shook.

"I can cook for you," I say, before I can remember I don't really know how to cook. She slowly looks over at me and then smiles, like she ain't sure about my skills.

"I mean, I love to help cook and maybe we can make some of the foods you miss from Trinidad. What you eat there?" I ask, raking my fingers through the long grass we were chilling in.

"Roti, doubles, pelau, pumpkin, callaloo . . . ," she says with her eyes closed in yummy reminiscing. Then she sucked her back teeth with frustration. "Steupse, man, I ain't even want to think about it, yuh see? I miss it bad! I been eating more Ital lately."

"Eat all?"

"I-T-A-L, Ital."

"What is that?"

"It's da way de rasta people eat. Just clean, it de best food. It give you life. Me cousin Epi is a rasta and he de best chef, next to me grandma Queenie of course. He food taste like pure love from de earth. He tell me, 'Yuh food should be yuh medicine,' and he right. Queenie feel that way too."

"What's Ital like?" I ask.

"No animal nuttin', everyting clean from the earth. Fresh. Ital stew, lentil loaf, green salads, smoothies, fresh juices. You would like it," Audre says, her eyes excited behind her glasses while she twirled her fingers in her hair, her whole mood seems to shift.

"Let's make somethin' tomorrow! Can you come through?" I blurt out, suddenly thirsty, like her excitement changed my whole body. We agree to meet up the next day after her dad takes her to register for school in the morning.

That night, I lay in bed. Audre is on my mind. Real hard.

She was another molasses altogether. She was sweetness, but also slightly bitter and slowly dark. And I could tell nerdy AF. She came to the crib with two books and a journal—I guess in case she may have to entertain herself if I was goofy or something. Neither were Bibles though, just a vegan cookbook and a color healing book, which sounded dope whatever it was.

I whisper to myself, and it feels good on my lips. Delicious and dark with a chew at the end. Aww-Jreeeeee. Pretty and slow. The moment she came in. Warm rain in a lightning storm. Soft and dangerous. Even thinking of her I feel something sweet in the world find its way to my heart. I wonder about her skin and if she would feel as smooth as it seemed to promise.

AUDRE

"SO THEN I GO BY YUH TANTIE to see if she all right, 'cause she been complaining about she knee, that she ain't been sleeping good, she diabetes is acting up and this and that. I tell she, lemme come over there and bring you some of these herbs that will fix you good, help you get your blood better and feel to get up and move so. She say she ain't want to be shitting all day like the last time I take care of she. And I say well, Daphne, you prefer the shit in or the shit out?" says Queenie over the phone, talking about her sister in Trinidad as I lie listening to her on my bed in Minneapolis, staring at my ceiling.

"Let yuh body rest, eh? Purge it out. I tellin' she to heal she self through she food. Them doctors will put all kind of chemicals in your body before they tell you to go drink a coconut, sit under the sun by the sea, watch the water, and cry. Or grow and fix yuh own food. But she go to the States for all them years and is brainwash and only trust them doctors and they stchupidness. She knew how we grandmother, from Saint Vincent, used to heal everyone with bush and ting and now she seem she is forgettin'." Queenie sighs. My grandma is a respected healer to people from all over T & T. She sisters seldom consult her for she healing wisdom, much to her frustration.

We been talking every couple days on WhatsApp, like I used to talk to my dad when I was in Trinidad. Hearing she talk—even if it's about she fussing with she sister—make me feel peace, like I home. I imagine she with her phone on speaker (she say the cell phone melting everyone brain) sitting in she backyard eating mango she pick from she own tree, wiping the juice from her chin as she buzzes on about Tantie Daphne. I miss mangoes from home, especially the sweet julies that is better than candy.

Queenie always tells me that, if need be, she could live forever on she land and survive off the food she eats—and eat like a queen too.

"You hear anything 'bout Neri?" I ask Queenie after we check in about she day and mine. She steupse and then breathe out long.

"Yuh tink I woulda hear something and go on about Daph and we ol' woman ting, like I dotish and ain't have no sense? It woulda been the first ting hot out my mouth, gyal! I ain't hearing a ting and you know I always listenin' for tings . . ." I hear an engine drive up to she house. "Oh, guuushh, hold on, baby, here come Larry to pick up some of my kombucha. I make a real nice sorrel-guava-cinnamon one," she says, and puts me on hold. I hear a deep and distant voice talking with her. "It on the porch there, Larry. Yes, see she name on it? Uh-huh . . . Oh-ho . . . Eh-eh. Mm-hmm . . . Well, nuh. Tell yuh mummy I call she later, I talking with my grandchile in the States," then she's back in conversation with me.

"I sorry, baby, I wish I had some news." Then she pause for a second and with excitement she share a next idea. "Maybe is there an app or one of dem tings from the internet to help you find people in y'all age? What about dat bookface thing you put me on for finding people, where I speak to my cousin in Toronto? You think you can find Neri there?" Queenie offers this idea thinking she uncover some hope for me.

I tell she, "I already looked just in case, but I feel that she wouldn't be allowed to be on social media. I just want to know if she fine." I been online searching her name and trying to figure out where she is in Tobago. I ain't even know if she have an email. Next thing I know tears is coming. "I get scared, 'cause I have no idea how she life is like, Queenie. A-a-a-and as 'fraid as I was to come to the States and live with my dad, it ain't been bad, but Queenie, I ain't know how she being treated," I say, my throat thickening with each word. Queenie is quiet and let me cry and then start to tenderize me.

"She is okay, baby. Try and not worry, okay? You talk to she anyway, you hear? Just talk to she in the trees, in the breeze, send her love. She will receive it, my baby. And you know I will discover what going on, I always do. Stay strong, my dahlin'." I almost feel Queenie is there with me, she love shooting from the phone all the way from Trinidad. She says this every time, and yet, my heart still hurtin' and feelin' low.

"What happening with you today? What the weather like?" she asks to be lighthearted, I can tell. I get up and look out the window and it's a little gray, but I can't tell if it going to rain or not, I can't read the sky like home. The window is open and it feels warm and wet in the air.

"We just registered me for school this morning. Weather is okay. It's gray but it warm too," I say, leaning into the window's opening and tasting the texture of the air on my face.

"You staying inside, then?"

I pull back from the window and lay back on my bed. "No, I is hanging with Mabel, my dad's friend's daughter. We had dinner at their house yesterday."

"They cook better than yuh father, I hope? The way you talk is like he Chef Boy-a-Grief!" My grandma always know how to bust a joke on someone.

"No, nothing like he, thank Goddess! It real good, actually. It was tasty food all from their garden and no animal, nothing. Roasted beets and sweet potatoes, a Brussel-sprout-and-kale salad with pistachios, I think? And then also some black-eyed-pea fritters with a good spicy and sweet sauce, which remind me of something Epi would make. And the daughter who is my age—Mabel—is cool. We talked about school."

"Eh-eh . . . well you sound like you having a good time there, it seem." Her voice lilts in a way that seem to say she hopeful for me.

"It better than being inside home all day," I say, not ready to give up completely on being miserable.

"Yes, well, that's good, nuh? You been up in that house like you hiding from the damn law, gyal. I know yuh feelin' sad, but you must get your bum bum out and see where you is living. My man Prince from there, so it must have some hotness to it." I roll my eyes since she mentions Prince every time we talk like I forget the Purple One from here. "Go be in nature, ground in Spirit and your purpose and lessons for there. Try to enjoy what you can, okay, my baby?"

I take off the glasses that were once hers and wipe my eyes with the corner of my shirt. I take a breath and clear my throat.

"Yes, Queenie, I is. We gonna lime by she house and then I don't know. What plans you have for your day?" I ask, more to be polite, because it hurts me to think of her life in Trinidad going on without me. Between missing Neri, Epi, my grandma, the ocean, and the island itself, I feel heartbroken and exiled in America. And alone. She say she working in the garden, then she going out to Queen Masani Bay by Las Cuevas to lime with she sisters, Tantie Daphne and Tantie Pearl.

I feeling tears cup up in my eyes again as I remember all the times I have been to the beach with them as they laughing and gossiping and teasing and fussing and steupsing at each other, all squeezed up in Queenie's convertible with the top down. Tantie Daphne in the front seat next to Queenie, sweaty and frustrated. The wind messing she hair and she is complaining about how low the car sit and how fast Queenie drive. "QUEENIE! Yuh act like we is late to give birth! Slow down, nuh? Let's arrive ALIVE, eh? And who de hell decide to get a convertible when ya almost blasted sixty?"

Tantie Pearl in the back with me and she already buzz, sipping on a big cup with straw with juice and rum. She whisper to me about how she never leave for the beach this late, and yell to Queenie if she can take off this old-time music and play some soca to get the party started.

"Can I listen to Stevie Wonder for once, Pearl, and you ain't talkin' about some soca?" And Queenie starts singing along loud to remind all whose car it is. My tantie Pearl steupse and is still treated like the baby sister by Queenie and Tantie Daphne. She think the best everything come from Trinidad, the best music, food, beaches, fetes, and men (yes, she say that), even though she ain't got nothing to compare it to.

I'm thinking of the smell of them all in the car, baby powder, oil, perfume, Florida water, warm skin, and perspiration. A party of wild women and a tagalong teenager. Tantie Pearl always ask if I have a boyfriend yet, since I pretty and my bum bum so big. I be in the back seat, deep in a book in my own world. All I have to reply is, "Books before boys, Tantie," which satisfies every adult in the car.

"Well, baby, have fun with ya new Yankee friend," says Queenie, snapping me out of my daydream. "I will tell yuh tanties to keep you in they heart and spirit."

I say goodbye to Queenie on the phone, asking her to tell everyone hi, not specifying my mother. I speak to my mother briefly when my dad was on the phone with her last week. I still ain't feel to say more.

My dad drops me off at Mabel's house at noon and gives me some cash. "In case you both decide you wanna go somewhere. If Uncle Sequan or Auntie Coco can't drive y'all, call me and I will. I'm home all day working." My dad smiles at me in that goofy but sweet way that he do. Despite he cooking, I like how he ain't ever tight up, like he always just got done puffing a spliff.

"Thank you." And I slip out his car and head to their house.

In truth, I feeling a little excited to be hanging with a friend. Mabel. I mean, I ain't know if she is really a friend yet. She may be just hanging with me because our fathers are friends and she dad is making she be nice. But she do seem really nice, even if she kind of mellow.

Mabel opened the door before I even ring the bell.

"What's good, Audre?" She lets me onto her porch, which has a big dark-green couch with pillows that are different sizes and shapes and shades of purple and lilac. There are plants and it smells really good. We sit on the couch together and look out the window. Mabel has jeans cut off at the knee and lace-up sneakers, and a T-shirt with no sleeves that say BLK LVRS. She hair was back in a low braid, really simple and pretty. I like she style, very cool, Black and edgy.

"This a nice porch. Very peaceful," I note as we step inside she home.

"This is one of my favorite places. I can always come out here and feel chill." We sit down on the couch and don't really talk much at first. We just quiet and sitting there for a while, and I feeling the wind move across me and slide the hot feeling from my skin.

"You hungry? Should we start cooking? I picked some things from our garden this morning," she says, playing with the fringe of her cutoffs. "Last night I was researching Ital and found some recipes."

I smile and say yes, feeling it was nice of her to learn about the way I eat. We walk into her house, and I take off my shoes at the entrance as is the custom in their home. We are standing in the tight hallway leading from the porch to the living room, when Mabel leans in, quietly speaking into my ear.

"Yo, Audre, so content warning: My mama is wearing booty shorts—or pum-pum shorts, whatever you call it—doing yoga in the backyard. She is very comfortable with herself and her body and all a that, so you been warned, fam." She giggles and shakes her head.

I smile at she funny words about she mom.

"Why you laughing? I'm serious!" She still giggling and walking me into the living room of the house, which has deep orange walls with a large framed painting that is colorful and abstract and other framed black-and-white photographs of beautiful and different-looking Black people. "I'm used to my mama's booty, but other people's mama's booties in the air can throw some people off. And my mama don't be caring, she an artist so she is real body positive and all a dat . . ." On a side table are pictures of their family. Her parents getting married. Her family dressed in all white in front of a garden. Sahir as a baby dressed as a bumblebee and Mabel as Missy Elliott. School pictures of Mabel, one with her missing teeth and her pigtails looking all crazy and another more recent one of her looking more like she looks now, a slight smile and an Outkast shirt. We walk into the bright yellow kitchen spilling with light.

"I just laughing 'cause my mother ain't like that at all," I say, looking around the space.

"My mom is different in a lot of ways, dope ways, though, I think. But she a free spirit, that's fah sho." Mabel tugs she shorts as they sagged below she waist. Mabel have a style that is boyish. It looks good on she though. I like that she is very laid back and smooth, which makes it easy to be around her. She looks me in the eye and I realize I been kind of staring at she and I look away.

"My mom definitely wouldn't even try yoga. If it ain't got to do with Jesus, she ain't interested." I remember how me mother was upset when Queenie first started taking yoga with Sarya, because she say Christ ain't "believe" in yoga. Sometimes, I really ain't understand how my mom come from Queenie, at all.

"Are you looking for a church community up here?" Mabel says, while leaning back on her kitchen counter.

"Church?" I say, wondering if she was joking.

"My dad said that I should ask you if you looking for a church, 'cause you was about that life in Trinidad or something," she say, and then I realize she is serious and trying to be helpful.

"I is cool for now on church. You does go to church?" I lean on the kitchen doorway as Neri cross past my heart for a second.

"Uhh . . . to be honest? Not really. Just a lil' bit, here and there. My parents kinda do a little bit of everything and don't really do Jesus all like that. I go to church every other year or so. Mainly, when my nana—aka my mama's mama—come from Chicago and presses my parents for us to learn about 'the Lordt.' My mama don't go, but my dad will take Gramma and us to this church his gardening mentor is a deacon at," she says. "It can be lit, when the choir sanging, I ain't gonna lie. Me and my daddy be jammin' up in there. You want me to get you the hookup?" She sway back and forth a little, pulling down pans and pots from above her head onto the counter. I think of the last day I was at church, the last day I see Neri, and I wonder what stories my mother tell my father about me and church all these months.

"I giving the church a break for a while." I barely able to respond because my heart hurting, remembering any of that type of thing.

"All good . . . SO! We got cabbage and okra. I went to the mercado down the street and got you some plantains and avocados, since they had it in a lot of the recipes," she say, bending into she fridge and emerging with the veggies.

"I love all them things—know how to make them real good too." On their counter is sweet potatoes, thyme, onions, garlic.

"Cool. Up here is all of the oils and spices and other stuff we may need," she says, opening a cupboard to the right side of her stove. "I'll do whatever you want. I'm not the best cook, but I'm a good helper." She smiles in a way that was both kind and earnest.

"I'm a good helper too; can I help?" says a little voice. Her little brother, a sweet little dumpling, with short dreads bouncing from his head and sneakers that light up as he walks, emerges from another room.

"Where your manners, homie?" She is teasing yet gentle to him, not really frustrated at all. "How do we treat guests? Remember Audre from last night? Show her some love, bro." She turns him toward me and he smile, a beautiful gap where two front teeth are missing.

"Excuse me. Hi, Audre. How are you? I like your hair." I give him a high five and he gives me a hug, which is real sweet. All three of us get to work. Mabel and I help Sahir measure the herbs and spices, and he cuts the okra with a butter knife.

"Oooh, what y'all girls up in here cooking?" says Coco, and she comes in from the garden with a yoga mat under she arm and smells our sautéing herbs and vegetables. "I know this ain't my daughter who hook all of this up." She Afro is out and she's wearing the promised pum-pum shorts on the big bum bum that Mabel spoke of. She comes by the stove to see the fried plantain, curry cabbage, and okra with coconut milk and nods her head in approval. "Audre come through with them Trini cooking skills, boy! Imma have to learn some of your recipes, love. Oooh, and y'all made limeade! So refreshing," she says, taking a sip from the glass in Mabel's hand without asking. "All right, sweetie, come by anytime!" Mabel shakes her head and giggles at her mama.

"Yes, I will." And I'm truly happy to be welcome. This was the most fun I had in weeks, just getting to be myself and cook food from back home. Also being with Mabel was real cool too.

"Sahir, come with me and let these big girls have time to themselves, all right, my baby."

"I'm big too, Mommy," says Sahir.

"I know, honey, but I need someone to hang out with too. I was gonna ride my bike to the lake and wanted a big kid to ride with—" Before she could finish, Sahir zooms out the kitchen to get his bike.

"All right, girls, have fun and leave me a little sumthin' sumthin' to try, okay?" she says, kissing Mabel on the cheek and smiling at us.

Mabel and I decide to take our steaming bowls back to the porch.

"I just started liking okra, like last year. Before, I used to think it felt too slimy in my mouth, but now I like it." Mabel eats each piece of okra slow and pensive.

I savor each bite, dipping my spoon in the corners of the bowl, meticulously collecting a piece of plantain and the stew from the coconut milk and cabbage in each bite. After a couple of nibbles I notice Mabel sit back in the couch, breathing deep and looking uncomfortable. "You all right??" I ask, wondering if she liked the food really or if she was just being polite. I place my bowl down on the floor and turn toward her.

"It is really good, actually. I just don't feel hungry sometimes, but what I don't eat now, I'll finish later," she says and places she bowl down on the floor next to mine. She bowl is nearly full, while mine was almost done.

"You sure you cool?"

"Yes, just not that hungry, I guess," she says, looking still a little uncomfortable. "How is it, living with Uncle Sunny? He seem like he would be real chill." She eyes and she question make me lose words for a second.

"Umm, well . . . It's okay. He is nice and is trying to make me feel comfortable. We is getting to know each other a little, I guess." And it's true. I start playing with the tassels on one of the couch pillows.

"Are you missing Trinidad a lot?" She curls toward me, hugging another pillow.

I take a deep breath and pause for a second, hoping I can answer she question without tears in my throat or out my eyes. "I miss Trini a lot. Mainly my grandma, Queenie, my cousins and aunties. And the beach." I think of Neri but don't name her. I ain't say my mom, since I don't even know if I miss she. She ain't seem to want me no more, especially now that she got Rupert and she new life.

"So was that stuff that went down with your mother—which you don't have to talk about—the reason you decided to come and live with your dad?" she asks, like I, a teenager, make decisions for my life, in my mother's home.

"It wasn't my decision. My mother decide for me to live with my dad," I say quick, and my eyes start to water. I get up off the couch and walk to the window to wipe them. I know I must seem stchupid, but I ain't know what else to do. How could I tell her my mom sent me away because I shame she? I can't imagine Ms.

Coco beating Mabel like a dog and sending she away. I start feelin' my familiar sadness spread through my body and anchor in my stomach.

"Hey, girl, I wasn't trying to be all up in your business. You don't have to talk about it. I was just trying to make conversation," she say, and stand up next to me and put her hand on my shoulder, a little shy, but I ain't mind it. We looking out the window together and just watching at life. Watching life quietly.

"You wanna pick some berries with me? I know you like them raspberries and we got so much, fam, and it's going to get out of season soon anyway. You should totally take some back for you and Uncle Sunny."

I nod my head, trying not to cry anymore like something is wrong with me. "Sure, I'll take some," I say at the offer of raspberries, and find a genuine smile creep up.

"Cool, Audre. And then you wanna roll to the mall? I wanted to hit up the shoe store. We can take the bus there, which you should know how to ride too. You down for that?" She looks at me with some shyness and hope. It is cute.

"Yes, I'm down. That would be nice," I say and turn to her and give she the best smile I can find in my sadness.

"Cool, I'll text my mom and let her know where we going."

We gather the dishes from the porch and bring them back inside, and the kitchen still smelling like we cooking.

VIRGO SEASON

in the body, temple of sacredness within our flesh and bone
the meticulousness of magic
the healing in the flowers and herbs
the toiling and the work
the grains of life, the harvesting of perfection
the healer and the need to heal

i unlayer the layers.
the wheat, the chaff, the stem
the harvest brings forth the elements
the ancestors of our work.
fine-tuned finesse
the clarity of our calculations
the quality of our hearth

wisdom moving through the pathways of the body
the brother who pays attention to every twitch
and movement of police and overseers
calculating the bales of cotton until escape
and he moonwalking like a seed underground to freedom

she the sharecropper in the fields
the protagonist in oppression's fairy tale
a deity, master of underworlds

she sugarcane fields and unemployment lines
she bussing yam to fufu
she tap-dancing what the drums used to say

toiling 'cause she understand the inherent
perfection of her existence is healer and the ancestors are trees
connected in roots growing towards stars

MABEL

"I'LL BE OUT HERE READING, baby girl, if they got any questions about your medical history or whatever . . ." He trails off. My dad and I are at the doctor's office for my annual physical. He gets so awkward for stuff he thinks my mama should be doing. Woman stuff. But she was at a voice-over gig, so he was on deck.

When we first got there, the office assistant was for sure flirting with him when he was giving my insurance information. Leaning over the counter, giggly and boobylicious and lip-gloss lipped and asking him about whether his wife usually brings me, which was just plain thirsty. And he still was oblivious, afraid she was gonna ask him about my period.

"I think I got this, Dad. I'm sixteen. Some kids my age got two kids by now, I can handle this," I tell him, and his face falls. I laugh and motion for him to sit down in the waiting room.

Dr. Cloud has been our family doctor forever, and I love her. My mama found her clinic when she was pregnant with me. Dr. Cloud started it with other indigenous and women-of-color doctors. It's got beautiful artwork everywhere, some by Dr. Cloud, and all of the walls are shades of pink, brown, and beige. She has long silver hair in a braid down her back and always wears intricately beaded earrings.

"Hey, Mabel," Dr. Cloud says as she enters the exam room. She has golden skin with freckles and the warmest brown eyes, and her smile always reminds me of getting free scratch-and-sniff stickers and fruit leather. She reminds me of an older auntie, who nosy and ain't afraid to ask about your period and if you having sex. When I first got my period, she recommended some books for me to check out from the library about relationships, bodies, and sex, which I told my mom I ain't want and then low-key, totally checked out from the library.

"So how is school going for you this year?" she asks as she looks into my ear (for some reason I have always found this medical procedure soothing, even though I don't know why they do it). I was in my socks, bra, and drawers and a hospital gown and feeling all extra naked.

"It's good so far. I'm a junior this year, and ready to be out," I tell her, closing my eyes as she peered into my mind through my ear canal.

"You grown now, hunh? Here, lean back while I listen to your lungs. Breathe in a couple of deep breaths." She puts her cool stethoscope on my chest and back, and I breathe in her soft smell with each inhale.

"Everything sounds fine there. You looking at colleges yet?" she asks. I tell her I want to go to a historically Black college, an all-girls' one that's supposed to be good, or maybe a school in California. She nods and smiles at me while she sits at her desk, taking notes on a clipboard while listening to me.

"I can't believe you are almost headed to college! I remember little baby Mabel *coming* into the world and now you are going *out* into the world. I'm excited for you." She turns around to me and slides her reading glasses off her face into her hands. "So, Mabel, when was your last period? I heard you have not been feeling the best lately around it." Apparently, my dad asked her to ask me about it. I explained that I just feel like I have less of an appetite, been having a hard time waking up and working out and been needing more sleep. She asked if it was before, during, or after my period, and I told her it is kind of all the time. She took some notes.

"Mabel, are you currently sexually active or interested in being so soon?" she asks all calm, like she ain't all in my business. That question always makes me want to vanish into thin air, leaving the itchy, pale gown in a pile on the examination table in front of her.

"Mm-hmm, nope, I'm not," I said and I wasn't.

"And it would be okay if you were, and I would give you the rundown, so you can be safe," she says, pushing the issue ever so gently.

Crickets.

She gets the hint.

"But that does eliminate some possibilities. I'm not sure what the change in appetite and energy could be, but I will order some blood work and do some tests," she says, sliding her glasses back on her face and writing some more notes. "You could be anemic, which just means you have low iron. It's not uncommon in young women. In that case, I could prescribe some vitamins for you. That should make a difference."

She gets ready to leave the room. "You can get dressed now and then one of the nurse assistants will grab you to do your blood work. I will send you and your parents an email with the test results. If anything seems out of the ordinary, I'll call." She winks at me, swinging her silver hair and body around toward me before she opens the door. "But like I said, it's probably nothing serious. Whoops! I almost forgot!" She grabs a small basket from a cabinet by the door. "You want a sticker and fruit leather?" she asks, smiling.

I nod and take a shimmery dolphin and concord grape fruit leather. "Thank you, Dr. Cloud."

"All right, sweetie, tell your mama and daddy I said hi."

When the door closes behind her, I start to change. I look up and notice myself in the mirror and walk closer to it. Then for a second, I just stand there and look at my face.

Do I look like I have sex?

I can't tell. I know I ain't have sex. I've barely kissed or made out with anybody except Terrell. I can't ever tell who is for real about that in school, because most people talking shit either way. I look at my dark eyes and my wide nose. I wonder at myself. Am I attractive? I kind of feel like I am sometimes, and other times, I don't know. I give myself a smile, then I stop. I don't know if I like my smile. My two front teeth are a little crooked, like a book that's wide-open but wants to shut a little bit, or like a butterfly mid-flutter. I lift my chin up and try to look chiseled with swag. Now, I think I kind of look like my daddy. A little bit, I see it. I wonder if he sees it. I look at my cornrowed hair and my little diamond earrings that I got my last birthday. Daddy say all time that I'm pretty like my mom, but I can't tell.

"Are you ready? We just need some blood samples and then you're done," says a voice from the other side of the door. I'm startled and remember where I'm at.

"Almost, give me one more minute. Thanks."

I put on my jeans and white T-shirt and gray hoodie. I put on my Chucks, tuck in the laces and head out to find the nurse's station.

MABEL

"DANG, GIRL, LOOK AT THIS FLY BIKE YOU GOT! Uncle Sunny hooked you up. I'm low-key jelly," I say to Audre when we meet up on the corner by the football field as we agreed last night over the phone. Her bike is an old-school Schwinn, dark green with a basket that holds her backpack. She beams, proud of her new wheels. We slide off our bikes and walk up the block to where all the racks are. Kids is coming from all directions, headed to our first day back.

"We went to this bike shop he friend own and this one was perfect for me and they fix it all up and shine it up for me. And then me and my dad ride around for a while so I could get used to it." She locks her bike next to mine, and I take an opportunity to stare a bit as she fiddles with the combination. She is wearing a light-pink T-shirt and high-waisted jeans over her curviness with a brown belt and brown loafers and of course her thick glasses. Her hair is in two cornrow braids that come together in the back of her neck. She is looking natural and fly in her own way.

"I love riding," she says as she stands up, and I avert my eyes.

"I feel so free when I is out here zoomin'!" She does a little hoppy dance. "And I figure out how to reach here by myself too, gyal. It wasn't that hard at all." Her gap-tooth smile radiates her pride. I feel happy for her—that she is getting used to Minneapolis and riding around the hood.

"Oh, I had no doubt," I say, offering a fist for her to bump and adjusting my backpack on my shoulder.

"I forget to ask you what classes you have. I hope we have one together," she says, and I dig in my pocket for my schedule.

"My first class is trigonometry, which I know I'll probably be too sleepy for that early in the morning, so I will see if I can change that up. After that I have poetry with my boy, Mr. Trinh, then chemistry, US History, ceramics, and weightlifting. Lemme see what you got," I ask, and she hands me her schedule. We have chemistry together after lunch, but her first class is World History with Mr. Burns.

We walk toward the gray-and-beige boxy structure of education, South High School. The building was built in the early seventies and is rumored to have been designed to be riot proof with slim windows and labyrinth-type hallways. It is also said that the same architect designed prisons, and I believe it. In the nineties they added a third floor with windows, which made it a little better. As we walked closer to the entrance, we floated on a flood of teenage commotion. Audre gets quiet, looking around at all of the first-day cray. Students figuring out classes and where they friends at. The excitement of a new year is buzzing through me as I guide Audre ahead.

She is a junior like me, but probably feels more like I did as a freshman. Her spirit seems like it is suddenly pulled in tight and timid amid all of the people.

"Mabel! Hey, sis, what's good?" asks a voice as soon we walk through the school doors. Ursa. Looking fly in all black—black button-up, black skinny jeans, black Jordans, and her pretty brown face shining in her loosely wrapped black hijab.

"Hey, what up, what's good? I missed you, playa! You been ghost this whole summer, is Jazzy your new bestie or something?" And we hug it out with each other.

"Chill, fam. I was about to say the same thing to you! You looking fresh for the first day. Oh, hey, I'm Ursa," she says to Audre. "I see you got new friends now, Mabel," she adds.

"It's not even like that. Dis my homie from Trinidad, Audre. Uncle Sunny's daughter and she moved up here this summer and I been showing her around. Audre, this is Ursa," I say, tucking my thumbs in my pockets.

Ursa turns and bows her head toward Audre.

"Hey, Ursa, nice to meet you." Audre shakes Ursa's hand, friendly, but her attention is somewhere else—maybe on the flow of loud-ass students coming down the hallway.

"Good morning, Audre. Your dad is cool. And Mabel coulda BEEEEEN introduced you, but she musta been busy," says Ursa, pretending she is hurt and wiping away a fake thug tear, hand gripping her chest dramatically.

"Awwww, Ursa, it wasn't *even like thaaat*! Dang. You know how the struggle is real in the summer in Black Eden, and how my dad get so emotional over his garden." I grab her and link our arms. "And you *know* that is why your booty was a ghost from by our crib: My dad woulda had you weeding and paying you in the strawberries that you picked for him," I say.

"I ain't afraid of yo' daddy, girl! Agnes Marie, you know I woulda been told massa, 'Hell to the no,' and that we was both phasing off the plantation." Ursa smiles, knowing that ish was a fantastical fantasy and that her mama woulda magically materialized to whoop her ass for being rude to my dad.

"Ha, Ursa, got jokes this early," I say, laughing hard.

"Just saying, I thought once you got sixteen and was working that little jobby job, that woulda been your cue to exit the garden. Your daddy's a real gangsta for that one." Ursa shakes her head. "Hey, Audre, you like poetry? You should come to this open mic. You may have heard I be rapping too," says Ursa, winking, knowing I ain't said nothing about her being a wannabe rapper, but she can't help but exude swag.

I love Ursa like she my fam, like my sister. When her family moved to an apartment on our block, we was in sixth grade. Her mama wanted to know if she could grow some things in our garden, and my parents was cool with it. Her mom is Oromo and wanted to grow special things from back home for her cooking. She would even share with my family, so we all bonded over that.

Ursa and I were inseparable from jump, especially when we was both stuck gardening with our folks. We would work "the fields," which is what we would call Black Eden, and would sing "We Shall Overcome" and pretend we was enslaved Africans looking for the North Star.

I would tell Ursa, "One day, Lil' Puma (Ursa's slave name; she came up with it), we finna know the sweet taste of freedom, and we won't have to deal with massa's evil ways no mo' or break our backs in his fields."

"You finna get us kilt, talking all of that freedom mess, Agnes Marie (my slave name; I did research). You know these fields got ears and eyes," Ursa would reply, looking around cautious and all scared.

"You think I'm afraid to die, Lil' Puma!? I won't have the white man's hand around my throat one mo' day, you scared Negro! I gotta know life!" I would say dropping my shovel dramatically.

"Y'all can play around and make fun of y'all ancestor's oppression all you want, but y'all gonna thank me one day," my dad would say, side-eyeing us while focused on weeding around the herb patch and overhearing our performance. "Black folks should know how to grow our own food, even if the white man done made us associate being with the land with being slaves. Our ancestors lived with the land and grew their own medicine and food, and we trying to teach y'all how to love and be comfortable with the land. And 'We Shall Overcome' is from the Civil Rights movement, you know, right? I know what y'all gonna be writing your summer essays on." My dad always managed to kill the vibe and assign me and another innocent child summer homework. He know how to drop some good ol' Black history on a playa, whether you felt like it or not.

Ursa and her mom and siblings gardened there until they moved to their own house a couple of years ago. Ursa got two older sisters, Ifanii and Jeeynitti, and an older brother, Birraa, who look out for her, which I was kinda jealous of, only having baby Sahir, but her sisters and brother treated me like I was they little sister too. My dad would tease me about liking Birraa, which was annoying and not true. Birraa is handsome and kind, but he was like my family. Ursa and I were basically inseparable until high school when we got more busy and into different things, but we always got love for each other.

"What's your first class, yo?" I ask Ursa, wondering if we have the same one.

"AP Calc, but Imma try to switch that around. They got me twisted. I'm barely awake now," Ursa says.

"Dang, I forgot you a math prodigy and all a that. I'm going to drop Audre to her first class and I will find you at lunch. You got second lunch, right?"

"Fah sho, but I'm rolling out with Jazzy, 'cause as you know the food here is garbage, so we going halfsies on a sandwich. Nice to meet you, Audre." Ursa adjusts her hijab and extends her hand to her chest. "We will look out for you here. This school can be poppin' in its own corny-ass school way and I'll introduce you to Jazzy, who is dope too." And then she walks away.

As we head down the halls, I can see Audre is wide-eyed, taking it all in: from the spectacle that was Ursa to all the folks reuniting with friends, teachers welcoming students back with new-year energy, and security guards roaming and encouraging folks to get to class on time.

"How do you feel? Is it a lot different from Trinidad?"

"Yes." She doesn't elaborate. I pull her off to the side of the hallway to get space.

"How you feel, for real?" I ask, when we stop for a breather. She is quiet for what seem like a while, before she speaks.

"I guess it's just real, real overwhelming. It's just a lot, being in America, everything is different. I can't describe it . . . ," she says, looking at the ground and playing with the strap of her backpack. I lean on the wall next to her as she fiddles with her stuff.

"Well, you know I got you. Whatever you need, girl. Folks here are cool, for the most part. There might be some haters lurking, but if anyone messes with you, just let me know, okay? That shit ain't right." I'm feeling protective of her, which is a strange feeling. Like nobody better come for her, 'cause she new or got an accent.

"I'll be okay," she says as she composes herself, closing her eyes and breathing in deep for a couple of moments. She opens back her eyes. "I ain't here to make friends, anyway," she says, like she is convincing herself, but it still made me feel some type of way. Wasn't we friends? "I is here for me studies and to get to know my father. If I can get good grades and behave myself, hopefully my mother will let me come back."

This was the first time I heard her speak of wanting to go back home for sure. I thought she was starting to like it here. The idea of her going back to Trinidad was surprising and made me feel some type of way again.

We get to her first class—World History with Mr. Burns, who also taught when my dad went to school here. I told her I'd see if she can switch out of his into Ms. Sharkey's class, Afro-Future Feminisms for a New World. She has us read stories from Assata Shakur (not Tupac's mama) and science fiction by Black women and reflect on what a "Black feminist future" might look like according to the ideas in their work. When I bring her to Mr. Burns's class, I tell her I will find her at lunch, and then I run to trig.

After trig is Taking Your Poetry from Page to Stage, a class with my favorite teacher, Mr. Trinh. He is the creative writing and theater teacher—and a poet in the real world too. I scan the room quickly and looking for a seat. His classroom is fly and moody. He, like Ms. Sharkey, has lamps and a couch and pillows everywhere, but he also has a record player with all of these records he got donated from some of his DJ homies and from his own collection. He got mad posters up in his room. Of Biggie, Grace Lee Boggs, June Jordan, James Baldwin. He also has a poster that says THE TIME TO BE HAPPY IS NOW, which always calms me. I slide in quietly, right after the bell.

Mr. Trinh doesn't even notice I'm a little late since he busy getting things together for class. He loves to drop bars, which are actually really bomb, and he's also good at clowning students who trying to be too cool to be smart and getting them to participate. He and Ms. Sharkey are the funniest and chillest teachers. There was even a rumor that they was together, but then there was another rumor that Ms. Sharkey got a girlfriend who got a Mercedes and play for the WNBA, so I don't know what to believe.

Mr. Trinh is pacing the front of the class like a first day of school hype-man. He is wearing a T-shirt with Geordi La Forge from *Star Trek: The Next Generation*, a dark-green blazer, some all-black Chucks, and his determined enthusiasm for the spoken word.

"Who ready for this new year? Where my real poets at? Where my slick talkers and ish droppers at? Who been catching up on that Lucille Clifton? Bao Phi? Joy Harjo? Nikky Finney? Let me hear you say, oh yeah!"

Crickets. Then some chuckles.

"Oh, I see y'all, wait till I start dropping these new poetics on y'all." His smile got many of his students crushing on him, low-key.

I open my notebook and am taking down notes while he goes over the syllabus. I keep thinking about Audre and how she did in Mr. Burns's class. I'm so deep in thought, it takes me a second to look around and notice Jada has this class too. She smiles at me a little smile and I wave a little wave.

Before Jada ghosted me this summer, we used to chill together in geometry. We would always be cracking jokes and study after school sometimes with other kids in class. One night she called me to ask about an assignment, and we ended up staying on the phone for three hours, talking about our classes and music. She likes BLK LVRS too, she said she thinks QWN Asantewaa is the finest one in the group. I was, like, *mmm-hmmm*. We started talking on the phone a lot more, until the summer-rain-hug thing. I also think she started talking to this dude, Eli, who is kinda basic. I guess I felt some kind of way, but then was like whatever.

"For kids who are new to taking class with me: Every day we will begin class with a free write with a prompt. It's just for you to generate and get in your writing vibe. You may not find the flow right away, but eventually you can find your way to the poetry in you. All of us got poetry in us, 'cause our lives are in constant motion and unfolding, and when we observe it and behold it, it becomes poetry. A place to reflect, a prayer, a possibility for your existence to be connected to all that exists. Even if it is very sentimental or not your best, let it flow out of you and be your own personal gospel. Okay, y'all?"

All of us is paying attention now.

"Aight, so the free write prompt for the day is, 'In that moment it all changed . . .' Let whatever flow out and see what you come up with, okay?"

Mr. Trinh then goes to the corner of his classroom where the stereo is set up and puts on a record of some hip-hop instrumental music, quietly in the background. I look at my notebook and write the prompt down. *In that moment it all changed . . .*

I can't think of anything right away. And then I think of Jada in class and come up with something to write.

In that moment it all changed.
How you saw me.
You couldn't see me anymore, I disappeared.
And you materialized into another phase.
I phased out, and you were glitter then gone.
Like a dragonfly, emphasis on the dragon.
Burning my heart and flying through the sky.
Why? Didn't I try?
I can't deny, 'cause it ain't even a lie.
So I'll just say bye-bye.

I look at what I wrote and cringe. It seems both bad and thirstily in my feels. Whatever. It's what I had off the dome and I ain't wrote all summer so thank goodness we don't gotta share these out to class because this wasn't my best work.

"I encourage each of you to consider contributing to the student lit journal this year and join spoken-word club, aight? Y'all know I will have cookies, popcorn, and whatnot. Lemonade on payday. But before the bell rings, I want to share one more thing with you. From one of my favorite poets, Donte Collins.

"My love is as ancient as my blood.
And of course my blood is still mine
because a woman, sweetened black
with good song, pulled me from the river
like an axe pulled back from the bark.
I learned *love*, first, as *scar*.
And of course my love is only mine
because I found the nerve to say it is.
Ha, My love is mine.
But was first my mother's. Not the *how*
but the *why*. But was first her mother's.
Not the *how* but the *why*.
Not the how; Not the how; Not the how;
Not the how; Not the how; Not the how.
I am bored with this beat. I seek
a different dance toward death.
Lord, listen up. Lean in:
I crave a love that happens as sweetly
as it was named. If love must be swung,
let it soften. Not split."

He closes his book and looks at us.
"Have a good day, y'all."
The bell rings, and it is time for the next class.
"How was your summer?" Jada asks me, as we are leaving
class and walking down the hall. She got a big Afro puff over her
smooth and pretty coffee skin. She's wearing a denim dress and
pink lip gloss and lookin' cute. Or whatever.

"Cool. I worked my little jobby job at the community center with the kids and helped my dad in the garden. Kicked it with the homies. How about you?" I try to seem chill and unbothered.

"It was aight. I went to Chicago with my parents and brother to check out schools and hang with my grandparents. I spent a lot of time at the lake with the homies. I wish I coulda seen you a little bit," she says, and my heart sinks a little.

"I was around. You shoulda hollered," I say, trying to smile naturally and like I ain't even care what she was saying. We are walking when she stops at Ms. Sharkey's class and sees her homie, Nevaeh.

"Hey, Mabel, what's good? Where you been?" Nevaeh looks at me with a little too big of a smile. Jada and Nevaeh hug each other, throw a bye to me, and head into class. Whatever.

In the cafeteria, Audre is picking over the taco casserole. Only school would take something as good and perfect as tacos and mash it up into a weird, soft casserole. I plop down next to her on the bench. Audre starts telling me about her first classes.

"So, I is looking at the class syllabus and I ain't seeing nothing 'bout Trinidad and Tobago. But dis supposed to be World History? Steupse. I look in de book, go to de index, I still ain't seeing nothin' so I go and see Caribbean, all it say underneath is Columbus in Hispaniola and Napoleon in Haiti. I raise my hand, real respectful, no attitude or nothing, after the teacher give his introduction to the syllabus. I ask, 'When will you be covering the twin island republic of Trinidad and Tobago?' Some kids in class giggling as if I say somethin' funny. And I see Mr. Burns laughin' low under he breath too, like I is the stchupid one. He say that he just covers major global events." Audre leans back, shaking her head no with her eyes closed, looking irritated.

"At the end of class, I go to his desk and ask what determines a global event is major? He explains that he covers the events that have global impact and not regional incidents such as what happens in the Caribbean. Before I could ask a next question, he asks me if they have detention in Trinidad and tells me to run along to my next class so I ain't late," she says, looking pretty irritated, both at the casserole and at the bigotry of Mr. Burns.

I can't think of anything to say really. "Yeah, that joker is stupid and he a little racist. He been here forever, like since the nineties. And he was the one teacher who gave out detentions to folks after the walkout protesting the Native kid who got shot by cops last year. He thought folks was just trying to skip," I said.

"What you talkin' about a walkout?"

"When folks walk the heck up out of class when some real stuff has gone down. Mainly police brutality and political ish. And some kids just do it to skip, but I don't blame 'em, since school be wack anyway, sometimes," I say.

"That would never happen in Trinidad. The teachers would be in dey hallway cuffing the kids down and de parents would be at the school, beating they children back into the building," she said all chill about it, but personally it seemed messed up to me a little that they couldn't stand up for their rights.

Next to her casserole, she was looking through a pamphlet for new students with all of the sports teams and extracurricular clubs, like theater, debate team, the Latinx student group, the Native kids group, the Black Student Union (which I was a part of a lot last year). She pointed to the rainbow flag for the PRISM group for the LGBTQIA kids and allies at school.

"That's for the queer kids at school. I know some kids in it. Ursa goes sometimes, 'cause Jazzy is a part of it. You don't got to be gay to go, though, I don't think. I never been to it though," I say.

"Oh, I see. I ain't ever hear of nothing like this. They don't have anything like that in my school in Trinidad," she says, and looks at it for a long time. I don't know what she thinks about it. I know she is kind of religious, but I don't know if that means she thinks that club is evil or anything. Lunch is almost over, and I notice that both of us barely ate our food.

"The food here can sometimes be aight and sometimes nasty as hell." I nod at her tray. "But just so you know, you can get chocolate-chip cookies three for a dollar, and they fresh and they fyah. We can split them if you want—I'll pay."

She looks up at me and smiles.

"Thank you. I would like one. That sounds tasty." We head to the cafeteria's kitchen to pick up cookies before I take her to the counselor's office to see if she can switch out of Mr. Burns's bullshit class.

AUDRE

I CAN'T DESCRIBE THIS AIR. It has a feeling to it that I have never known. It is still sunny during the day, but it getting darker earlier, and the evenings get so cold, I had to ask my dad for another blanket so I wouldn't be shivering through the night. And then I ask for a next one.

This week, he took me to get some more clothes that were appropriate for the colder weather. We went to the mall to look for some sweaters, turtlenecks, thick socks, boots, and long underwear, which is like thin pajamas to wear under your clothes, because he say it gets so cold and freezing during wintertime you need to wear a layer underneath your actual outfit. Steupse. What kind of place must you wear two sets of clothes to not die of cold?

At the mall, besides the socks and boots, I wasn't really finding anything I was too liking. All of it seem too basic or for another type of girl.

"You ain't feeling these clothes, honey," he ask after a while of me trying on clothes and not finding anything. We were walking through this overwhelmingly fluorescent and sterile mall that had to be five times the size of the malls at home. I was beginning to feel blinded by all of the brightly lit intensity of stores filled with things.

"Not really, I guess. But I can just pick something. I'm grateful you are taking me shopping," I said, not wanting to seem like I ain't appreciate what he was doing.

"I'm your dad, and it's my honor and pleasure," he said in his cheesy yet sweet way. "Hey, Audre, how about I take you to my favorite vintage store to get some stuff? I notice you have a bit of a funky style, like your dad." He popped an imaginary collar from his dashiki. "You might like the stuff that they sell there better than the mall. What you think, honey?" he asked, as we stood talking in front of another annoying shop of clothes for teen girls with no bum bums.

"Sure." It felt a bit weird to have him describe us as alike in any type of way. But it's also kind of nice.

And he was right about me liking the vintage store—just like he was about me liking my velvet friend. The shop—called The Lion, the Witch and the Wardrobe—was inside of what looked like an old house, and it had floors filled with cool, old-school, and eclectic clothes, shoes, and all kinds of accessories and jewelry. He told me to explore and find what clothes I like and he would be wandering around if I needed anything. I kept on expecting him to say something about what I was picking out, but instead he was just letting me do my thing. And for some reason I was feeling awkward, not having any critique from an adult figure to help me determine my outfits. Every time I would show my dad something, he would say nice but unhelpful statements like, "That's dope!" or "I can see you rocking that" or "It's whatever you like, Audre." It was hard to make a choice when I had free rein.

The shop clerk was very friendly and she pretty, with steel-blue hair. She have a skinny black line on she upper lid that look a bit witchy. I liked she style. She offered to help me find sweaters in my size that were my style.

"If you don't mind me saying, you have a pretty accent," she said, selecting a couple of items from the sweater rack for me and I felt shy a little bit by the compliment.

"Oh, thank you. I'm from Trinidad," I said, glad she ain't guess Jamaica like most people.

"Ooooh, I heard of Trinidad—and its carnival and music. Is this your first winter in Minnesota?" she asked, and I told her yes. "Okay, love, I'm going to make sure I hook you up then. I was born in El Salvador and came here as a teen, so I know the struggle." Her smile was pure kindness. "I had to figure out how to dress warm and be cute at the same time. You want a pro tip?" I nodded again. "Get cute tights that are thick, and cozy chunky sweaters to wear over dresses. That way, you can still wear your fly summer clothes, but add some additional layers and still stay warm."

She helped me find some maroon corduroy overalls that fit my big bumper, funky old-school sweaters, and a super-soft green cardigan that I could wear over dresses and that pop real nice against my brown skin. I also got a black hoodie that says *Goddess* in gold cursive letters that she said goes good with jeans or a cute skirt with sneakers. She then helped me pick out some thick cabled tights in black, navy, and a turquoise color, which reminded me of the sea. When we got home, I went into my room and laid out all of my new warm clothes on my bed.

My winter clothes.

I know I ain't going back to Trinidad anytime soon, and this leaves me feeling suspended in an impossible reality. I keep hoping that my mom will call me back so I could be home and with my family. In my last conversation with her, she made it clear that she thought I seemed like I was doing fine with my dad and it's good that he and I are connecting. Like she whole intent in sending me away was for me to get to know him and not disappear me from she life.

I sit on my bed, on top of my new wardrobe of thick and scratchy layers, insulation for my new life, and I start to feel like my room is closing in on me, with sadness rushing into my ribs and on my lungs. I feeling heat flare in my throat and eyes, and I tearing up. Before I overflow, I pick up the Goddess hoodie, put it on over my dress, and zip to the garage to get my bike to ride to see the sky and fill my head with it.

I ride fast and I's aggressive. If I can't stop my tears, then I need to feel my body, feel in control of it in other ways. My speed brings a wind to my face that is pleasing and I find a way to forget myself. I feel traces of my tears along my now-dry cheeks. My knuckles grip the handlebars tight and I feel kissed by the breeze that I'm cutting through, wiping the dark-cloud vibes that envelop me. With each push of my pedals I exhaling some of my sadness. I hearing Queenie's words: "Let the pain leave out of you with each breath. It want to be free too," she would say whenever I would get hurt, or if I was feeling sick. Even if I was sad, she would say these words, and through my tears and pain, I would find my center again.

I ride until I seeing a creek and the water feels like it calling to me. I walk my bike alongside the water, and I wonder what it is rushing toward. The rush and movement of energy feels like how I feel. I want to shake and roar and fly around. My body still zinging from my ride and all of the trees roar and sing to me in the breeze. Spirit. I lie down with my bike under a cover of trees right by the creek and on the dirt itself that is layered in leaves and the little green sticks from the pine trees. A little cocoon for me. I let all of the layers of earth beneath me and all of the wild, crying winds above me envelop my body and just breathe and be still. I speak prayers to myself.

"I love you, Audre. I love you, Audre. I love you. I won't let nothing happen to you. This is your body. It belongs to you. These are your hands. They belong to you. These are your feet. They belong to you. I love you, Audre." I say things to myself, like I is a sweet grandma. Like I is my own ancestor. And I say it to me from me.

"I love you, Audre. You are safe."

MABEL

DR. CLOUD WASN'T RIGHT. I didn't think she could be wrong ever.

I feel dry up inside of me. Every day feels like I'm falling deeper into a hole of myself, one that ain't got a floor or even a hell. Just a nonstop falling flight into my insides. Every night, I cry until I'm weak and sleep catches me. I wake up every day and I hurt more than the day before. Like my skin is made from iron, my blood is lava, red-hot, breaking and moving. My bones are a magnet to the core of the earth, locking me to my bed. Every feeling is too much, and I am too little to feel them. Through my curtains, I see the sun is shining, too hopeful for the life I'm choking on.

My mom is standing and looking out the window. My dad is on the edge of my bed and he won't look at me. Or he can't. We are home after the third opinion and several weeks of confusion and medical professionals and blood work and tests and late-night research and being picked up from school early and missing classes and then whole days. He could look at me after every other time and say something hopeful and lighthearted. This day, we are all in our own worlds, and we can't look at one another.

When Dr. Cloud called and didn't email, I felt a little nervous but also not that bad. She had even assured us that sometimes second tests are needed to clarify results, but that she also wanted us to see an oncologist—which I had no idea what that was until I searched it online and saw that it had to do with cancer. Except, it seems I don't have cancer—at least not a regular one. They don't understand what I have but from all of their tests, it seems closest to some kind of leukemia-like cancer, and it is moving through me aggressively. "Aggressively" is what the oncologist said. The main expert, Dr. Johnson, at a youth oncology facility an hour away, had suggested I start taking radiation and chemo right away, but my chances are still not clear.

I could have a year, he said.

That's when the earth opened and swallowed me. I had been pushed off a cliff of myself, and the free fall was numbing. I don't think I have landed yet. Having a year doesn't seem like anything. How could I "have" a year? A year is all the life I have left in this world, and it feels like nothing.

My mother comes and sits next to me. She pulls me into her and is rocking me. I fall apart and crumple in her arms.

"Sequan, come here, baby," she says, motioning my dad to come to us. I look at him and he is quiet and leaned up with his eyes watery. He's wearing one of his IT WAS ALL A DREAM Biggie Smalls T-shirts. He is breathing slow. He comes over and is on the other side of me, and my mom pulls him and me, both up and into her arms.

Every moment is swallowed up in the next and lost immediately. My mom tells us we should all get some rest. Sahir is at her sister's, my auntie Niiki's house. My parents surround me again in their arms. They are holding me up like they did when I was a little girl, but I feel ghost already. I can't see or feel myself, I come in and out of focus. I feel empty inside. I fade into them, like I have my whole life whenever things were scary. I feel fear in them, which scares me. At least we are broken and scared together.

AUDRE

I RIDE AND I IS RIDING TO NOT FEEL MYSELF. I riding so that life can't catch or find me or hurt me anymore. I escape into the night because I need to disappear, to fly beyond feeling. My bike whisper itself my chariot, and I harness it towards freedom from a beat-up heart. I is tired of the lost feeling. Neri. Mabel. My mommy. Queenie. Port of Spain. Ocean surrounding my home. I'm tired of feeling. I don't want to remember something. I remember still.

The classroom phone rang and Ms. Sharkey stopped lecturing me about how the classroom is a no-phone zone and picked it up. I notice her face looked concerned and then all of a sudden Jazzy pulled my chin in her direction. "So, who you texting, though?"

"Yuh is nosy," I said, opening my notebook on my lap and pretending to get distracted in it.

"You already knew that." She laughed and snuggled into her corner of the couch, extending her legs out and pulling out her notebook too.

"I was texting Mabel. I ain't heard from her in a little while and I was just making sure she cool."

"I'm sure she's cool. You don't gotta worry about her. She'll be back in school once they figure out what's up with her," Jazzy said. "So you have any idea who you going to research?"

"Not sure. Ms. Sharkey suggest I think of someone from Trinidad. I might study Calypso Rose, since she is a feminist calypso singer from Trinidad and I ain't really know much about her."

"Yes, a little something for the island culture, that's a good look. Me and Ms. Sharkey was talking yesterday, and I'm gonna make a documentary about Missy Elliott's Afro-futuristic influence on Black feminisms and sexuality. So Imma watch Missy videos on repeat, and interview my mama and them—"

We noticed Ms. Sharkey was off the phone and walking toward us on the couch.

"Hey, you two. Can you stay after class, please? It's important. I'll write you a note for your next class." She tried to smile nice, but she also look a little nervous.

After the bell rang, Ursa walked in with a woman who is statuesque and stylish in a hijab and dark-red henna designs on her hands. Then another boy from my math class—Terrell, I think. Then my dad walked in next with Mabel's mom and our principal. The energy is heavy and sad, and I feel it hit my body.

Before anyone spoke, there was hugging and crying, like we all knew something bad was coming.

Ms. Coco's eyes looked so sad when she finally stood to speak. "Hey, sweeties." She took a breath and then another. "As you know, Mabel has been missing a lot of school lately, since we have been figuring out what is going on with her health.

"Y'all have been so supportive of her, and she has appreciated y'all reaching out, even if she hasn't always been able to respond. A couple of days ago we received a diagnosis of a rare leukemia-like illness that is moving aggressively and unpredictably in Mabel's body." She paused and I realized I was holding my breath. She voice got more heavy. "The doctors, specialists, are not sure how to cure this and are trying everything, but are not sure if they will be successful. They are not sure if she will survive it."

My heart dropped. The room got still and without air.

"What? Ms. Coco? What are you saying? Is Mabel dying?" Ursa sounded broken, and Ms. Coco went to hug she and she mother. As they hold her, Ms. Coco looked again to the whole room and started to talk again.

"The doctors have said that this can end her life, but me and her father are not accepting that and will be doing everything to heal her so that she can live a long, sweet life. Our baby is going to need the love and support of her friends right now, even if she isn't gonna know how to ask. She is taking this hard, as you can understand, and may need some space. But of course she still needs love. Check in on her from time to time, and keep her in your prayers and thoughts. Imagine her healed and pain-free." She broke off, looking at her hands. Then she was quiet.

In that moment, my body feel like it want to collapse, but my dad was right there with a hug and was helping me not disappear.

The steel between my thighs is lightning, and the breeze on my back is my wings. The blackness is an oil spill of indigo and cosmos spread before me. I is fire in my lungs, and each breath feel like it almost want to drown me or levitate me. I is riding so fast, I hear every conversation of every winged thing that prevail in the night. They gossip and laugh, and it shudders a sparkle into my spirit, and I can go faster. My skin is glowing, and I is levitating over life, over myself and the hurt, but then over the trees and the streetlights.

I ain't understanding how gravity release me from the earth, but I is flying somehow and I is not stopping, 'cause I ain't want to. I wanna feel this levitation until the pain stop. Somehow I am like Queenie, but I ain't understand how so. But I is pumping my thick thighs until they tingling, pumping and taking the sky into my chest and my legs and it is effortless, like I always know how to do this.

I sit by the lake, my steel wheels of flight beside me. I'm looking out on the water underneath the trees and leaves of changing color. I talk to the water and my spirit and my own sadness. I pray to everything that loves me, my eyes closed and body huddled close to myself. I'm a tight bud and I try to melt a little, so I can open.

I pray for Mabel and beg for she healing from any and all malady. I pray for Neri and beg the spirits to protect she, wherever she is. I look at my skin and it is glowing with constellations of ancestors. I ask them about escape and freedom and listen for revelation. Mabel is my friend, and I ain't want she to die. It can't happen. I can't let it.

MABEL

LAST NIGHT I COULDN'T SLEEP. The night before it was the same and the night before that. I stayed in bed and cried. Or maybe I am asleep and this is all the dream?

My parents have been bringing me tea and my favorite foods: chicken soup with dumplings; roasted sweet potatoes; fruit salad; and pineapple fried rice. I don't touch it. I mostly just lie there.

"You need anything, honey?" She or my dad seem like they are always asking me that. I don't know what I could want except for my life and they already gave me that one time.

"No, I'm all right, Mom," I say from under my covers. I'm lying, of course. My face feels soft and ugly from crying, like it's going to fall off and betray me like the rest of my body already has. Nothing feels good to me anymore. She comes and gives me a kiss on my head and then leaves. A little while later, I hear more footsteps, then a knock.

"Mabel, can I come in?" It's Sahir. I say, "Yeah," and he enters. He squeezes in bed with me, like he has since he was little. I can tell by the way his eyebrows are squinched he wants something.

"What you doing?" he asks.

I think about it. "Nothing."

"You wanna come outside with me and watch me ride my bike?" He looks sad and desperate, his bottom lip quivering. "Mom and Dad both yelled at me. I ain't even do nothing. I did my chores. All I wanna do is ride my bike." He leans in real close, holds my face with his eternally sticky hands, and brings his forehead to mine, making his and my eyes cross the closer we are to each other. I hug him real tight and he hugs me back.

"You look sad, Mabel. Mama said you ain't feeling well." And suddenly, I wonder how he will be in a year when I'm gone. He kisses me on my forehead.

"Yes, I'm sick, but I'll be okay," lying to him.

"Are you tummy sick? You got a fart stuck in your stomach? When I got a fart stuck in my stomach, I do this dance." Sahir climbs out of my bed and puts his hands on his stomach and starts doing a Minnesota version of the Harlem shake, with extra squatting. He farts almost on cue. Sahir's eyes are surprised at the effectiveness of his technique, and I bust out laughing. I laugh so hard, I start to shake. Sahir still looking a little shook, starts to laugh too and then jumps back in bed and hugs me again. I tell him I'll meet him outside. I'm feeling a little better and decide I can watch him ride. He starts doing his dance again, running out the door.

I've been wearing the same blue-and-white polka-dot onesie for the last two days. Sahir, my mama, and my daddy all got matching ones for Kwanzaa. I put on my Chucks and my hoodie on top of it and head outside. As I walk through our hallway, I pass my parents' bookshelf and kind of feel like getting a book that might help distract me from my sad and cray thoughts. I haven't been on my phone or computer for the last week. I ain't been to school, neither. My dad passed by school and picked up my homework, but I haven't felt like doing it and they ain't made me. I wonder what they have told my teachers. Or Audre or Ursa. I don't know if I want anybody to know, because I still don't feel like it's real.

I read most of their Octavia Butler, Alice Walker, and Maya Angelou this summer. I look at a book by one Japanese author my mama likes, Murakami, and grab that. As I'm looking at the bookshelf, I remember, dang, my mama got a lot of self-help and spiritual books. One about healing your body catches my eye and I snatch that. Most of my dad's books are history or gardening books. Then I see a book, *The Stars and the Blackness Between Them: The Memoir of Afua*. The title grabs me for some reason. I pull it out, and on the cover, I see a drawing of a full moon, with the silhouette of a Black man with an Afro and nebula and other cosmic imagery. It's kind of cheesy looking but intriguing. On the inside cover in my dad's handwriting, it says, "For Coco, a beautiful sister. May you enjoy this book. Love, Sequan. '97" The inscription makes me smile, my college-man dad trying to be all woke and woo my mama. I realize this is the book about the dude in prison my dad had mentioned when I was working on my essay for the school-to-prison pipeline. I tuck that one under my arm as well and head outside to watch Sahir.

LIBRA SEASON

the leaves were raked up by an older cousin for us to dive into
and the impact was crunchy yet soft somehow

she gathered the splendor of changing leaves
rustling breeze and flamboyant descents
to afterlife and let us look at the sky from the softness

the expressions of love are a labor of love
hands at harmony with the heart
reminds us to be slow, decadent
working and toiling yields for balance
for pleasure and
luxuriating in it
she played a love supreme
on the turntable to set the mood for indulgence

and she rubbed the feet of the queen of the house
seeing the daily attempts to break her back in her eyes and walk

she brings her tea with extra sweetened condensed milk
to coat her belly and then she picks her afro out
so her head feels free

a radical adornment of care
auntie is a lover who allow the pots to simmer and set in flavors
passed down from tired hands whose names she don't remember
and never knew just the love is what she tastes
and the love is what remain

MABEL

I'M IN BLACK EDEN IN THE MIDDLE OF THE NIGHT and the half-moon is low and yellow. I can't sleep. I feel shitty. I have been really weak all day, because I can barely eat and everything I eat goes right through me with this weird medication and treatments. I came outside after waking up for the third time and having diarrhea. I'm glad I didn't wake my parents this time or else they might trip and get worried, and them being worried don't help me sleep or live. Being in Black Eden with the quietness and darkness feels like where I need to be. I end up by the raspberry bush that I brought Audre to when she first moved here from Trinidad. All of the raspberries are long gone, and that day feels like it was a me from forever ago, but it was just a couple of months ago. I walk over and sit beside the raised bed where we grow all the herbs. I rub my hands in the remaining dried leaves and flowers, bringing my hand up to my nose each time. Lavender. Mint. Rosemary. After doing that for a while, I bring my face to the dirt and place my cheek on it. With the cold and soft dirt on my face, I feel alive. I see my breath become smoke in the cold air. I am alive, my breath is proof, even if I feel like shit and all I can do is shit. I feel soothed, my body starts to calm down, and I decide to go back inside.

I crawl back into bed and round my body into a fetal position, hugging my stuffed lamb Jonika Jamison—JiJi for short. I have had JiJi since I was a baby. She is light pink and raggedy, her once-soft fur is matted and tufted and dingy. I banished her when she started cramping my swag at around ten years old. But after years of being able to sleep without her, I wanted her back and asked my daddy if he could find her, which was apparently easy, since she was in one of his Jordan boxes in the closet. He was crying and laughing at the same time when he gave her back to me. "I always thought I should keep her in case you changed your mind." JiJi is now back to ride-or-die status in my bed. Ride or die, for real.

I'm listening to my quiet storm mix to help me sleep and forget about how wack I feel. Initially after the diagnosis, the feeling of falling asleep made me afraid I would never wake back up. I still ain't been sleeping well, and the medication I'm taking makes me feel weird when I'm awake, and then on top of that, I just be thinking too much, feeling too much. And then other times, I feel nothing. Just empty and like I don't care. I turn on my reading lamp, and on my table are the books I found on my mom's shelf. I pick up the one from the dude in prison. I figure I'll read it until I fall out. I open it up.

To the constellations
of ancestors in our bones.
Thank you.

INTRODUCTION

Incarceration is a sustained, lifetime lynching, meant to discard your soul and make a shell of you in plain life. Make you into your monster self, the beast that comes out when you are forced to survive in the absence of love and safety. Never mind that most of us come broken and traumatized, we still are no longer worth our own humanity.

We are a criminal.

We need punishment and to be rehabilitated.

We need shame and exclusion.

We are not worthy of control of our own lives; we are hopeless and evil.

We are not individuals or of a womb or a family.

We are not absent from anywhere else; because we are here, we simply non-exist.

The world is better without us.

In this society we are taught our crimes are the summations of our lives and define the limits of our possibility. Our only potential is to harm and destroy.

But I was a boy once.

And to be honest, I can't help but hold and carry him inside of me. Most of us in here is holding and carrying a scared and lonely little child in us. How could we not? I write this story for the little Afua in me that needs to know he is okay and worthy of life, even if my whole existence is a reminder that my breath will one day be taken away at a predetermined time by an executioner, whose house I live in. I protect that young boy's soul by reminding him he is infinite, like the stars and the blackness between them.

AFUA

FULL MOON

In 1989, my best friend, James, was in college in Philadelphia to be a lawyer. We were both from the same block in Harlem. I was my mama's oldest of three sons and he was an only child. James was two years older than me. Outspoken, smart, and helped me in school.

You ever know anyone who was everything you wanted to be?

That was James to me. His mom, Ms. Valerie, was a literature professor at City College, and James went everywhere with her. She was a very creative and intelligent woman, who would take me along with her and James to experience the city when we were around twelve and fourteen. His mom would take us to see free music in Central Park or all the way downtown to walk across the Brooklyn Bridge and get ice cream and look at the Statue of Liberty lighted up. I remember once she took us to see Alvin Ailey Dance Company in Midtown and I still remember it vividly. I had never seen Black people look so free. I remember the feeling of seeing brothers like me move with grace and control, flying through the air like demigods, half heavenly and half terrestrial. It was a thing that I didn't know we were allowed to do, and it gave me a possibility for my spirit that I didn't know could be. Seeing them made me imagine myself airborne and carefree.

I, on the other hand, was afraid of the world and learning that the world was afraid of me. I was shy, a quiet dude, who liked to blend in so I could observe the world. But as a tall and kinda chubby Black kid, I never really blended in, and standing out made me feel like a target of people's assumptions of me, whether it was police or a woman crossing to avoid me. Hanging with James, though, I always felt free, and when we got older we would go on adventures all over the city, wandering around the Museum of Natural History or watching folks play ball in the Village.

When James went to college, he was ready to leave New York and expand himself as a scholar. I was seventeen at the time, and he would invite me to campus for the events that the Black Student Union would put together. I would ride the Greyhound from the Port Authority to visit my friend in his new digs and new life. James introduced me as his "little brother from the hood" to his friends from school, many of whom were young Black activists on campus that James was getting tight with. What James discovered when he went to college to learn how to survive professionally in this world was that, instead, he needed spiritual and cultural knowledge of himself as a Black man. James would kick it in Uhuru Books, this Black bookstore and café near campus, and get schooled by older cats who put him onto all kinds of new ideas and books from Kemetic spirituality, I Ching, Yoruba, and Dogon cosmology. Everything he learned he would share with me too.

"The Blackness between the stars is the melanin in your skin," he said one night when we were hanging out in the middle of the quad, lying out on blankets, looking at the sky on a crisp and restless night.

"I read it in book. I take it to mean that as Black folks we are limitless. That, maybe, our blackness holds our ancient cosmic memory. What if our wisdom can come from our dreams, not just churches and Bibles?" he asked, looking away from the stars and looking at me, and I could tell he was serious.

"I always loved the stars," I said. I looked at the ink sky and the silver scatter of stars above us. After that I started to pay attention to the stars and if they held messages for me.

After that, I would repeat those words to myself, "The stars and the blackness between them is the melanin in my skin," when I was on the block and think of the stars above me, the few I saw and the millions I couldn't.

James said I was smart and limitless and helped me study when I kept getting bad grades, because I was babysitting, selling weed to make some money, and not doing well in school. He fell in love with a dude, and he was happy and confused. He told me about it and I told him that he was my brother and nothing would change between us, that he deserved to be happy and in love. I told him I loved him, and we hugged. He gave me books, and I started saving up for college; he told me I should save up and go to Africa first. I started researching and decided I wanted to go to Senegal and see the castles they put my ancestors in when they decrowned them of their own lives. I also started reading my horoscope every day too to see if I could anticipate weed business and the moods of people in the streets.

One day, I was going to a Stop Police Brutality rally with James on campus and sliding nickel bags around. The night was hot and electric, filled with the voices of conscious sisters with Afros and nose piercings on the mic calling for justice, as well as brothers in dashikis and dreadlocks getting folks signed up for cop watches. James was a junior at this time and one of the event's main organizers. That night, he looked with pride at how well things had turned out, despite the anonymous threats the organizers had been receiving. James wasn't scared though. In that moment, his smile was humble and hopeful and I will never forget it.

And the moments that change your life forever are indeed only a moment.

At the end of that night two men were dead. One a policeman, Officer Travis McConnell, and the other was my best friend, James. The events of that night were vivid as well as a whirlwind of trauma and violence that I hate to remember. However, there are two things about that night, I will always remember intensely and with certainty: I had borrowed Jordans on and the moon was full.

AUDRE

IT ALL STARTED WHEN I WAS NINE and had all of these dreams. These nightmares.

I killing in my sleep, swinging machetes and running.

I tied to a trunk, I is screaming blood out of me, blinded and choking on smoke, and fire is a lake of hatred I drowning in.

I running wild through the woods, then by the water, then into a mountain.

I jumping off ships, bleeding from between my legs and plunging into ice water and darkness.

I pulled into the air by a rope swinging from a high branch, and I see the tops of green trees, fire, smoke, and a river with blood.

I can't scream, because I already feel the night won't hear my prayers.

I wake up crying and running out of myself. My mom comes into my room with she Bible and has me recite passages to cast out the devil. She tell me a demon has got me and Jesus can help me. It ain't work.

• • •

One Saturday when Queenie was taking me to the beach, my mother tell she what is going on with my dreams. Queenie was quiet, listening, and then said I can stay by she, away from Laventille, for a little while until school start back up. Where Queenie lives is more country and closer to the sea. She said that the feeling of being by the water would help soothe my sleep and clear the dreams, and it would give my mom a chance to rest.

My whole life, I always loved my grandma's house. She lives on top a hill away from the action of Port of Spain. It's the house Queenie grandma lived in, a brown brick-and-cement structure that used to be just one room when Queenie was little, but she added rooms over the years. In her house, everywhere you lay your eyes, you see beauty. In her bedroom she has a big window that look over the hills of Saint Ingrid's Bay. Each wall is painted in multiple shades of purple. "One day I woke up and wanted my room to feel like an amethyst," she told me.

Her bed takes up most of her room. It's a canopy that she built from driftwood, discarded rope, and sheer, white mosquito netting. She soaked the netting in the ocean and let it dry in the sun all day and all night in the full moon. When I sleep in her bed, I feel suspended in sea foam. Her bed is my favorite place on the planet; it smells like her skin and her dreams.

She living room is all white except one wall, which she calls her "living installation." It could be covered in gold, with a haze of thin white lines, streaks of black, and clouds of blue. Or dark green splatters that have slunk down to the ground in long wet drips.

In she home, everything has a story. A statue carved by a

brother she used to dance with in Harlem, a mask a teacher from Mali gave her when she returned to Trinidad. An ornate weaving of raw yarns, hand dyed, with rocks, sticks, and beads made by Mahal, whom she loved "and who was a shaman of my heart." Mahal could wield and understand dream medicine better than anyone Queenie ever met. They used to live in the same building in Brooklyn, and became friends when she knocked on Queenie's door, curious about the aroma of curry chicken coming from the other side. Queenie say she believe I, like she own grandma and like Mahal, was born with dream medicine in me.

On the wall of Queenie's mango-yellow kitchen is a picture of my mother as a girl wearing a gray-plaid school uniform with pink ribbons in she hair. My mom was raised first in Trinidad with her grandparents and her father, and then in Brooklyn with Queenie, who spent years living in the States as a dancer.

One corner of she living space is devoted to her massive record collection and her record player. But on nearly every wall throughout the house, there are pictures from Queenie's performances all over the world, in all kinds of costumes—headdresses and Afros and cornrows and lashes and feathers and leathers. She has posters from concerts of Stevie Wonder, Bob Marley, Chaka Khan, Fela Kuti, Prince (looking too sexy, bare-chested and in black panties), and all kind of people whose records I have heard all my life. She also has photos of Sparrow and Kitchener, who Queenie listen to as a kid, and who she still love to wine up to when she got rum in she cup.

Then there is Queenie's African cloud. It's a big, stuffy chair with an ottoman that she upholstered in mud cloth. "I got this Bògòlanfini from a fine Senegalese brother on 125th Street." He had a crush on her, according to the story she often told. According to my mother, Queenie think everyone is attracted to her. I think Queenie probably right though. She does her sketching and daydreaming in this chair. My favorite picture in the house is next to this chair. The picture of Queenie, my mother, and me at the beach when I was a baby. My mom and me had just moved back from the States to live in Trinidad. She had three-quarters of a college degree and a full baby girl. In the picture, my grandma has a big floppy hat and a bathing suit that consisted of three white triangles that cover her nipples and pum-pum. Barely. She is looking seductive and elegant, staring straight into the camera. My mum is next to her, hair cut short and sleek, like Toni Braxton back in the day, wearing a black swimsuit. They look more like sisters than mother and daughter. My mom is smiling big at me as I, butt naked and half out of the frame, begin to run away from them toward the water. My love for the ocean was instant, according to Queenie.

In another corner of Queenie's living room is her altar, a table with a white candle that is always lit. A tall glass of water. White shells. A vase with white lilies from the woods behind her house. Pictures of her parents and her grandparents in Trinidad from back in the day. A black-and-white image of my great-great-grandmother in her carnival costume, a headdress, a bodice covered in shells, a skirt with beaded tassels. Another picture is of my great-grandfather in a sepia silhouette, dark and chiseled cheekbones and as pretty as Queenie.

Queenie has more magic than her walls can contain, so some of my favorite Queenieland things are in the huge yard surrounding the house. When I was having the nightmares as a kid, she would fill her outdoor claw-foot tub with water and let it sit under the moon and heat up under the sun. She'd add oils, dried flowers, and herbs. When I would get back from playing all day with my cousins and the kids from down the road, she would soak me in the water while she prayed, sang, and danced over me. She rubbed coconut oil we'd made together into my skin and hair.

"When I is young, Audre, I feel I ain't fit in nowhere on this earth. I always was different and I struggled with my existence," she said one evening while we having tea in she yard, watching the moon glow on she garden and on the ocean. "I decide for myself that I going to just start talking to everything that speak Spirit back to me. I going to make a spirituality that loves me as Queenie. I going to be in conversations with Goddess, the universe, my ancestors, spirit, dance, and dirt and see the divine."

Queenie know every song and story of every leaf, grass, bush, pod, tree, bud, seed, fruit, and blossom that grow 'round she land and she said I must learn them too. Queenie gave me special teas to sip and prayers to sing to the sacred powers in all of existence, not just that in the Bible. She said, "Sing your prayers, Audre, before you sleep, so you have power in your dreams, in case they get scary." The dreams mellowed out the more I took my special baths and prayed with Queenie.

"Audre," she explained to me, "I believe dreams hold the memory of all the places where a soul has traveled since the beginning of existence. So, my baby, you must listen to your dreams, that is where your work will happen. Listen to your intuition and the feelings you get when you are awake too. You will one day know how to bend them the way you need to."

After the ninth moonbath she gave me that rainy season, she

and I had a ritual together. It was at night and the air warmed my skin until it humming. I bathing in the black dirt, lying out in Queenieland, on the hill amidst the dasheen bushes. We each had on white dresses that we had been sewing together the last couple of weeks whenever we went to the beach with Tanties Daphne and Pearl.

"Audre, see how the moon fat and full? Ripe. That's when it have the power of an old wild woman. The moon is a euphoric warrior now. Shining she light for we to witness our true self, eh."

My eyes were closed but I felt she come down low by me, smelling like only she do. Like soft and spicy and earth. She put she hands on my temples and start singing and humming.

"Put that feeling inside you, right in your bones, follicles, heart, hips, and toes."

I felt Queenie dancing around me, burning a sweet, dirt-smelling bush. "Breathe in, baby. Be quiet and feel all of the sensations in your body. You paying attention to how you body is feeling, Audre?"

"Mm-hmm."

"How you feeling?"

"I feeling safe and free, Queenie."

"Take your feelings and hold them with softness, but also with power. And whenever you feel afraid, know you can ask your fear about itself." And as she said this I felt the humming within me get stronger. "Why your fear know you and how it find you? What it want to heal? Who in yuh blood is arriving in this fear?" I opened my eyes and saw she was shaking the bush, with each question. She moved gracefully, and I saw light reflecting on her gap-toothed smile, bright like the old warrior moon.

"Who ancestor needs sweetness and love inside of you? In your skin, in your beautiful darkness?" she asked over me, breaking smoke over me and under the moon. I closed my eyes 'cause I feeling so alive with she words, she very voice is holding me. Then I felt a strange feeling between me and Queenie. Like the air was too easy to breathe, like I was floating, and like I was getting warm from within. I opened my eyes, and Queenie was dancing up high over the dasheen bushes and me, in a rapture of she own. I looked at my own body and I saw it glimmer, glowing like I was made of light. I believed my eyes and I believed my heart, because I was seeing what I have always felt:

That Queenie is God.

I started shaking, the feeling was so strong between me and Queenie. I felt as if I were up there with her. And I was, floating feet above the ground. I felt myself in my grandma's body and she in mine. I closed my eyes and fell backwards into myself.

The next thing that happen is that I woke up in Queenie's sea-cloud bed and Peter Tosh was singing really loud. And the air was hot with the smell of saltfish and bake. I climbed out of she bed and walked out to the kitchen and there is a plate of cut-up mango and a pitcher of juice in her breakfast nook.

"I thought you was going to leave me with this saltfish and bake to eat myself, sleepy gyal. Epi pass through looking for you to see if you want to go to the beach, and I tell him we would meet up with he later. Have some juice. It passion fruit and cherry." I sat and watched my granny move about the kitchen, fixing me a plate.

"Queenie?"

"Audre?"

"Are you God?" I was feeling so many feelings, including a tremble that become tears. Queenie started to giggle and came by me.

"Oh, dahlin'. We all divine, remember I tell you? All of we. I just happen to give birth to your mother and what is more God then that? But don't forget, eh? If I is God, we all are," she say and sit down next to me.

"Audre, what you see and feel is true; who you are is divine. All of this is God. The mango, the bake, each bush in the yard. Sacred, each chicken crying at dawn. Each lesson that hurts you, and each hair on your head that reach for the stars is God." She told me to eat my food and headed out to the yard to pick some fruit for the beach. I picked up a piece of bake and put a piece of saltfish in it. It was oily, hot, and chewy, and I ate it real slow.

On the night before school started and I was to go back to my mama, I snuggled against Queenie. I didn't want to leave. We were in her backyard and had just finished drinking tea and toast with honey she get from the rasta man down the road, who take care of the bees and collect their sweetness. He is one of Queenie's old boyfriends, Dawitt. She helps him with the bees, and in return we never pay for honey. We were looking over the hills of the island, the houses tucked into the land, handmade brick squares of dwelling, and the streetlights slowly glimmer awake into the night. I leaned on her lap and she rubbed my back and I started to cry, because I didn't want to leave she home to be with my mom, who was too tired all of the time to be with me and can't cook like Queenie.

Queenie told me that she will always be here, so don't worry. She also gave me my sky-blue pouch and taught me how to use my oracle stones. She let me know that I would begin to feel Spirit and not to fear it when I do. That was seven years ago that I began to understand how to read the medicine in existence.

AUDRE

"GOOD MORNING, QUEENIE. I need your help," I say, as soon as she gets the app open on her phone. I am sitting in my room wrapped in a blanket and snuggled up in a chair by the window, listening to distant morning birds sing as a slight sun warms my room.

"Good morning to you too, dahlin'. You is up early, so I figure yuh must want sumthin'. Is this about Neri again this week, gyal? I tell you, you would be the first one to know if I hear a ting." I hear her bracelet clanking the teakettle and running water in her sink in the background.

"Queenie, this ain't about Neri this time. I need help to heal my friend who dying."

"Which friend dying? Your friend who sick?"

"Yes, Queenie, yes." I feeling urgency and I waiting for she to feel it too.

"Oh, I ain't realize it was that serious. What is it, dahlin'?"

"It some kind of leukemia or cancer or something they ain't really ever see." It still feel vague and scary in my chest as I say it.

"What? I is shock, this is so strange."

"I need your help, okay?" I fiddle with the fringe of the blanket.

"Audre, let me think about what can be done, okay, dahlin'." I hear something like unsureness in she tone of voice.

"Queenie, please help me. I ain't trust them hospitals a-tall."

"Audre, dahlin', calm down. The hospitals have they work that they do to help people. Remember, I used to work in one." I can tell she is trying to ease me down, but I need she help.

"Yes, and you say it run by a whole bunch of fools and all the true healers got paid half as much and had to go around fixing they mistakes." My mind is racing. "What if one of them stchupid doctors is assign to Mabel, and there ain't no Queenie here in Minneapolis to heal she and something happens to her?"

"Oh, gahm, I just don't know, if I ain't there, and I ain't never encounter whatever this thing is." I hear she breathe deep and exhale deeper. "I have a next question . . . you consult your stones yet, my love?" she ask.

"No." Of course she is asking me about my stones. But I had hoped when she hear the extreme nature of the situation, she would see why I need she to take the lead.

"Why not?" I envision her sitting at her breakfast nook, sipping tea, and watching out she window at the sea.

"Queenie. I don't know, it just so big. I is afraid I will hear something I can't handle or understand . . . So that is why I is asking you."

"Well, Audre, I understand it scary and hard, but just start off with reading your stones. You must trust yourself. You have nothing to be afraid of, okay?"

I ain't say nothing back.

"Okay?"

"Yes, Queenie." I huddle into a ball, pulling tighter into myself, feeling a little frustrated and dismissed by Queenie.

"I will try and help, but I also wan' you to believe in your own powers, dahlin'." She's trying to be motivating, but it still feel like I is being deserted to figure out such a big thing, alone.

"And you must also listen for the spirits and ancestors of your friend Mabel."

I just still and listening.

"I ain't sure what she destiny is but if you are to try and help her, you must listen for the love and power that is around her. You must understand some things before you go into any space of healing, Audre," she say.

"Like what, Queenie?" All this is feeling too big.

"If you even afraid to cast your stones for wisdom, you might need to work with your own spirit first and make sure you strong and clear."

"I strong, Queenie, you know I am."

"Yes, you are, but when you heal, you must know your heart in a real way, so you can feel how Spirit wants to work with you as a healer, yuh understan'?" As she speaks, I touch at the pouch on my chest and breathe deep. "Healing is like falling in love, but deeper. You unite with someone so that you can work alchemy with they soul. So that they might elevate and revive them and heal not only them but their ancestors. And like love, if you don't know how to protect yourself, it could consume you." As she say this, I know it is true. "So," she continues, "I need you to consult your stones and then let we talk and see what you should do."

This is not the answer I want to hear. We hang up from each other after saying our goodbyes.

Next, I call Epi.

"Wha' the scene, Epi?" I ask as soon as he pick up.

"I dey, I dey. Making some breakfast for Sarya. It good to hear your voice, Aud. One sec . . . It's Audre. Oh, Sarya says hello and she miss you."

"Tell she I miss she too."

I ask Epi about the most healing foods he know, trying to inspire his most top-notch magic. I'm up and pacing around my room and I hoping so much that Epi is down to help me in this mission.

"Aud," Epi says and I can almost see him pause mid-chopping of his onion. "That is a BIG thing you talking. Healing from death is what you talking!"

"Remember you make me that syrup for when I had the horrible cold? And also that time you gave me all dem juices and teas when I was cramping bad and I got better in less than a day, remember?"

"What you is talking is two different things, Audre. Even if you was feeling you was going to die, them was cramps and bloating, not a serious illness, dahlin'—"

"Epi, man, you going to help me or not? Just tell me anything to do, I'll make it happen."

"Wha' Queenie say? You know she know every bush and thing for anything happening wit'cha."

"Epi, please, I is asking you, okay?" The desperation in my voice is hard to suppress. I hear a big breath of contemplation from Epi's side of the phone.

"Okay, you got something to write with? I ain't saying this will heal she of death, but it will certainly give she body some life." I grab my notebook and start writing down everything he say, detail by detail. As he is talking, I touch my chest at where I keep my pouch under my shirt and ask the ancestors for strength to not feel too afraid to heal my friend.

MABEL

IT'S FIVE A.M. and my room is hot and my face is sweaty and stuck to a page of the book. The book I been reading all night. At some point I musta fell out. I look at my phone and see that I have a missed call and text messages from Audre.

> Hi Mabel.
> :)
> You doing fine?
> You want to do homework? Together?
> How you feeling?

Audre keeps texting me and I don't know what to say, so I ain't been saying nothing. Ursa had texted a lot initially, and now it's here and there, as has Terrell, and Jazzy hits me up too, but after I've been ignoring them, their messages are slowing down. Except Audre. I feel like if I respond, she will want to stop by and I'm not ready to see anyone yet. My mom has asked me if I want folks over, and I have told her no, not yet. I like my friends but I don't want to talk about nothing about school or life, and I don't want them looking at me like they sorry for me. I already feel icky and weak from all of the stupid medicine and treatments I have to take.

I also feel like I'm losing my mind with this diagnosis. All I want to do is read or listen to Whitney or watch cartoons in bed with Sahir and André 3000. My dad and mom take turns taking care of me and checking in about how I feel. I really haven't been able to talk to them about the diagnosis either. My mother has been more pushy than my dad. She wants me to go to a therapist to process how I'm feeling. I told her I ain't ready yet. My dad still seems numb. Distant, like the news is still reaching him.

I pick up *The Stars and the Blackness Between Them*. I look at the front cover, then the back cover, and then I flip through the pages to the last page of the book.

If you would like to know more about Afua Mahmoud's case or are interested in expressing your support or connecting to Mr. Mahmoud, please send all correspondence to:
Friends of Afua Mahmoud
P.O. Box 70981
Amherst, MA 01059

I look at the address and I get an urge to write him. And tell him what? I don't even know if he is alive, and if he is alive, he probably don't got time to read my letter. Or probably don't want to. The book was written in the nineties, which was so far back in the day, if he is alive the address probably don't work no more. I push the idea out my head and start to fall back out.

MABEL

I'M WAKING UP AGAIN and hear a light knocking on the door to my room.

"Mabel? Mabel, it's me, Audre."

It takes me a second to recognize what's happening. I see my periwinkle walls, my Lynx WNBA championship and my *Warriors* movie poster, my dream catcher hanging above my head, my nightstand with tea and water. And Audre's voice in the midst of my four-walled world.

"Come in." She enters my room and I feel my cheeks and mouth do something weird. They smile, from some place. To my surprise, I'm instantly so happy to see her, and I forget everything messed up that's going on, for a moment. Her hair is in little twisted knots that make her look from the nineties or Africa. She looks pretty, and even though she's standing in front of me, I miss her so bad. I thought of her a lot since my diagnosis, but I had never felt like it made sense to reach out. To her or anybody. I know she had texted and called, but I never felt like talking. What would I say? But now she is here and I really want her to stay. Bad.

"Hey, Audre . . . how you doing?"

"Your mudda said I should just pass through and bring dis ting I make for yuh," she says, motioning to a bag in her hand. She looks around my room a little bit nervously. "I hope you ain't mind I just come by. If you want me to leave, I will . . . I had miss you." She smiles. "I miss you, gyal."

I feel it. Her eyes look sad and I wish I hadn't been so distant, but to be real, I couldn't do anything else. I didn't even know who I was these last couple of weeks. My words come out in a stupid rush. "My bad, I didn't hit you up. I thought about it, I missed you too. Come in, Audre. I was gonna holler. But . . . I . . . couldn't figure out a good time . . ." I pause and can't figure out what to say next. I don't know how to talk about what is happening to me and my body. She walks in and sits on my bed. I start leaning up in bed, and I feel my stomach tighten and then comes pain, but I try to look smooth, like I'm just chilling.

"But . . . I'm glad you came through . . . It's really good to see you . . . How is school?" My mouth feels coated in powder, and I remember this is the first time I've spoken today. I have no idea what time it actually is. I look at my cell and it says 9:17 a.m. She had come by early to see me.

"It's good. I glad you get me to switch to Ms. Sharkey class. Jazzy in there too. I like everything we studying and Ms. Sharkey letting me do research on all the Caribbean women who helped lead resistance throughout the islands. Ms. Sharkey is so beautiful, natural and nice too. So anyway, I like she, she real, real dope," she says, and I smile. Hearing her accent all pretty and melodic and then hearing her say "dope" all cute made it hard not to feel some good feelings.

She goes on to tell me that she likes Mr. Trinh a lot—his jokes and his writing and that he asks about me, which makes me happy and sad. I miss his class and getting to write and read good poetry and obscure hip-hop. She tells me that she been making her own lunches now, and Uncle Sunny's cooking is not as horrible as it was at first.

"I see Ursa too; she been looking out for me," she continues, and this makes me feel some type of way, which is weird, but true. It just feels unfair that I introduced them and they get to bond or something when I ain't there. I mean, they can do whatever they want to do. Whatever.

"Me, she, and Jazzy usually split the three-cookie deal at lunch and walk to fourth hour together. Ursa say she really wan' visit you, Jazzy and Terrell too. They say they ain't been able to reach yuh, either."

"I'll holler at them," I say, feeling unsure of how I feel about Audre, Jazzy, and Ursa sharing the cookie deal at school. I feel left out or something. Maybe I'm being petty for no reason. Why should I care? Ursa is my homie, and Audre is a cool girl who need good peoples. We are looking at each other quietly. I don't really have much to say. The only thing that has been on my mind is the diagnosis, and it's the one thing I don't want to talk about.

"When you ain't respond to my text, I call up your mom every day, to see if you feel for company. Today she just told me to come over. I think she tired of hearing me all miserable and missing you." She grabs my right hand with both of hers.

"Audre, I, um . . ." My throat feels thick and tight, my eyes start to get wet. "I have some stuff going on, but Imma need to wait to tell you and everybody more. I just need some time, okay?" She nods and starts rubbing my hand. Her touch feels so good, I can't help but feel something feel good inside of me.

"I understand, Mabel. It's okay. Your mother share a little with me."

I look at her and see that she looks like she may cry too.

"I bring you green juice I make for you." She pulls a jar out of her bag.

"What's in it?" I stare a moment at the swampy neon-green concoction she done brought me, and when I look up at her, she is smiling with her pretty space in her teeth. I'm glad she don't got braces. We can have non-braces teeth together.

"Listen. You see how all the Rasta women and men them get real old and never age? They look young and vibrant and strong? 'Cause they drinkin' things like this." She puts the mason jar in my hand as if it was a sacred elixir. Even though the substance looks intense, the fact that she made me something makes me feel kinda special.

"You can't tell me what's in it, though?" I lay my head back in the pillow, trying to make my face act right, instead of looking scared of the greenness of it all.

"Drink the damn ting already, nuh?" She's laughing but insisting. Any unsureness I have disappears because instantly I just want to make her happy. I open the jar and take a sip.

The first sip hit my mouth and was like all the dang feels. Pineapple-y, sour, spicy, citrusy, gingery, and even tasted like it was, literally, damn green. I can't help myself: "Cyyyyaaaackkk!!!"

"Whatever, gyal . . . I know it good, steupse," she says, sucking her cheeks around her back teeth in a long hiss, like she's annoyed but she's laughing at me too.

"Hmm. Actually, you right, it ain't that bad," I say, as I take another sip. I feel and taste the greenness again, and this time it almost tastes good. Damn, she done got me to like this stuff. My mom has been juicing things for me here and there, but I barely can sip it. She is smiling at me and looks satisfied with her gift.

"See, good, ain't it? It got kale, apple, lemon . . . oh, and I put pineapple, spinach, celery. . . ."

"It's actually really good," I say, enjoying the next sip even more.

"Parsley, ginger, lime, sea moss—"

"What?!" I say, almost spitting out a green sip.

"He-he-he-he, dat is good island healing, trust me, okay?" Her cheeks spring up again, reveal the gap that I had been missing since I been sick and ain't even know I did. Her smile gives me life. It gets me so emotional, like Whitney said. I just stare at her and then catch myself. She snuggles closer to me on my bed. We are both awkward and I keep sipping my juice—juice she made for me—grateful that she rolled up on me, even though I realized I must look really rough, since I got my du-rag on and ain't brushed my teeth yet.

"What book is this? It looks interesting." She looks at the book tucked under my pillow.

"One of my mama's books, by this dude named Afua Mahmoud. It's good, actually, I fell asleep reading it." I don't mention I've fallen asleep reading it seven nights in a row now. "I think it's my new favorite book."

"What's it about?" she asked.

"It's about this guy and his growing up, life in prison, about the universe, the stars, and Africa and Black folks and what we been through." I worry I'm not breaking it down the best. "I guess it's spiritual, but not Christian or with any religion or anything like that. But hearing his story helps me feel less . . ." And it takes me a while to pinpoint what it is I was feeling. "I feel less . . . wack or hopeless or somethin'. Like I'm a part of the universe, when I'm reading this book." I know I don't make sense, but whatever, I just feel a connection to his story.

"Since you like it like that, Imma get that book soon and read. My father has so many books, I sure this in there, somewhere." She picks up the Whitney vinyl that was leaning on the side of my bed and gives it a look and starts tracing alongside Whitney's face and lips. Audre's nails look like the color of lemon pudding.

"I like your nails," I say.

"Thank you, Jazzy do it for me. My toes too. The yellow remind me of a friend I miss," she says.

"A friend in Trinidad?" I ask.

She is quiet and then nods in her secretive way, which I learned means she doesn't want to talk about something. She stares out my window and then lies back down next to me with Whitney on her chest and looks up at the ceiling. She is filling my bed with the sweetest smell as she lies there. She is wearing skinny jeans, and they make her big thighs look even more powerful and pretty. We lie there quietly, together. After a minute, I try my best to match the pace of her breath for no particular reason.

"Sahir!!" my mom yells from downstairs, all hood and loud. "Saaaaaahiiiiirrrr!! I ain't gon' tell you again! Come clean up all this hot Lego mess that just busted my foot up. I'm 'bout to keep all of these for me and hide 'em, since you ain't taking care of 'em!" My mama screams this empty threat every other day when she jack her whole foot up on one of his Legos. But she never do since Sahir loves two things the most: André 3000 and Legos.

"Is it all right with you if I pass through after school and lime with you? I miss you and I can try and bring you stuff that would make you feel better," Audre says suddenly. I smile at her and her slang from home, but I'm not sure how to answer her. I don't know if I want her to be seeing me sick.

"My grandma Queenie has taught me a lot about healing and I can make you some of the tings she show me." Her eyes hold mine for what seems like a long time.

"Okay," I finally say. "That'd be okay. I'm glad you stopped by today, and I'm sorry I been acting weird." Suddenly I'm fighting my eyelids meeting and yawning. I stayed up late listening to Whitney and reading Afua.

"I ain't vex at all. I see you fallin' asleep. Dream sweet."

I can't help but close my eyes and follow her guidance into the other side of darkness.

MABEL

NEXT TIME I'M AWAKE it is in the middle of the night, and I get the urge to write Afua. Maybe he still uses the P.O. Box, but whatever, for some reason I can't rest until I write him. I pull a notebook out of my backpack that is lying by my bed, it got Whitney on the cover of it, of course—all my notebooks do. On this one, she is a teenager with her hair pulled up high and she's smiling sweetly into the camera.

I start writing.

Dear Mr. Afua,

Hi. My name is Mabel Green. How are you? I hope well. There was an address in the back of your book. I don't even think it works no more since you wrote your book way back in the '90s. I feel strange writing this, but I feel like I need to, because I really feel alone and need to talk to somebody. I don't even know what I need to say.

I guess I just needed to say your book changed my life and thank you for writing it. Even though I am young and in a different situation than you were, I felt like you wrote it for me.

I also need to tell you something else. I'm dying. Of some rare shit. (Is it cool if I cuss?) Anyway, that is the first time I said I'm dying out loud. Even if it is in a letter, I think it counts. I don't even understand the disease all of the way, but dying is all I can think about. I'm only sixteen, and my life hasn't been very long or as significant as yours. But my life matters to me, like I'm sure yours matters to you and I don't wanna die yet. Even though I know this can be a messed-up world, I want to know it more.

When the doctors first told me and my parents, I felt like I died right there. Dying is the loneliest feeling I didn't even know could exist. But on top of that, my body hurts so bad all the time too. I used to love eating. Now I always feel like I am going to throw up. I can't really play ball for real no more or help around the house. Every day is long and every night is longer, but every day my life is getting shorter, which makes me more scared and more sad.

How do you deal with knowing you're gonna die? I just had to ask you, since it is so hard for me. What I feel most guilty about is that before this diagnosis, when I was younger, I wondered what people would do if I died. I guess sometimes I felt so sad about my life and no one seemed to get me. I regret all those feelings now. I don't even know who I am yet in life and soon I won't be nothing.

My parents are scared too. They don't wanna give up hope on their "baby girl." But I don't feel like a "baby girl" no more. I feel old and weak and sick all of the time. In a weird way, their hope makes me feel bad, since I feel hopeless.

One thing that is good about life, even if it is kind of random, is Whitney Houston's music has been really getting me through. She is my favorite, always has been. Another thing is, I have a friend who understands me. Her name is Audre. She is from Trinidad so she talks real pretty, and she is weird and nerdy like me, but in a different way. She makes me feel like I can just be myself. I still don't talk to her about being sick, but she don't make me. She takes care of me and makes sure I try and eat things and I keep my head up.

This may be a weird letter from a strange teenager, but if you get it, I hope you don't mind. I don't even know if you are still alive. I ain't search you online or nothing, since I didn't want to find out. As long as I can read your words in your book, you are alive to me. I think if you were dead, I would be broken in a way. Reading everything you wrote, you ain't deserve to die. It seems that you, like me, had no chance to be anything either. Thank you for your words and helping me feel not so lonely.

Sincerely,
Mabel Green

SCORPIO SEASON

i desired to see myself in the nocturne of me
night vision to look into my shadow

the secrets and shames of my daddy's DNA
his tears coming from a wetness deep inside that was all hid

my mama's womb is encrusted in rubies
of calcified blood
heirlooms of mothers and grandmothers
whose womb never got to belong to them

they sit with me so I can see the root of things
a sacred death is the climax of life and all death is rebirth
a soul's portal into parts unknown

i deep dived to our ancestors' Atlantis
they jumped middle passage to immigrate underwater
and accumulate wisdom from deep-sea sages
wise in liquid intelligence
when to flow, float, and sink

i went underground
i grew an armor to protect my secrets and inner delicate

i was magic and ritual and communion

and goddess and rain

and orisha and ancestor

and fire and dirt

AFUA

ANCESTOR SONG FOR THE BROKENHEARTED

As a kid, I wanted to be an astronaut. My mom, dad, brothers, and I used to go to the top of our apartment building on 143rd Street and look through a big telescope that my dad found at a pawnshop downtown. On a clear night, our family would take this telescope, our dinner, and a boom box up to the roof, and we would take turns looking at the stars and planets and moon while we listened to tapes by Smokey Robinson, Chaka Khan, Earth Wind & Fire, and John Coltrane and others. I used to love it so much, I never wanted to go back inside. I was so obsessed, my mom got me a book all about astronauts and space, planets and stars for my ninth birthday.

In the book, I was inspired seeing the women and men of NASA in orange jumpsuits hover in tight and orderly space. They would travel in space capsules and shuttles with dials, buttons, and levers that they knew how to use to command the travel of these vessels through the last frontier. They could watch our planet Earth, floating in the distance, suspended in an expanse of quiet blackness. Our planet seemed inherently gentle when viewed from space, a rounded, smooth and simple Eden, innocently hovering in galactic murkiness. Maybe, as a kid, I subconsciously thought distance would make the heart grow fonder of the life I had. The reality of our planet. My hood could get fuzzier and more tender, the more distant I got in my spaceship.

Home on Earth was Harlem, glory of creative Blackness and revolution that, in the 1970s and 1980s of my childhood, became depressed and embattled, transformed from a tight community of Black folks into a province of suffering under broken dreams and high unemployment. Many of our families were susceptible to the escape, violence, and enterprise of crack cocaine, and my dad devastatingly succumbed to this addiction. My mom, brothers, and I were drained in the mayhem of his jonesing. Stuff we loved, including the telescope, disappeared, and his gentle nature mutated into the anxiety of addiction. I saw my mom try to love and be united with a man who was shackled to his own destruction. My brothers and I all coped in our own way; I mainly escaped to the streets. And to my best friend James's house.

But more than one thing can be true. In all of that heavy, I still remember times when my dad would be clean, and home was a place that was filled with the love of our parents, and the cacophony of our joy and laughter. I understood from an early age that people have many sides and aspects to them. And as I have grown older, I have been grateful for astrology in helping me love and see my dad and mom in their complexity and cosmology.

On death row, in some ways, I feel like I *did* become the astronaut of my childhood aspirations. I live suspended, distant and hyperaware of all existence. I'm alien, yet affiliated, living like a satellite, away from all that I have ever known.

I know more about human life now that I have moved my research on planetary existence from the streets of Harlem and Philadelphia to my Spartan spaceship of four cement walls, steel commode, and a cot. The space travelers of my felonious legion are drafted from our streets, vulnerable and afraid, some innocent, some guilty, all trained and broken in this system. We are sensitive scientists of the soul who stumble into a laboratory of the self we can't figure out how to escape. We spend our days rereading our star maps, trying to understand how we ended up at this unintended destination. The solitude of these walls allows us the time to explore the vastness inside of us in ways that our survival on planet Earth never could.

I don't glorify this irony.

One thing I learned in the book my mom got me is that, by the time you see a star's light shining bright, it could be dead already. Its brightness is a remnant of ancient creation. The star is the bright pinprick of heaven shining through darkness, an imploding message sent from a burning ancestor. Its illumination offers an arrangement of meaning from the sky. Sometimes, I think that is what astrology is: wisdom from our ancestors, the stars.

What is it like to be an astronaut of incarceration? It's stomped wings and a choked heart. The sound of my mom's screams in that Pennsylvania courtroom made me deaf, like I was actually being pushed beyond and into the stratosphere. She swallowed all of sound into her pain. I saw my dad poured out of himself, shriveled, his breath hijacked, trying to be a pillar to my mom, as he crumpled.

A couple days after I turned nineteen, I was sentenced to die. That moment was my death in a way, everything else afterward has been a drawn-out formality of the state.

When I got to my prison cell, after the impact and awe of the verdict and the trauma of being processed to my death, I couldn't sleep. I cried like a baby for my mama. I grieved James till my lips were dry and crusted from the salt of tears. I starved myself to bone. I felt so sick and afraid, sweating and shaking like I was dying already. My best friend was dead, and I was in jail because they said I did it, a jury of my peers. Peers who were all white and not from Harlem. That first night was the longest night of my life, and every night after was a century long. When that first darkness descended on our cell block, there was noises coming from every direction, noises of agony and repressed life. And I had no idea how I got there. Why did I let James leave with that cop when I had that feeling? Who killed my friend and that cop and why?

I would lie in bed, close my eyes, and see the stars. I would imagine James laughing and remember how falsetto and silly his joy was. In my mind's eye, I would see the castles that I saw in books about Ghana, Senegal, Nigeria, and the slave trade. I would think of other worlds. I would think of the stars and what they would say to me now. What wisdom from before life, from before pain and death and existence did these stars have for an innocent kid on death row? I talked to James in my head, because I didn't know what else to do. I prayed that if I could feel the stars in me and ask them for guidance, I could solve the equation of my pain, my innocence, and my captivity. Then one day the stars spoke back.

One day I got a package of books in the mail. My mother and

Ms. Valerie had sent me mine and James's books. Ms. Valerie had sent me a letter saying that she believed me and that she knows I would never hurt, let alone kill, her son. She said she knew we were like brothers and that I will always be a son to her and that she knew he would want me to have his books and she will send me more whenever she could afford to. This is the one thing that I think helped me live even this long. I knew I didn't kill him, but having her believe me made me feel free in a way, even if I was still going to die.

Among the books sent to me were two astrology books of James's as well as other spiritual books. He had read and dog-eared all of them. I opened up the astrology book and saw his notes and underlines and started to cry. It was like he was there reading the books with me.

I read and reread the astrology books. I memorized each sign, its element, and ruling planets. I studied the characteristics of each sign and what each symbolized. I learned how to make charts. One of the books had a chart for all of the movements of these planets and where they would be until the year 2050, which gave me hope that maybe I could be around that long too.

I heard that during the Attica riot, the prisoners who were a part of the rebellion slept in the prison yard so they could be under the stars. I totally dig why.

A man on my cell block started a fire one night. He must have wanted to destroy this place, bring it down to flames; it consumed him too. He could have waited for a final supper and an IV of a supposedly painless demise, but he was an Aries Sun with a Sagittarius Moon, Scorpio rising, so you do the math. In the middle of the night, an alarm goes off and I'm not sure what is happening. Moments later, a guard calls my name, handcuffs me, and pulls me out of my cell and into a hallway that is filled with smoke and commotion. I'm coughing and my eyes are tearing up, smelling burning flesh, mattress, and building. I cover my face so as to not vomit or absorb any more agony from the stench. We are evacuated into the yard, and I go from a suffocating anxiety into a crisp, chill air with an open sky with stars.

It was the first time I'd seen night in years.

How do you explain the feeling of seeing the night sky after years and years of artificial light and darkness, a life of walls? It felt like I was arriving to this planet for the first time. The sky looked brand-new. There were so many stars and mists of galaxy above us, I heard gasps from some of the other captive cats, and then silence from the awe of it. We were convicts of earth entering a cosmic cathedral. As an incarcerated man who studies astrology, I felt like I'd arrived in Mecca, awakened into the most beautiful pilgrimage, a night sky on planet Earth. The sight filled my eyes with water and my chest with hope. Hope because I realized I was among this limitlessness the whole time, even if caged within a finite box. I thought of James and how we would chill outside in Harlem and then in Philly, seeing a sky with a sprinkling of stars, most of the sky darkened by city lights. Now, I was in the middle of nowhere and the stars couldn't hide. I looked at the drinking gourd, the big bear constellation that was the astrology that helped Black people on the Underground Railroad find freedom in their own unthinkable enslavement. I asked those stars in that moment to sprinkle my heart with any hope they had left.

MABEL

I FEEL SOME PARTS OF AFUA'S BOOK RIGHT AWAY. How he loves his family. How much he loved James and how he looked forward to loving him more. But Afua also wrote a whole chapter about doing an astrological reading for a guy with actual swastika tattoos—a real fucking Nazi who killed a couple because the guy was Black and the girl was white. I didn't know what to do with this when I first read it. I still don't.

In some ways, reading Afua feels like being back in Mr. Trinh's class, struggling with a new poet. Afua even writes some of his own poems:

> Remember that you are from the stars and that you can return
> to them.
> Remember you are a sacred being of love, no matter the
> darkness of an earthly life.
> Remember you come from light and return to freedom.
> Remember you are the healing of your ancestors, that you are
> Chiron the wounded healer.

You heal through the compassion you give to yourself.
Remember you are an astronaut of the soul.
May you find solace in your travel to another star.

I started using this poem as a prayer for myself at night and any other time I was feeling scared. He had written this poem to recite to the other men who were on death row with him to give them hope and as their astrological final rites as they left the block to be executed.

Sometimes this book is real hard, but it's worth it. Not hard as in reading it, but hard as in feeling it, the unfairness of life and how it impacts people who could be something else to this world. I had never read a book that had so many feelings in it and it made me think of all kinds of things and mainly not think about being sick.

I thought of this one time my dad came home from picking up Sahir from daycare and was stopped by cops and Sahir wouldn't stop crying because he was teething and my dad was afraid to turn around and soothe him in case the cops reacted with bullets. The traffic stop was just to tell him that he didn't signal and he was getting a warning. But I think something about Sahir being in the car with him made it so that he couldn't stop shaking after the cops were done. He was still shook even when he got home. My mom started cursing up a storm and rocking Sahir, who was still hysterical. I remember going over to my dad to kiss his forehead and he looked at me and was crying. And I just hugged him and started crying too.

MABEL

IT'S MY SEVENTEENTH BIRTHDAY and I feel like shit. My parents must have blown up at least one hundred purple balloons; our house is swimming in them. They made an epic meal of tacos with all kinds of fixings and toppings and cremas and salsas and roasted chicken and sweet potatoes and black beans. They made watermelon juice and limeade. My mom made a homemade banana cake, my favorite.

Ursa, Jazzy, Audre, and Terrell were all invited to celebrate. Not my idea. I wanted to stay in my room and chill by myself as usual, like any other day, and wait for snow to fall on Black Eden and listen to music. But my parents kept insisting that I celebrate my seventeenth birthday with a party, even when I told them I didn't see the point.

So now the homies and I are in the living room amid the balloon flood my parents created. I'm feeling awkward and in pain and wearing my du-rag to cover my hair, which is falling out from treatment. I look sickly, and I could tell that Ursa and Terrell were shook but trying to be cool. Terrell started crying a little bit when he saw me but then got it together when Jazzy pulled him aside for a pep talk.

And I swear I'm trying but I can't really figure out how to be nice to anyone. I'm not being mean, but I'm not able to fake the feeling of happy or grateful. I can't seem to muster up pretending I'm into this birthday party for the convenience of everyone's good time.

I switch up the music to play Frank Ocean. It's my birthday and I'm feeling emo, so I'm playing that dude.

"Hey, Mabel, you look like you are doing okay." Terrell approaches me, lying from his sweet little concerned face. My armpits start stinging with sweat. "How do you feel?" He looks scared that I'll tell him the truth.

"I'm fine." I hate people being sorry for me. I don't know why he even asked, but I guess everyone feels like they have to.

"Hap-pyy Birth-day to ya. Hap-pyy Birth-day to ya. Happy BIIIRRRRTHDAY! HAAAAAAA-PYYYYYYY, BIIIIIRRRRTH-DAYYYY!" My mom comes holding my cake, sanging loud as hell the Stevie Wonder version of "Happy Birthday" (of course) with Sahir dancing in behind her and my dad filming on his phone. I blow out the candles unenthusiastically.

The whole thing just felt kind of extra—as well as disappointing and kinda depressing. I feel my eyes wanting to cry and that makes me feel dumb on top of sad. I hang out for a couple of minutes and then make an excuse to my mom about not feeling well. I go to my room to cry alone.

I know folks are trying to act like everything is normal, but that only makes things more awkward, because everyone knows

I'm sick. And celebrating my birthday just reminds me this is probably my last one. I hear the rustling of people leaving the house, and I'm relieved.

Someone knocks on the door and I tell them to enter. My mom enters the bedroom with a piece of cake that she puts on my side table. She sits on my bed and starts rubbing my leg. Her gentleness makes me cry harder, and I feel bad for not liking everything that they did.

"Mabel, I love you, honey. I love you too much." She combs her fingers through her Afro, like she does when she's thinking. She leans down and kisses my head. The tears are pouring out my eyes and are thick in my throat.

"I'm sorry, Mom."

"Don't be, Mabel. You told me you didn't feel like having a party and I didn't listen. I just wanted you to feel how loved you are." She sighs. "Mabel, I'm going to do everything I can do to be the best mom to you, and please forgive me when I don't get it right. As soon as the party started, I could tell you weren't feeling it." She laughs to herself. "It actually reminded me of your first birthday party. You hated that one too, girl. The noise, the people, the decorations! You cried so much we had to kick everyone out early then too."

I smiled through my wet face, imagining my baby self, being emo then too.

"Mom."

"Yes, honey?"

"I'm afraid. A lot." It's all I can get out of my mouth to say.

My mom sighs and nods her head at me, as I snuggle closer to her. "Baby, I can't imagine how you feel. I love you so much. I feel afraid too." It's the first I ever heard her speak about being afraid of what's happening to me.

"I don't know how to feel, Mom."

"You just need to feel how you feel, girl. You don't need to do nothing but be you." She looks down at me and strokes my forehead.

"Mom, can you snuggle in bed with me a little bit?" I ask her, and she laughs.

"I would love to." I make room for her and soon her Afro is on my pillow, smelling like amber and rose.

"Snuggling with you like this reminds me of your very, very first birthday, the actual day you were born. I remember having you lie on my chest, and I just couldn't believe how perfect you were. Your eyes, your fingers, even your little lips and nose. You were such a mellow baby. Like this regal old woman in a little baby." She pulls me closer. "Mabel. You are still perfect, baby. Remember, that. No matter what."

We spent the rest of the night chilling in my room and just talking. I took a bite of the banana cake and it was bomb as usual.

SAGITTARIUS SEASON

hood blocks are auction blocks
he took the noose off his own neck
he knew he deserved a gold chain and a Jupiter ring
b-boy philosophers
tenure on the corner
on blocks
ghetto institutions of knowledge
local community college
writing notes in his head and back pocket notebooks
hoofing through cement streets
Mansa Musa descendant got gilded memories in his blood

and asks every day, how many dime bags
does it take to bring back
stolen abundance?
how many dime bags does it take
so everyone can have gold dangling from them
and Jordans on they feet?
how we gon' cash checks earned
over infinite Black lifetimes?

she said stars bring everyone back to they own Mecca
satisfaction come from outsmarting the riddle
and she knew they hunted our bodies

and they would make us pay
if she ain't make them pay first
she utters under her breath
strategy

hunter of the mind, soul architect
she got pull like Ganymede and she use her fire for alchemy
harnessing the thin line between tool and weapon
let the fire become lava and it will create lands for Eden

MABEL

I WAKE UP AND I DON'T KNOW WHAT TIME IT IS, but the room is dark and it is dark outside. I feel confused, twisted up inside, and dry. Before I'm all the way awake, I remember the moments before I fell asleep and the fight I had with Mom and Dad. They came into my room with an envelope, demanding to know why I was getting a letter from an inmate—a letter they decided to open, even though it was for me.

"Y'all was the ones that had his book and told me to read it. Did y'all even read it? And now y'all seem almost mad that he is alive," I shouted, my body shaking in anger.

"Baby, don't be upset. We ain't mad at you," my mom replied, obviously lying because they clearly was feeling some type of way and that's why they came up in my room all rah-rah, talking about it.

After another minute of arguing, I told them I was tired and, like that, I was asleep. One of them must've turned off the lights.

I sit up and turn on my lamp. My eyes focus on a rectangle of white that I realize is the letter from Afua. I grab it and look at it closer, it is heavily stamped and already opened. I see *A. Mahmoud* and his handwriting in blue ink. It is square and tight and orderly. Neat. I see my name written out by him in this same blue ink and it gives me chills. That the words that have been sacred to me and the man that is its source knows I exist and wrote me. It hadn't ever occurred to me that he would actually write back, and now this envelope is in my hand. I open it up.

Dear Mabel,

    Thank you for your letter. It meant a lot for me to receive it and hear about your current journey and the challenge you are facing. Whoa. So heavy, young one. Honestly, I don't think I know what to say, but I knew I needed to write you to tell you that you and your family are in my heart, meditation, and prayers, which may not feel like much, given what you all are going through, but still I give it fully.

    I don't necessarily know what I should say about dying. I been "dying" so long, I must be good at it (laugh). I guess, in a lot of ways, I try not to think about it too much, 'cause it is a fact: We all die, we all gonna die. I remember when I was first sentenced, death scared me. Death felt like it was the clothes I wore every day. And someone so special to me, my friend, was taken from me and that felt like my death too. I guess life has a lot of little deaths before we leave this planet officially.

    I remember what it feels like to be young and feel like you are alone in this world. I used to feel alone even before I was in here. And in ways we are always alone, and in other ways, we never are, since there are feelings and beings that are unseen and unknown in this world that are around us and protect us. All the old heads will say that there ain't nothing new under the sun (or moon or stars), which is true in a way. But still your life is new for you. How you deal with something for the first time and the way you feel about it is new and yours and sacred.

An old head, Rashad, who was on death row when I got here and is an ancestor now, told me, no matter what, to never let them institutionalize me. It took me a while to understand that but then I realized I been doing it my whole life. I never let this system take my mind and spirit and shape it into whatever lie they designed for me to become. Even when I was out on the block, I knew it was 'cause I was helping my mama out and saving to go to Africa. I decided after about five years in here that I may be locked up, but this is still my life and no one else's. Not the police, this country, these guards, these judges. Even my family, who loves me even through everything, it ain't their life, it's mine and I get to cherish it. I hope you feel that your life is yours, even in this sadness.

I am so sorry that this diagnosis is a thing you have to hold. Nothing in life prepares you for death, and the certain promise of it. Whether it is your own death or someone you love. And nothing in life prepares you to live, truly live, knowing that death is near. Another thing to remember is, you alive until you ain't, so live in any way you can. I know that may not seem that deep, but it is just what I have learned. I been on death row for longer than I haven't, meaning I have been told I was a dead man before I ever even became a man. I got diagnosed with death as a boy of nineteen. I had to find life on death row and I will live until my moment comes to reunite with the essence of the divine.

Mabel, you have the power to live your life with attention and intention. Whether any of our souls continue to journey into other stars and worlds (which is what I believe) or if this life on this beautiful and bitter rock is all there is, you get to choose your relationship to life. And it don't got to look like no one else's. I'm happy you have someone like Audre, who makes you feel like you are not alone and who brings joy. Enshrine that in your heart, it's a gift.

And Whitney Houston is the greatest of all time, still to me and I'm an old man! I'm glad the young people still feeling her. She a wild and limitless Leo queen. She forever in my heart, looking like a goddess and sanging like an angel. Man, I used to have a crush on her! I always thought her smile could command ships and her voice, whooo, it could melt knees . . . nothing like it. When I first got in here, I wore out my cassette tape of "Where Do Broken Hearts Go?" It was my favorite of hers and really spoke to me and how I was feeling in here. I remember it was a single tape (Do you know what that is? It's when a tape got only one song on each side). I don't even remember the B-side. Your parents know what I'm talking about. Anyway, that song is an old one—and kind of sappy, now that I think about it —but that song made me so emotional (pun intended).

And all of these years later, the question still stands, don't it? Where do broken hearts go? In this country some might say prison. To be honest, in my life I have met a lot of broken hearts, inside and outside these fences and walls. We stay wondering where we will go. The answer I found for myself

*is that we must go within. Within us is a universe that no
one can touch. When you can find that inner spot, even for a
moment, that is Goddess.*

*I hope that you can feel solace and joy in this moment and
every moment. Thank you for your spirit and being so honest.*

Blessings,
Afua

P.S.

*Do you know your sign? Get your astrological birth chart
and study your stars and what they have to say. Your friends
and family too.*

I read the letter three times back-to-back. I feel a lot of
emotions—from the letter and my argument with my parents. I
couldn't explain why I needed to write this man, but now that I
got his letter, I'm so glad he is alive and wrote me. I think about
the stars and living with attention and intention as he said. Ever
since I got diagnosed, I haven't known how to be with life. Life
had become my biggest fear. But I'm still alive, even if I'm dying.
In this moment, I am breathing and my heart is beating. I put on
my speaker and found "Where Do Broken Hearts Go." I turn off
my lamp and let Whitney's and Afua's words fill the darkness.

MABEL

"I THINK THIS WILL WORK; let's just try it, eh? We will keep track of any changes," says Audre from the other side of my closed eyes. It's warm for late fall in Minnesota and it hasn't snowed yet, so we decided to head outside and absorb the feeling.

She has me lying in Black Eden in a bed of dirt that we didn't get to plant tulip bulbs in this year after I got diagnosed. It's in a secluded part of his garden, farther from the house and in an area with a little shade. She is bent over me and holding me around my shoulders and head and breathing slow and I'm relaxed by it. The air is warm and a little crisp. The leaves are changing color and have started falling flamboyantly to the earth. My last fall. I'm so nauseous and weak, I can barely think. Every time I have to go to the hospital for a treatment, I come home feeling sicker and less like me. But, as I lie here, I feel Afua's letter in my pocket and it makes me feel strong.

"As you lie in the dirt, imagine that the land can hold all of the feelings. All of the sickness and hurt. Confusion. The earth can take it all. Don't feel like you is too much. You are okay and loved by creation." Her words come slowly and her voice is a little shaky.

Audre always kicks it with me after chemo. After the first couple treatments, she created "dreamo" treatment for me. Her and her witchy concepts . . . It's supposed to help heal me from chemo, help me remember dreams, and also *dream* myself healed. Her grandma Queenie taught her some of these techniques, and she said she is going to figure it out. It's kind of an experiment of healing, and I don't mind being an experiment of hers.

Even though I think this dreamo stuff is weird and doesn't always make sense, I do end up feeling something different after each dreamo session. I feel less scared and more alive. Or maybe that's just Audre. Either way, I'm just glad she cares enough to try the healer stuff she saw her grandma doing as a kid. (And if half of Audre's stories about her grandma are true, she's got as much swag as Whitney did back in the day. No complaints from me about having her techniques help me out.)

I feel how tender the dirt is beneath me. I love dirt—always have. I feel Audre hovering over me, and I smell her scent mixed with lavender, Florida water, rose water, bay rum, and some other things we got at the botanica together on a day I was feeling up for leaving the crib. She presses into the insides of my feet with my thick wool socks, and starts rubbing them. A good feeling comes all over my body, even though I don't know how she ain't grossed out by my feet.

"Queenie always say I was the best at rubbing she feet. I always like she feet," she tells me. I open my eyes and see the shake of leaves that are sheltering us, and Audre attentively bent over my feet. "It just seem like she was always made from nature anyway;

they were her roots. She told me her feet was like that 'cause as a kid, she had to walk everywhere barefoot 'cause she could only wear her shoes for school and church." She softly kneads her knuckles into my heels, and I relax more. "They are also dancer's feet. She the best dancer. I stop wearing shoes as a kid, because everything she do, I wanna do like she."

My body is tingling all over. Audre's hands are gentle, and they are putting me in my feels. I want to tell her how nice this all feels, but I don't trust myself to form the words right now.

"Your feet can receive healing from the earth. I is imagining I activating their receiving powers."

Receiving powers. Sounds like something Afua would write about. This makes me laugh just a little, and I risk a few words. "I can't imagine rubbing anyone's hard feet, even if it was in wool socks or my favorite gramma."

"I can tell. Yours is always ashy like you don't even like rubbing yuh own with a lil' cocoa butter." She giggles.

"Oh, snap, you came for my feet like that, girl? You had me thinking I had some cute model feet." I start rolling too, because she is right. In general, I kind of skip lotioning them and throw on my socks and sneakers.

"I like to take time and just rub my feet in the morning and give thanks for them like my grandma does," says Audre, holding and rubbing my heels, ankles, and calves. Hmm, feeling her that close, I just want her to lie down next to me. The pain from chemo in my body gets sharper and starts to move through me again. I feel like it is trying to split me. I turn on my side and pull my body tight to myself, I close my eyes, trying not to cry. Audre looks at me, and I can see her eyes are scared. She starts rubbing my back and talking to me real quiet and low and stuttering a little bit, like she was scared.

"I is here, Mabel, just let me hold you, okay? Breathe with me, o-okay? The pain always want to leave you; just breathe it out. You still here, Mabel, I still with you. Okay? So you'll always be here."

Slowly, she slides down next to me, holding me from behind. She rubs my stomach real slow and breathes with me. I start to relax into the ground and into her body.

She sings that her love is my love, that it would take an eternity to break us. Whitney. I close my eyes and I just feel her arms wrapped around and holding me and hear her voice and I feel myself disappear into sleep.

When my eyes open up, the sun has shifted completely out of the sky and it's twilight. My favorite time of the day, when I can see the arrival of stars. I look over and Audre is still lying next to me, looking at the sky. And then she looks over at me and smiles.

"You sleep hard, gyal. Snorin', talkin', and everything! Do you remember your dream?" she asks.

And I do.

I look up at the stars in the sky and it all tumbles down into me, I remember it all.

Audre and her grandma were in it (though I don't know what she looks like, so I think my dream brain just substituted young Anita Baker), and I was walking behind them in these woods, up this hill. No matter how much I tried to keep up with them, I was falling behind. I tried to speak to her and I had no voice, even when I tried screaming, it was gasping and silence. She got so ahead of me, she was gone, and I didn't know which direction she went and the wind was picking up. Next, I was in the midst of a hurricane. I was in love with the hurricane, with the annihilation of it, the power of it. And it felt good to be a part of that power, to be able to move myself into the void of destruction and feel like I was safe. That I was loved. Then all of a sudden, I was at the top of this mountain and Afua was there, but he was someone else too. He was the watcher. I don't know what that means, but that's what it felt like. He was just the feeling of peace. And there was still a hurricane, but instead of destruction, it was the swirl of cosmos, it was just the everything. And nothing. Then there was nothing. Just a limitless feeling.

I finish describing my dream and look over at Audre, and she is looking at me kinda shook.

"Whoa, gyal, all that? You dream me? Queenie? And you dream Afua? That's weird. What yuh think that mean?" she asks, peering at me through her thick lenses.

I realize I hadn't mentioned the letter to her, even though it has been on my mind. Maybe because I felt stupid to be writing it in the first place. Telling a random stranger things I haven't been able to tell Audre or my parents or the therapist at the hospital, things my mama been trying to get me to say.

"I wrote him a couple weeks ago and he just wrote back. Maybe that is why he was in the dream?" I try to be chill about it.

"Oh."

I can tell she is feeling some type of way by the way she gets quiet. It is an awkward quiet.

"Audre, you cool?"

"Yes, I cool," she say in a way that I can tell she ain't cool.

"Mabel. Yuh never seem like you want to tell me important

things. I ain't the only one who is private about my life." She looks away from me to the sky.

"It wasn't a secret, Audre. I just didn't know why I was doing it, so I didn't even really think about it like that. I didn't even know if he was still alive, to be honest. I wrote it when I was bored." It seems like everyone has feelings about me writing Afua. There is more awkward silence.

"So . . . what it say then? Is you going to tell me that?" she asks, still seeming a little irritated, but curious.

"Of course! You can read it, if you want."

"You sure?" she said, sounding softer.

"Fah sho. I wanted to share it with you, anyway." As I reach down to grab for it in my pocket, I realize I'm covered in a soft blanket that she must have placed on me when I was sleeping. It smells like her and it makes me smile imagining her tucking me in. I stay quiet while she reads the letter.

"He sounds real, you know? And real sweet!" She is smiling, sitting, and using her phone for light to read by. "He said we gotta learn the stars, astrology, and thing. He mentioned me. You told him about me?" She looks up at me and I nod. She smiles bigger and continues to re-read the letter.

"And you tell him about Whitney? You is a nerd, for real! He favorite song is 'Where Do Broken Hearts Go?' Awwww. I don't know why that is so, so sad to me." She hands me back the letter and snuggles under the blanket with me. I put my arm around her, even though I'm self-conscious about how skinny it is now, yet she melts into me. It just feels natural. It feels good to be this close to her, on the dirt, under the stars and trees.

"How do you feel? You going to write him again?"

I think about it for a second. "After that dream, I think I'm supposed to."

"Yes, I think so too," says Audre, snuggling closer to me. We fit perfectly. My skinny, tall self, and her short, thick self. The pain is still there, but there is also Audre and the way I feel when I am around her. Just warm and safe, but wild too, like the hurricane in my dream. Lying there with her, I feel like if I could be as perfect as nature, maybe I could live forever.

AUDRE

I WAKE UP FEELING EXTRA COZY and sleepy under my blankets. It's Saturday, and since I ain't got school, I feeling to stay in my bed longer and I do. After a while, I feeling restless and I get up and put on my glasses and look out the window.

Everybody has been telling me about it, like it a bully that I have to keep my eye out for, but this bully never show up, despite all the talk. Until now. I can't believe what I'm seeing, and I start jumping up and down, it's so glorious.

"Dad, Dad! Look, you see it snow!?" I come out of my room, and he is sitting by his altar, meditating. "Oh!" I quick turn back to my room.

"Audre, it's all good—I was almost done anyhow." He smoothly rises. "And either way, this is your first snow—some kind of special rite of passage as a Minnesotan. What do you think about it?" He joins me at the window.

It takes me a minute to find words. "It's like nothing I ever experience. Like an overnight monsoon, but it accumulate like a sandstorm. I mean it is unbelievable and just so much of it.

And it keep coming down." I see our neighbors across the street, bundled up like rotis, waddling around and cleaning the snow off their car.

"Dumpling, I have to shovel our walk. Want to come outside and help? Really experience it? Make your first snowperson? Or snow angel?" He cracks a little smile and does the old shimmy dance he does when he is excited.

"It look cold, Dad, I is good watching it from in here." The idea of leaving the warm cuddle of his home for an adventure in knee-high snow and cold is not appealing.

"Okay, girl. You going to have to introduce yourself to it one day, though." He begins putting on his boots.

I watch him from the window slide the shovel underneath and then lift the big piles of snow from off our walk into our yard. I watch him for a while and then go into my room and lie in my bed, but the window catches my eye. I look at the snow coming down some more on a tree that had just lost all its leaves and is now holding snow as their replacements. It's truly beautiful. I decide I want to go outside.

When I finally conclude I have enough layers on, I is already sweating and it's difficult to even move. I step outside the door and onto the first step.

"Look at this snow queen! You look like you from here, girl. Actually you were born here, remember that? Minnesota girl!" he says, leaning on he shovel and cheering me on as I step out into the whiteness, like I is just learning how to walk. The cool air grazes my face wherever there isn't a scarf or hat. Meanwhile, Dad must be hot from shoveling; he has unzipped he own coat and stuff he hat in he pocket.

The sidewalk feels funny under my boots, like the ground got a cushion on it. Snowflakes hit my glasses and melt. I step into the front yard that yesterday was green grass and leaves and is now a jungle of snow. I keep walking and when I bring my hand down to touch it, I feel something whizz past me and land. I look back, and my dad is giggling.

"Try making a snowball, honey. This kind of snow is perfect for it." He packs the snow into a ball in he gloved hands, then flings it into the air, letting it land and disintegrate on impact.

I pick up a handful and start patting it down in my gloves. It makes a nice little ball, and I throw it into the yard, where it sinks through the surface. Magic. It feel like living inside a snow cone. Real strange, like a different planet altogether. I never imagined how snow would actually feel like.

"You know what?" my dad said, watching me and my island-girl apprehension at all of the snowfall surrounding me. "I have a surprise for you. Let me finish up and we going to have a little field trip," he says, and starts shoveling again before I can answer.

I soak in the tub and think about my first snow day. It's barely evening but it's already black like deep night and the bathroom is dark except for a candle. My skin is cold and clammy and welcomes the warmth and plunge of the bathwater. I can't believe I went sledding today—and that I loved it.

From the trunk of his Volvo, my dad produced a purple plastic-tray-looking thing with a rope dangling from it. We walked into the park and I felt like I was walking in a desert of snow, each foot dragging and heavy.

"It's like sit-down skiing?" I asked him, looking at a small crowd of people basking in the snowy mayhem, with no fear. "You want me to do that?"

"It's called sledding, baby. Here I'll go first, okay?" My dad somehow managed to get he hard-back self into the sled with he big ol' boots. He rocked forward once and then dropped over the edge of the hill, zooming down into the snow at what seemed like extreme speed. When he hit the bottom of the hill, his sled spun around and he let out a yell of joy. I couldn't help but smile.

"You scared?" said a little voice that pulled my attention from my dad. She looked about nine and was brown, cute, and nosy. "I been doing this since I was three. I ain't scared, it's fun. Why you scared?"

"Umm, I ain't scared. I just watching."

"You know this the baby hill, right?" she said.

My dad walked up and offered me the sled. I decline.

"I thought you said you wasn't scared though?" the little girl said. "You want me to go down with you?"

"No, thank you, I'm fine," I said.

"Do you, boo." Then she got on her sled and hits the hill without hesitation.

"Dad, okay. Let me try it once. Just one time."

He smiled and handed me the sled quick, probably afraid I'd change my mind. I placed it on the edge of the hill. It slid around when I tried to sit in it. My dad centered the sled and started to give me more advice.

"So, Audre. All you gotta do is get over this little edge and gravity will do the rest. You got this, honey."

I took a deep breath, rocked forward a tiny bit, and then I dropped off into the snowy abyss, my face whooshed in the cold, and snow flying all over me, my stomach instantly releasing a tribe of butterflies. I zoomed and swished and leaped through the snow. When I landed at the bottom of the hill a few seconds later, I fell back and looked at the sky. It was washed in gray clouds, puffy and drifting down flakes on my face, as I felt like I was floating on the snow beneath me.

I giggle and wiggle around in my hot bath. The candlelight glistens onto the water, giving the room a glow. I can't wait to tell Mabel about sledding when I see her next. The water is warming my body and skin. I try to get as much of my skin under the water as possible and stretch my body underneath the liquid surface.

MABEL

SINCE AUDRE'S DREAMO EXPERIMENTS, things have been weird and I can't explain it, how real it feels. It feels like I'm been traveling to other worlds and times. To be specific, the world and times of Queenie, Audre's grandma, and it's vivid and I feel it all over me. In this world, I am hearing and feeling the experiences and spirit of Queenie. Last night was the weirdest one yet...

I following a tall and handsome stranger through the woods. She song is trembling the leaves, grasses, and trees that was laid out in this hidden city bush. Mahal is slim and wild, like my boy Marley (my biggest love, my heart still broken he gone—two years already). She look like a man from behind, her back strong and broad, and in the front she got less tut-tuts than me. And she face is sweet and pretty while still being handsome in a way that I want to stare but I try not to look at too long. She got a small guitar that she call a cavaquinho, that reminds me of the cuatro that they have back home, swinging and strapped onto she back. Also slung on she was a leather bag she made for she self from back home.

The air feel soft, and like it can reach all the corners of my chest every time I breathe. I feel so happy, I start to hum a song to myself, just to feel the rumble of my voice pour through me alongside hers. Where I is walking is green and alive. I feel each tree is my friend and wan' tell me something they been holding in for a long time. I is tuck up in a forest so big you ain't feel like it amidst this harsh city that still ain't feeling like my home after ten months.

I used to listen to Bob Marley sing about a "Concrete Jungle" when I was in Trinidad but ain't understand it before I move to Brooklyn. Hard glass surfaces, high-rises, stone-gray cages, sidewalks that are harder than bitterness. Brownstone and limestone homes that hold the fury of lives in this city. In winter, the cold and the underground of this city will depress you, like a damp blanket on your heart is what I discover after a season of subways of snow and ice into Manhattan and working in a hospital that is old and white and with matching old and white nurses, who tell me to repeat myself slowly so that they can understand me "thick accent." Steupse.

But this is lush green. It is almost like home, and I is grateful to feel close to Spirit. Mahal is clearing the forest ahead of us, and as we step through, she creates passageways with her strong arms. She is taller than me and walk with power in she legs and back, yet she feet hit the ground soft. She nineteen like me too. She skin copper and dot up with freckles of she grandpa's cocoa skin, her mama's daddy who raised her after her parents left for work and never came back. She tell me later that her grandpa was an Afro-curandeiro, a Black healer, and taught she how to play the stringed instrument that looks like she borrow a child's guitar, but it sound like a conversation between angels when she sing while playing it, I would soon discover.

We reach the top of a hill and see the roofs of trees as far as we can see and much further away, all a Brooklyn and Manhattan. From she bag, she bring out a quilt that she lays out before us. Also from she bag is a feast for two runaways: almonds, raisins, grapes, apples, sorrel, lime juice, a chocolate bar, and four doubles (two for each of us).

The whole time we is talking real mellow and nice, like we ain't just meet the night before.

"This, I can do all day, every day. For real, Queenie. Be in nature and read clouds, read all of the songs of life in the wind," she says to me. She is leaned on her side, biting into an apple, looking at me, and I is avoiding she eyes and watching at the sky. I is thinking that meeting Mahal is the most interesting thing that happen to me in 1983.

The night before, my sister-roommate Daphne is working the late shift at the hospital and I have our place to myself and I feeling real irie, for once. I was home-cooking curry and playing my reggae records real loud like I does like it and which Daphne ass always complaining about. I was singing loud and wining my hips and stirring up all dem vibes in my food.

I almost ain't hear a knock at my door, but this knock wanted to be heard. Probably one of them church women, ain't wan' hear people jammin'. But when I looked out the peephole and I saw a face that familiar, but I ain't quite remember how it is I knew it right away. Next, I realized, I had started seeing this person in passing in our building recently. Some mornings I would see them waiting for the subway at the platform or walking away with a small guitar on they back. They was handsome, masculine, and always dressed sharp in slacks or a buttoned-up shirt, colors and patterns that made them look royal and artsy. And like they from a home of mine I ain't never been to yet. I kind of surprised myself, when I opened the door with small hesitation. They got thick, midnight curls surrounding a smile. I mean they face was a smile mainly. You see *a face like that and you notice eyes that soft and you know this not just a handsome person but a friend. We stood there watching at each other for a moment before they remembered to introduce they self and I recall to be annoyed.*

"Yes?" I ask.

"I, uh, live above you, and my name is Mahal," a voice pure and deep and an accent rolling from underwater.

"Mmm-hmm?"

"I a single woman, new to this neighborhood and ain't got no friends here," she said, smiling.

"And so?"

"And so, tonight what'tchu cooking made me need to know who was creating that smell. I could taste its healing in the air." She grabbed her stomach to prove it was empty. Her eyes were laughing and un-ashamed, like they had only known yes her whole life. She spoke in an accent that wasn't Yankee or West Indian. She look like she could be Trini but from the country, not a city girl like me, but she don't feel quite like she from Trini neither. She wore a button-up shirt made of blue, green, and purple patterns and intricately beaded symbols on the chest, almost like Egyptian hieroglyphs. This shirt was tucked into dark-green slacks that fit better than Marvin Gaye's on Soul Train *and shiny white-leather shoes. And she smell like sweet fruit and a fresh, manly type a cologne.*

"Well, you ain't even ask me my name before you come begging for me food?" I asked, remembering who I is and where I is from, but I feel-ing my tone is more nice than vex.

"What's your name?"

"Queenie. What yuh fix upstairs?"

She smiled and I could tell that smile ain't know how to cook.

"Well, nuh . . . so you come to make friends, 'cause you wan' food, but yuh come wit' yuh two arms swinging with nuttin' for yuh new friend?" I put a hand on my hip and point with my wooden spoon.

But somehow, I gave she a plate filled with curry chicken, curry melongene, and on a hill of rice, a sliver of avocado with plantain, and a dash of pepper sauce. We decide she would trade me a plate for an adventure.

The next day, I feeling excited and a little silly, but I is in front the little grocery on Fulton, down from the A train station, waiting for her end of the bargain. I ain't tell Daphne where I is going because she always got something sensible to say that result in no blasted fun. Even though I is nineteen and have a baby of my own, she still treat me like I is a chile. Since we kids, she sniff and scare away fun. She always act like she ain't know what it is like to be young and want to feel good and sweet tingling in your body, like when I used to climb trees, or swim out far and float in the water, or make a new friend for the purpose of unexpected joy. If I tell she I headed out to adventure with a strange stranger, who is more handsome than any man but is a woman, I would still be sitting in the apartment, hearing she mouth now.

Mahal was from Brazil, foreign in this land like me. And maybe she could be my friend. I ain't really have much friends 'cept some of the other West Indian women at my job at the hospital, but many of them are married or have kids and don't always have time to lime. Maybe we both need a friend?

Red apples are pile up high on the fruit stand, between oranges and green apples. The sun heating the sugar in the fruit and filling the air with they sweetness. The apples remind me of Daddy buying apples around Christmas as a special treat. He would bring them home after work, then pull his knife from his back pocket and would cut it in four, a piece for he, Daphne, Pearl, and me. I looking at the oranges and remember how he would peel skin off them in one long swirl for us to dry for tea for when we belly aching. I imagine Makeba, my daughter, hanging with him in the backyard, picking passion fruit and asking questions, and he patiently bending down and explaining all the different bush and herbs and what they do, like he did with us when we was little.

I sense Mahal before I hear she footsteps, and then I see her. When I see she walk up, I realize I feel something. And I realize it's I feel that I like she walk. Something about the way she move—strapping but also joyful, light. It reminded me of my favorite uncle Vincent who got the prettiest dance to his walk and the prettiest stutter when he talk, that all the women does love. When she come close, she smell like fresh shower and frankincense and swinging a small guitar on she back.

"You know yuh late?" I say, but she face is full of joy and she walking free and then she get serious and sorry.

"I know and I apologize. I no good with time," she say, and I realize I ain't really care. By how she face look, she seem sorry for real.

"No worries. . . . I is usually the late one. Good morning, Mahal," I say and try to be mellow.

"Good morning. Where I from, they say, 'Bom Dia!' or just 'Dia.'" Her eyes was looking in mine and we both looking too long. "You look so beautiful. I love you hair and you dress. I can't cook very good, but here is something I made after I ate you food." And she hands me a handkerchief of fabric that matched her shirt and was tied in purple ribbon. I open it up slowly. Inside is a bracelet with yellow and golden beads in a simple pattern, fastened together by copper and leather. Different, yet so pretty. No one had ever made me something like that.

"I sorry I late, I lose track of time. You like it?" she ask.

"I love it," and I really do. She offered to put it on my wrist and I let she.

"Let me get you some fruit, pick whatever you want," she say, waving her arm above the bounty and we pick out fruit for the adventure.

On the way to the train, she bring us to a Trini spot that was really just a door, a window, and the smell of curry. There is a line down the street of empty bellies waiting for their turn to order. When we get close, I see on the other side of the glass stew chicken, curry chicken, plantain, provisions, pumpkin, channa, dal, macaroni pie. I wasn't hungry till I see all my favorite food from home is there, even fry bake and okra.

Mahal looks over at me and we smile at each other. Then we giggle. I feel shivers when she places her hand on my waist to guide me in the tight quarters.

"How you know this place?"

"One day, I was on the way to work in the city—I wash dishes at a nice soul food restaurant in Harlem. One day, I will bring you food—and anyway, I see a line down the block, I get nosy and see why," she say. "Get what you want, I buy for you. Get drink too."

And suddenly I feelin' shy or good or something strange. Like we on a date.

"Please, let me. Remember I came to your door hungry last night? It's the least I can do."

I smile and don't refuse she. "Hmm. You know . . . I feel for some doubles."

"I love doubles," she agrees and licks she pretty lips.

"Mmm-hmmm, yuh love doubles?" I ask, surprise a little.

When we get to the counter the woman working behind it had she hair tie up in a scarf, her cheeks and eyelids peppered in moles, her mouth pursed up, looking prepared to put someone in they place at any given moment. She had on a bright-red shirt, red apron, and a big, wide bum bum—*a bum bum you could trust knew how to cook up something real good.*

"Eh-heh?" *she said, impatient at us already. She unprovoked vexness made me miss home bad.*

"Two doubles, please."

"Wit' pepper?"

"Slight." *My mouth feeling ready to eat.*

The lady grabbed two pieces of wax paper, and put two barra bread on each of them and then scooped up channa and pour it on top of the barra and then she put tamarind sauce and pepper on them. Everything she doing, my eyes chasing and seeing. Then in one move, she grabs the edges of the wax paper and flips and twists them into little soft pockets, just like back home.

"Umm, actually two more, please, same everything," *says Mahal, looking at the magic trick and leaning over like a hungry child. She then looks back at me and we giggle at each other for no reason. We just happy. The woman behind the counter look like she thinking to be annoyed with us, but then she face make a little giggle at us, like she catch we happiness too.*

"What you wanna drink?" *Mahal asks. I say water is fine. Mahal orders a sorrel and a limeade, which is actually what I did want. Mahal hands the auntie her money and a tip in exchange for the warm bag filled with home. We head to the train.*

Our walk in the park feels good. To be sweaty and be breathing deep good clean air and be amongst trees feel good to my soul in a way I ain't know I was missing. Once we reach the top of the hill and settle in, I take my first bite into my doubles, and I feel as if I is going to cry for some reason. I feeling emotional and foolish for it. For all the cooking I do, I almost never fix doubles and I think this is why. It reminds me of Bamba Rose, who help raise us. She pass a few years ago. She made she money selling doubles in the market and Daphne, Pearl, and I would go along with she while our parents was at work. Each bite, I overcome with missing home and Bamba.

After a bite, I chewing and I look up and see Mahal smiling at me like she know a secret.

"You look like you travelin' inside yourself," she say.

"Yes, whoever make dis, hand is real sweet. It's just like home, yes." I finish my first double.

"I like watching you eat. You eat like you know hunger for real. Me too. I love to eat. Food is a good healer. Make you feel like you have love." She fills she face with smile. "Like your food last night. Food made from a soulful place, is always healing." Then, after she finishes her own first doubles. "Do you miss Trinidad?"

I pause and think about it. I think about all of the sacrifices I had to make to be here, all what people had to say about me, mainly Makeba father. "I miss my daughter so bad, how she does smell and how we snuggle up. She laugh. I miss my mommy and being up early with she and walking by the ocean. I miss walking with my daddy up in the hills and picking herbs." I feeling my heart getting heavy thinking of Trinidad.

"What make you decide to move to New York?" she asks.

"My father and mother knew I had always wanted to see New York with my sister. They said since me and Ivan done—my daughter's father—if I wanted to try New York out, they would watch Makeba until I get settled and I could send for she. They ain't ever like Ivan since he is a bit of a ass. I think they knew he was the only reason I ain't travel the world. My mommy say, she knew I always have a spirit that want to travel, since I a little girl. I would look in my tantie's National

Geographic *and seein' all kinds of places and I want to feel how other worlds feel like. I is want to ride camels and play by the pyramids, I is wanting to go to China and walk all a the Great Wall and eat duck. When I little, I is dreaming of going skiing in Switzerland zooming down them mountains, boy." I wonder if Mahal think I sound foolish. Daphne think I is too dreamy and strange, and Pearl think I is always being too risky for no reason, chasing too much tings. I watch she face and she is watching me and I feel a zooook!!!! in my body. Like a feeling between us.*

"I love how you envision yourself . . . Back in Bahia, I play my cavaquinho and dream of soul music. I come here 'cause I wanna play music wit' my Black soul sisters and brothers in America. But, I also still sing Samba to myself, 'cause it remind me of home," she say.

She start singing a song in she language, and her deep voice become tender and full of emotion. I close my eyes and fall into she singing and the warm outdoor feeling.

"Why you choose New York City?" she asks.

"I always dream I would come here to dance. I love dancin' since back home. I taking dance classes and teaching myself moves I see on Soul Train *and at fetes. I always have my own style and pick tings up real fast. My tantie help me pay for my own ballet and modern-dance lessons in downtown Port of Spain, when I was a kid. I always wanted to dance in New York. Everybody go to New York and come back talking like a Yankee and making style with new clothes like it a perfect paradise. It ain't, I found out. But at least I dancing. I in dance class at least four times a week and I is going to start auditioning soon for a company. As hard as it is, I feel like it was meant for me to be here. I'm going to send for my daughter soon and then everything will be good." She so easy to talk to and I realize since I been here, I ain't really have anyone to talk to.*

"What's your daughter like?" Mahal asks me.

"You ain't tired of hearing me talk, yet? Goooosh, I feel I been talking your ear off, nuh."

"I don't want you to stop. The way you talk is pretty and what you have to say is helping me get to know you. So what's your daughter like? Is she like you?" She brown eyes blink slow and sweet.

"Makeba. She strong like she name. She a smart child. She understand so much even though she was only a little bit over two when I left home. She loves to snuggle and she smells like baby and fresh coconut oil. I miss holding she." My mom say how she would cry and look out the window for me after I leave for the States.

"I can feel how you miss her," Mahal say.

"Miss ain't the word. I feel lonely for her laughter. She laugh is so miraculous. I still can't believe this angel came through my body," I say. "She with my parents and she also spends time with she daddy, Ivan, sometime too. This is just until I can afford to bring she up here with me," I say. We are both lying down on the quilt Mahal spread down for us. We is looking up at the sky, breathing under its belly. It quiet and I cherishing every moment, being up there with she.

"Now that I tell you all my business, what bring you, Mahal?" I ask, leaning closer to her and holding my hand back from caressing her curls.

"When I thirteen, all records I listen to over and over, until it make me go crazy, Stevie Wonder, Marvin Gaye, Nina Simone, James Brown. I would be so full of hurt in my heart, I would walk in the woods and sing all night long praying for hope. I sing and I pray to feel heal after my parents were gone. I begin to have visions when I sing. Like I can communicate beyond what I can see. That my parents could hear me and I could see them. My dreams started to change and I was hearing and feeling things from a place deep inside of me and far away into other worlds. Sometimes, I would just close my eyes and all of these stories and voices and songs would come inside me, until all I could do was cry. I can see things in my dreams that tell me messages and no matter where I is, I feel I is being guided by a deep knowing inside of me. Like a old bush woman talk to me, like I is an instrument for the divine," she say, looking unsure of me.

"You is special," I tell she. "From when I first see you, I know that. When I was young in Trinidad, I see so much tings wit' my own eyes and in my own soul, that you would tink I telling stories. But I always knowing and tinking I was special too," I say.

"Can I tell you something else?" she say.

"Yes," I say, and Mahal smile and laugh a little bit, and she stay quiet and close she eyes. I close my eyes as well, liking that she silly and different like me.

I is there, behind my eyelids and breathing the stillness. And when I ain't seeing nothing, I feeling the thick heat on my skin, then breeze on my spirit. It feel so good to be still and quiet in creation. I feel my chest get quiet too, not racing and scared. Then I hearing Mahal, like she is singing from afar. And she voice ain't just human, but it from a bird that I feelin' trilling deep inside me. And there is a sadness there, a deep undersea sad. Without a seam, I fade into she voice itself. And then I is hearing ocean water and I feel I is lying beside it. And I is feeling the trees move in a gust, leaves singing a song about a child who is feeling abandoned by God and love and parents. A song of rainforests. A tree is a father in a long sad night. A night lasting weeks and months of tears and grief. The ocean becomes mother, and birth is the sun on the water. Mother let me float on she surface and I crying tears to add to she body and she rock me *in love and say it okay for me to bawl, and she carry me to the edge of she wet, never-endingness. And then that opens up from somewhere and I feel waterfall and the cool and everlasting healing of sky baptism, of good feelings opened in love. And I is in love with my own self. And I'm in water I can drink, and it sweet, like it got sugarcane soak in it. I start to giggle, 'cause I is almost drunk from its honeyness.*

I open my eyes and Mahal is giggling too. We look at each other.

I feel her hand find mine and when it does I settle my palm in hers. I is feeling her song in my chest and the breeze above me, and where she took me. I look over at she and she eyes is closed and she singing toward the cloudfull and unending blue above us.

MABEL

I DON'T TELL AUDRE ALL ABOUT MY QUEENIE DREAMS. Not yet at least. I got more to figure out first before I tell her about the potential side effects of her dreamo treatments. I use my chemistry notebook for my astrology notes and studies. It only has a few pages of notes in it from before I got sick and stopped being interested in doing homework. On the cover, it has Whitney and Robyn as teens sitting on a couch giggling. I pull out the two books I got on astrology from the library. One is *The Black Woman's Guide to Love Astrology* and the other is *Astrology Forever: A Complete and Comprehensive Guide*. I open up the first, which is poetic and easier to understand, with a lot of interesting pictures. I find the pages with my sign, Scorpio, and there is a painting of a brown woman with an ornate outfit and the pattern of a scorpion around her big Afro as well as beautiful beetles and bright red-orange flowers. I'm almost afraid to read about my sign because it's supposed to be the sexual and secretive one, and I always thought that was embarrassing. I remember the first time I met Jazzy, she was like, "Before we are friends, I need to know what sign you are." And when I was like "Scorpio?" she said, "Ooooh, girl, you a secret freak, ain't you?!" real loud in the lunchroom, which was so embarrassing because at that time I ain't even kiss anyone yet.

I read the first paragraph of Scorpio.

SCORPIO

OPAL, STEEL, CACTUS, ALOE, BURGUNDY, OYA, HEALING, THE UNSEEN

Scorpio is the second water sign in the zodiac and this rainstorm sista carries her magic and passion like sacred lightning. Very psychologically layered, this passionate sista is not afraid of the mysteries of life and all of whom want to share their deepest self with her. The sistas of this sign are intense and magical, in a highly intuitive and empathic way. They are intentional and tender lovers to all who are lucky enough to enter their lover's rock and will keep you laughing with their intelligent and penetrating humor. The shadow of her intensity is possessiveness, a side-effect of her deeply sensitive spirit and past broken trust. This star sign rules the most sacred and intuitive parts of our humanity. Sex, the occult, magic, pleasure, religion, death. She protects the divine that is within the shadow and in her own way protects the light. Scorpio symbolizes all that dwells in the magical essence of existence.

I stop reading and let those words marinate for a second. I'm not sure what it all necessarily means to me. I decide I'm going to read as much of these books as I can, even if I don't understand everything. All of the stuff about houses and planets and degrees is confusing but also a little like geometry with some mythology. I start to fill up my notebook with notes from both of the books and write up some info for each sign. I write another list and it's with everyone who is close to me, their birthdays, and sun and moon signs, which I was able to figure out from a chart in the back of one of the books called an ephemeris.

In my reading, I learn that people mainly just know about what their sun sign is, but that is only one part of who we are. That the Moon, Venus, Mercury, and all of the planets and where they were in the sky when we were born will tell us the story of who we are. I close my eyes and imagine little baby me coming into the world and all of the planets and stars are imprinted in me like cosmic DNA or something. I wonder if my dying or Afua's death row and all of the messed-up stuff in life is somehow controlled by the stars? Are the stars like God?

And I don't even think I understand God or how I feel about him or it. Or maybe she or them? My grandma talks about God and Jesus and the Bible, and my mama is more meditation and the Universe. My dad said he knows God through growing food from seeds and dirt, water and light, and he feels God when he tastes the miracle of fruit in his mouth. Audre told me a story about how when she was little, she thought her grandma might be God. I still don't know if I know what I believe yet, even now that I'm . . . maybe gonna be gone. I have been praying Afua's prayer anyway though, to any and everything that might, could help me live.

I look up the Sun and Moon signs for me, Whitney, Audre, Mama, Daddy, and Sahir, and write it down in the book.

I read that Whitney's sign is the sign of Leo, which is ruled by the Sun and is symbolized by lions and are powerful, creative, giving, and are brave. I write this down in the notebook too. That seems like Whitney. Reading on Audre and her sign is Aquarius, the water-bearer, and that sign is supposed to be freethinking, individual, and inventive. That sounds pretty accurate to her. I decide to skip to the part of the book that talks about the signs in romance and read the compatibility between Scorpios and Aquarius . . . out of innocent curiosity.

AQUARIUS AND SCORPIO IN LOVE:

Both signs are intense in unique and evocative ways.
Scorpio's intensity goes deep and soulful, while Aquarius's
intensity goes wild and into other worlds. They challenge
and awaken each other in ways that are curious and at times
frustrating. But no blessings come without lessons and love
without expansion is not the kind of love that satisfies either
of these signs. This love may not be the easiest but when
you combine the powers of Scorpio, who goes as deep as a
submarine made out of hematite and ancestors' bones and as
far reaching as Aquarius to the birthing of universe itself, you
find a love that is dangerous and divine.

The way they describe us feels intense. "Dangerous and divine." It's weird to see something written in a book that feels real to your heart. Kind of like when I first read Afua's book. Either way, Imma continue to write and read up on everyone's astrology stuff. If I'm going to be learning anything new before I die, I would rather it be stuff like this and other stuff that feeds my soul.

MABEL

MAHAL'S APARTMENT IS SMALL, *a single room with a tiny fridge, sink, and hot plate in one corner and a bathtub in the other. The walls are forest- and emerald-green swirls that look like the malachite she wears around she neck, close to she heart. She got a bed that she cover with mosquito netting in the middle and different blankets and weavings and wind chimes that she create in honor of her ancestors and spiritual guides, with collected fabrics, ribbons, copper, bamboo, shells, and branches. She has a sepia-colored picture of she and she grandfather from when she was little on the fridge. He a sturdy dark man with a machete in he hand and she a wild brown child next to him, with a smaller machete in her hand. She has thrift lamps with shades that she created from cutting designs and shapes out of beautiful handmade paper she bought in Chinatown. She fill the space with she spirit and it my favorite place to be. And it got the best heat—almost tropical.*

I sitting in my panties on she windowsill, peeking out onto the courtyard with the night snow, that looking like crushed crystal and sapphire in the full moonlight. I finishing a spliff of ganja, lavender, and tobacco. It's my twentieth birthday, and I is crying. I is officially no longer an adolescent or a kid. I ain't know why I crying, shouldn't I be feeling like a big woman? I feel like I is a stchupid lost girl chasing a dream in a strange land. And I crying 'cause I can't believe I is somebody mommy, when I still feeling so young myself. How is it I a year older and I feeling even less big? I dancing and living in New York, but I miss my own mommy. And I miss my little Makeba so much. And I just miss my island. I miss the smell of the tree and bush and flower and the way the sun knows my skin back home. Mahal brings me a plate of sliced pineapple. She kisses my lips and cheeks that are wet up with my tears like she been doing all day.

"Querida, I know how it feel when your soul is telling you what you need to do to be happy and it seem strange to everybody in the world. You feel like you gotta do it or a piece of your spirit will never be whole," she say, like we was already talking in our spirits, before she speak aloud. "But, it ain't easy following your dreams."

"I decide after I give birth that Makeba would know that she is loved and free to be she self." I is crying harder. "I just feel so far away from her today."

"But you're always with her, in your heart. Trust, even if it's hard." Then she kiss each of my feet. "Let's go to La Palais, in honor of you blessing this earth twenty years ago, and in honor of Makeba, who loves you," she say.

"Mahal, I ain't feeling to dance."

"Minha gatinha, it's bad luck not to dance on your birthday," she say swinging she lanky body around me.

"Is that right?" I say, feeling a little softness smile within my chest.

"You an old soul in the body of a young wild woman, and they both need to dance." She starts to samba for me in she underwear, in the moon's spotlight.

• • •

And that night, we reach to the spot after a journey in tundra, in snow higher than we ankles, colder and heavier and wetter, like sand made from ice. We maneuvering through snow and icicles and night. Mahal in a bright-red thrifted snowsuit and me, thick leg warmers over tights, under a golden yellow sweater dress and dark purple coat. We covered in hats and scarves. Snowflakes on my mascaraed lashes and my bright eyeshadow, lipstick, blush, and foundation bought at the only makeup counter that sell hues for Black woman on Fulton Ave. We making tracks for ourselves through the winter wonderland of Brooklyn, passing the other snow-drifters along Nostrand and Marcy. I feeling the snow on my face, frigid and intense, but invigorating. I laugh because in my core, I is an island girl, and somehow I find myself wrap up in a snow globe of a life. Mahal's and my brown bodies huddle close. We tropical travelers share a flask of ginger tea that we simmer in cinnamon, orange peel, and some apricot brandy to fill ourselves with hotness for the journey.

We knock on the door of Le Palais de Pum-Pum, also known as our friends Vipasa and Nuemeh's brownstone, and inside is a full house of people dancing to a blaring fury of organs, trumpets, percussion, and guitar picking scripture, while the Afrobeat King himself, Fela, sings and chastises the Nigerian government in broken English from their speakers.

"YESSSSS! You bring the birthday girl out'cha love den! I is glad you share her with us! Honor to the queen, QUEENIEEEEEE!" It's Vipasa, in a sexy and slinky satin emerald-green dress, a turquoise lace headwrap and big gold Fulani earrings hanging from her ears. She is a sweet woman from the Virgin Islands—a dancer like me—and as soon as we come to she door she squeeze we up in a hug. She and she lover, Nuemeh, run "SPEAK! Easy . . . ," a space for artists, for free-spirit type of people, for people who love like me and Mahal. It's a place to dance, share poetry, sing, shout, and be free.

The room smell like sweat, pelau, plantain, and joyful feelings. The room is filled with skin, in every adornment and sharpness and handsomeness and pretty. People is moving and graceful in they own bodies and rhythms. It is pure magnificence and love.

I see Nuemeh, a dapper and sharp older Cameroonian butch, who came to the States to study architecture. Every Saturday she is behind the bar she designed and built in their garden-level apartment. Behind her is all the elixirs she created out of spirits and herbs and spices, flowing into glasses and into hands and onto the dance floor. The DJ starts playing some house music and we hang up all of our winter heavy and is onto the dance floor.

Mahal bring she Brazilian samba feet and I is swinging and wining my Trini hips and bum bum. When we dancing, it like we souls been dancing together forever. It always feel so right with Mahal. She grab me from behind and snuggle me as we dance together. We sweating and hot, forgetting about winter and ice. In La Palais, it remind me of J'Ouvert in Port of Spain, when we all feeling our most colorful and sensual selves, where you see people evolve into a spirit they abandon their day-to-day selves to become.

On a slow song, me and Mahal wrap up in each other, my arms around she neck, she arms around my waist. Close. She singing along to one of my favorite tunes, "Distant Lover" by Marvin Gaye. It has to be damn near three in the morning, but the music so good it won't let me leave the spot before I sure I wear myself out.

Then, we is in the corner, sitting with Mahal arm around me, cooling down from the dance with some of Nuemeh's ginger beer on ice and feeling enchanted. I is tracing invisible designs in Mahal's skin with the sweat dripping from her.

"You give me the best birthday, thank you, dahlin'," I say, kissing Mahal on she dimple on she cheek, then she nose, then she lips. She smiling all silly and kissing me back with she soft and sweet lips. Our bodies are snuggled up tight when I notice something catch her attention and I looking to see what she is watching at. It's a young woman, tall and cinnamon, look like a model with her hair in a ponytail, blue jeans, and a light blue sweater. She smile is broad and intoxicating and I understand why Mahal staring a little. The girl's friends is pushing she to do something and then all of a sudden I hear something that lick me in the soul.

"I've got to be free!" The girl's voice is so pure, goose bumps lift up on my skin. She start singing to the inside of my heart. She is singing Deniece Williams, and it is a voice that you can feel in your toes, glory in each note. The DJ fade the music and give she the room to take over and she fills it with bewitchment. Her voice is coming from Goddess she self, and everyone is quiet and listening and staring at she. And she beaming wild joy when she is singing. She movement is energetic and excited almost like she blossoming fire from she chest with every note. She is singing and she overcome the room with her soul, and I realize, she is in she own universe. We is quiet, except for moans of feeling and "yes, chile" and "all right, baby" in response as we all filling up our soul with she blessings. When she done, we all quiet for a second and then we all clapping, yelling, and giving she love.

"Give it up for young Whitney! She is already a star, can't y'all see it?" the DJ says and there is more snaps and claps and yelping.

A coolness walk up behind this Whitney and wrap she up. This coolness was another girl, handsome and tall in a black turtleneck and *jeans, her hair curled, short and styled neat. She bring she a beverage. The chanteuse sips it and gives she a kiss and swings her arm around she lover's neck and they start dancing. With not a care, like she is free. The dapper girl smiles, kinda sheepish, melt into them love and kisses from she sweet singing lovey.*

"The soul in that voice . . . she know some blues and hurt," Mahal say.

"Why you say that?" I say.

"The prettiest voices are kites for the heaviest hearts," she say.

"Well, it seem she know some sweetness too," I say. The couple is dancing and watching each other, not noticing or even thinking of we. In La Palais, they were like all of us. All of we being our full self in a world where most of we is told to contort, lie, or die.

AUDRE

"**AT CARNIVAL TIME,** I does love Trinidad the most. Everywhere yuh hearing drums bumping bass and the pans is beating, and Soca music is everywhere. And everyone is themselves in a way that I wish they would be all year. Everyone acting free and dressing up and masquerading! You does have the jab jab, who paint they skin shiny night black and be talking a silly rough weird voice talk in the streets. And then there be them kind of masqueraders that wear bikini, feathers, and beads, in one of them big groups that is all about looking sexy and pretty and partying. I does love the moko jumbies, which is them on the two stick and they is high above the crowd, dress up like neon and blue aliens." I am telling all this to Mabel late one night in she bedroom after she shaking of fright and sickness and sweating out the chemo.

She was twisting and turning in she sleep and then she started to mumble and shake up while she was dreaming. When she started to moan and scream, I woke her up. I was awake and unable to fall asleep anyway. Once Mabel was up, she couldn't fall back asleep, so I decide to tell her about mas time in Trini.

"Carnival is very important to we, especially in my family.

Queenie tell me stories about how when she was a kid, her father, my great-grandfather Maceo, would be up all hours of the
night, tuning and rehearsing his pan for playing mas," I say, and
the picture of Queenie's altar comes to my imagination as I snuggle with Mabel and smell the healing mixture of sweet orange,
lavender, bay rum, and amber I made for her.

"Leading up to carnival, Queenie would pick me and Episode
up on evenings and take us down by the panyards to hear the different steel bands practice, getting ready for Panorama, which is
a big competition of all of the different steel bands to see who
got the best calypso." I close my eyes for a second and drift there
in my heart. We watching all of the different musicians, jumping
up and beating them rhythms, and we is dancing too. The night
does feel so sweet with them sounds. Queenie would get us Solos,
Trini soda, and she get she a Stag beer and of course we is eating
doubles. Gyal, the music is so sweet, Mabel—I mean, it just put
this feeling in the air." I feel my eyes getting wet from even imagining this sacred moment from back home.

"What does steelpan sound like? I don't think I have ever
heard it," she says.

And I wonder to myself, how do you explain the sound of
pan? I pull out my phone and find a mix of steelpan I have. I find
an older one, of a Stevie Wonder song, "As," that used to be one
of Queenie's and me's favorite. I play it for she and feel my whole
self tingling with each note.

She seems to feel it too, as she eyes closed with a smile to the
tune. "Do you got any Whitney on steelpan?" she says, and we
both start to giggle and I love how joy between us feels, especially
when she ain't feeling the best.

"Right, your best friend. I bet someone do one of she songs. Let me see what I find on YouTube." I look and find one and play it for her.

"Oh suki now. Girl, you found a cut too. 'Saving All My Love for You' is a classic. Hmm, this is sweet, like a lullaby," she whispers, her eyes closing. She leans into me and snuggles even closer and I feel she breathe softly on my face. I snuggle up to her a little too. I close my eyes and imagine myself back home in the pan-yard with Mabel amidst these sounds. I imagine Neri too and us all being there together. This possibility seems impossible for a lot of reasons, but I is imagining it anyway. I look over at Mabel and she has passed out. She looks peaceful again.

"I'm saving all my loving, yes, I'm saving all my love for you . . . ," I sing to myself and Mabel and no one in particular.

CAPRICORN SEASON

the greatest one of all was a fury of dance and jabs
in honor of those shackled and beaten
he fought for them and giggled while doing it
it was a joy

it was a reminder
that we can climb the mountain
sure-footed,
on crumbling foundations
boogie on them even

even if it is known that Kilimanjaro is surrounded by valleys
it is also known on the summits
we get a full view and when the clouds is below you
you can dream of heaven on earth

the crone got all silver teeth and she use mud to make her home
the pretty red dirt is her makeup
and her chewing gum
the mud got so hot it became ceramic
and endured for civilizations
underground, lingering earthly lifetimes

Olmec heads are proof
that we crossed oceans and we built and we remained
and embedded under every new civilization
is an earth that never forgets

AFUA

DISAPPEARING ACT

Sakeem disappeared while being injected. Entirely faded into space as the serum united with his blood. It was through the walls, whispers, and kites that this news spread. That he got more transparent until all that was left was the navy-blue attire issued to him that all of us convicted wear. The way rumors move around prison, it is hard to know what to believe, so you got to believe all of it and none of it, at the same time. It was never confirmed by the two guards I asked, but more importantly it was never denied. Instead there was always a look of curiosity at my question with uncomfortable laughter and then a shake of the head but never an utterance of the word *no*. They looked like men who heard of a miracle they refused to believe, and thus laughter was their only response. So then I had no choice but to believe it and ask myself, why couldn't someone just fly away? Remove themselves through magic or fear itself?

After Sakeem's disappearance, I would lie in my bed and think of all of the layers of life and magic I done experienced in my

lifetime. Even the bad stuff, over time had begun to reveal a certain silvery emergence within my soul and a recalling of lessons.
And sometimes there was no lesson, just an ambiguous abyss of
loss, like in the death of my friend and my own unjust incarceration. Loss, plain and simple.

Ms. Valerie sent me this book about past-life-regression hyp-
notherapy that up until that time, I never thought to open or read,
but Sakeem's disappearance opened up a channel of my brain
that I couldn't shake off and this book for some reason piqued
my interest. I started attempting to do some of the techniques.
I would lie in the bed in my chamber and breathe deeply until I
could relax myself. I recited the words over and over that were to
bring me to a liminal place within my consciousness. I felt kind
of foolish at first but I would just keep reciting these words until
they were cycling through my head in a loop. One day, I said these
words until I found myself perched somewhere high and above
this earth. I was where I could see the landscapes and doorways
to the lives of my soul. I watched cosmic reels of me journeying
through past existences that I had never known of. I felt the tingling of past bodies in my current one.

MABEL

AFUA'S BOOK and my dreams got me thinking hard about ancestors. Afua writes about his past lives all the way back to Africa—sometimes as a man, sometimes as a woman. I begin to wonder about if whether this was my first and only life. I have always been a kid people would call an old soul or like my aunt Niiki would say, I been here before, but I don't know if that means I have actually lived other lifetimes or will live again when I die in this one.

Afua calls going back in the past in order to embrace the present moment through meditation, mantra and hypnosis Sankofa sojourns. He travels and sees himself in a past life and watches it like a movie. One life that he spoke of, I remember in particular. He was a girl-child who was more indigo than night.

> *I was imprisoned in that life too. All of the women in my family were shamans and sensual healers and I was a warrior in this lineage. Women were powerful within my family and village. One day strangers arrived. They smelled like smoke and their*

skin was silver and thin. They offended our people by talking to my king grandmother's husband instead of bowing to her and giving her gifts. These offending men were sent away with machete and breast brandishing. Then that night our village was destroyed in an explosion of bullets as were our temples. They slit my grandmother's throat as well as her two wife-companions and three husbands. In all of my lifetimes and all of my losses, the loss of this grandmother put the largest break to my soul, I learned in my Sankofa sojourns.

I wish that he was free in this life and could walk in a cool mist of rain and feel it on his face or just be home chilling on the couch, talking shit with family. Stuff I'm going to miss and want to do, no matter where I end up. Even if his concepts or ideas might seem like he is a weirdo or crazy to some people, sometimes the only thing that gives me hope are his thoughts and words. I'm still scared and can't think about my future very much without it feeling foolish. And at the same time I feel like I can imagine myself being more than an afraid girl dying but a soul that can return again and be a multidimensional being.

I have had different bodies and earthly and otherworldly homes. I see this as a lifetime spent to study stars, meditate, and master myself. How else could I be here? Or is this what I tell myself to try and make sense of the darkness and destruction of spirit that prison has been to me? I guess I'm never really sure. I do know that I'm here and that I have been before and I will be again.

AQUARIUS SEASON

clay mold of structure and intellectual mastery

holding the wetness of our emotion heavy humanity.

the wisdom of the future

unfolding in multidimensional visions

in woke third eyes.

holding the expanse of emotions

the emotions of seas, the depth of oceans

hold it all

without succumbing

to the heavy of the feelings.

she the old lady sage from other worlds,

the precision of restraint

and the limitlessness of cosmic intuition.

AUDRE

We was fifteen and she was an underground railroad to my hidden self. Freedom, at the end of dark tunnels. When I met Junie in 1957 in my Harlem hood on the stoop of my uncle's brownstone, we was best friends on the spot. She was the first person who I ever kissed and told "I love you" to and my first real friend in the States when I move up from Port of Spain with my mother. Junie's father was Dominican and her mother was from Jamaica, but she born in America. In Junie's love, I learned that loving on a Black girl wasn't sinning, but something I lived to do, like painting or eating perfectly ripe plums. From when I was a kid, I had always wanted two things: to love on women and paint. Before I even know the words lesbian *or* bull dyke, *I fell in love with my best friend one Harlem summer on a rooftop watching clouds move and make shapes above us.*

Junie even as a young woman looked regal and with the cutest dimples. She was salve and rain for me. I never felt like I deserved love, because from young, I knew I loved and desired women and that it was supposed to be a transgression to God, so

I had decided not to love at all. But Junie loved me. No one ever tell you that falling in love with another Black girl would allow you to feel like you a part of an ancient and precious secret. When we spoke it was soul to soul. My body felt her stories and poetry, and I would just surround myself in her day after day. To see Junie, this brilliant black star, I couldn't help but love myself.

When we was eighteen, I started classes in plumbing at tech school, and it seemed like she was avoiding me. Next I heard about her, Junie got married to a Jamaican and moved away to Queens. It was an unexpected shock, to lose love and be betrayed all at the same time. When I tell you I felt like I was dying, I was so heartbroken. It wasn't easy being a Black lesbian then, or even now and she probably did what she thought she had to do. Yet, somehow at the deep-sea level of my grief, the seed of her love illuminated a desire for life. And a desire for pleasure and knowing my erotic, my bliss. Every woman I have loved has shown me Goddess and devastation and I thank them every day for the lessons and insights in their love.

—Ena Amethyst-Miel, *Black Girls Know How to Love, with Coconut Oil, Along the Cornrow*

I copied these words into my notebook. They come from a lesbian Trinidadian-American painter and poet I found to do my project on for Ms. Sharkey's class. She paintings is like she words, unique and vulnerable and it remind me of Trinidad. I read the words over and over. The words make me feel less lonely, just hearing someone else has experienced a big tabanca. I think of my life and how I seem to find some kind of pain, wherever. Whether it be in my dreams, with my mom, Neri, or Mabel. I feeling love for Mabel and I don't know how to stop it. All I know about love is how to find its hurt and its endings after I find its sweetness. I touch by my heart and feel my pouch and feel for the hardness of the rocks I find by the creek by my house, the sand from by the beach by Queenie, herbs, and my sacred stones and whisper my affirmations for Mabel's healing.

Sweetness is here. Kissing at all things. Broken or confused.

You are safe. Universal. Limitless. Sacred. Sensual. Divine. Free.

I breathing and trying to remember Queenie's lessons and incantations when I feelings so scatter in my spirit. I'm in the corner of Ms. Sharkey's room, feeling all of these feelings while Prism, the LGBTQIA+ and allies group is meeting like they do every Wednesday after school. Jazzy is in the front of class leading the meeting while everyone is chattering with laughter and ruckus. I is in the corner, trying to ignore everyone and to focus on my prayers and concoctions so I'll be ready to see Mabel right after the meeting. But I keep getting distracted by a feeling I can't shake: heavy and weak, stuck and hopeless, like the snow and the ice have taken over my inner world. Nothing feeling like it going right, just stuck in stone and nothingness.

After the meeting, I is helping clean up the room and pack up the snacks. Folks are leaving, and Jazzy is sitting on the couch and finishing writing up the notes from the meeting. Prism's meeting agenda is on the big white board. Jazzy's handwriting is big and loopy, each item in another color of the rainbow.

QUEER PROM
POETRY NIGHT
OUR ZINE

END OF THE YEAR TRIP TO ATL
SERVICE LEARNING
JUSTICE FOR MURDERED TRANS WOMAN
PETITION FOR INCLUSIVE LGBTQIA+ SEX. ED

She and I have become pretty cool, especially since we have Ms. Sharkey's class together. She invited me to lime at the meeting even though I tell she I have schoolwork to do and I is not any of them letters that the group is for. Like Queenie, Jazzy don't really care what you want to do when she wants you to do something. She said if I stay, she will give me a ride and I can do homework in the corner if it's boring.

"I'm glad you stayed. You always bouncing home after school or to Mabel's house—which I totally get, Audre. She goin' through it and it seems she really trust you," Jazzy says, as I finish organizing about the room and plop down next to her in the couch corner that is my favorite place to be in Ms. Sharkey's class. She finishes her note taking and looks at me and smiles.

"How you feeling about the group? I know you ain't 'any of the letters' as you say, but you know anyone back home who is? What is it like for queer folks in Trinidad?" Jazzy asks, and my chest and face start feeling hot and nervous and I is fidgeting with my fingers.

I um and uh and shrug for it seems like forever, but she won't let it go, so finally I say, "I sure there is people down there who is like that, but I ain't know . . . I mainly would see my friends from church or I is with my family, so I wouldn't know," I say, stumbling out an excuse as I curl up a little bit more in my corner. I wonder if she could see I ain't comfortable with she questions.

"Hm-mm," Jazzy says. "I bet you there some fine girls down there. One day you should let me go back home with you. That would be lit. I bet you I find me some queer family down there," she says, looking wistfully into the constellation of Christmas lights hanging from Ms. Sharkey's classroom ceiling. "Do you got a special someone in the islands? 'Cause people around here is asking about you . . . ," Jazzy says in her way that seem like she know something mysterious, whether she actually does or not.

"Asking about me?" Besides Jazzy, Ursa, and Mabel, I ain't thinkin' of no one else at that school unless they are a teacher who is affecting my grades. "I ain't interested, I just here to focus on school and I have my little crew. I ain't got time anyway," I say, and leave it at that, only slightly curious.

"All right, playa, all right. So there *is* a fine cutie at home?"

I don't know how she make her eyebrow rise like that. "Why there have to be a fine cutie at home? I just doing me." I try to act cool, adjust my glasses, and sit up a little bit.

"You right, you right. Sometimes you gotta just be *Living Single* like Khadijah. I feel you. I'll let the streets know, it's no nada for you." She seems finished with the interrogation, but I have a question for her.

She and Ursa been my main sistren here, besides Mabel, since I begin school. I is happy for this moment, with all of the starry Christmas lights twinkling around we. I like talking to Jazzy, and the room is deserted except for us.

"So, is you and Ursa something?"

Jazzy starts giggling and smiling really big the moment the question slip out my mouth. "Are Ursa and I something? I would say yeah, but we can't really be all out there with it, even at school 'cause she is concerned it could get back to her family, since her auntie work here. She is the youngest, and she don't know how her mama would feel or even her siblings. Her mom is really sweet though, and she don't know we a thing and I'm okay with that . . ." She pauses for a moment. "I guess, 'cause Ursa is my heart no matter what anyone else knows or thinks. Ursa said that she don't even know if her mom knows what being queer is, which I doubt." For the first time, I see Jazzy not seem so sure of she self, which I could relate to.

"How about your family? Do they care that you is a lesbian?" The word lesbian feels new in my mouth.

"I think they over it now. I came out when I was in eighth grade. My dad ain't really care too much, actually. My auntie who raised him is a big ol' dyke and they real tight. My mom at first thought I didn't know how I really felt and was doing it to be cool—like I ain't already dope." She laughs at the notion. "So, me and my smart mouth asked her if Auntie Alexis was just trying to be cool for the last forty years? I was really hurt she would even say that, Audre, you know? Like I'm simple. And I know she wouldn't have said that if I said I was liking some boy, so, why is liking girls a phase?" she asks me and no one in particular, and I feel she was right. I ain't never hear she tell me about she self in this way and I appreciated her openness. Then she starts to giggle again.

"And then WHY my first girlfriend had to be this FINE senior, when I was a sophomore?" I love how Jazzy say she thoughts like a question. "I had been liking Charmaine since I was in ninth grade and we was in Journalism together. *Whooo* and my mama wasn't ready for that, but I wasn't gonna lie since me and my mama is tight. For a while, she kept acting like Charmaine had 'seduced me,' which I had to let her know, it wasn't like that." She pulls out a pic and starts fluffing her hair wider.

"I get dudes hollering at me all the time, like I owe them my attention and body, but Charmaine wasn't even like that. She was so sweet and shy, she played ball, was tall and everything." Jazzy trailed away, giddy in even remembering Charmaine.

"How did y'all connect?" I is hoping she feel to share more, wondering how girls talk to other girls when it's not an underground church love.

"Oh, I was the one who hollered at her after one of her games. I was, like, 'What up, shawty?' I was so thirsty. I asked her if I could take her out for ice cream one day when she was free. I don't even think she knew it was a date. At first, she wasn't trying to talk to me 'cause I was younger, or whatever, but she got over it. It ended when she went away to school. She plays college ball and we still cool." She's quiet for a moment and then I see she eyes notice the clock behind my head.

"Let's get up out of here, girl, so I can bring you to Mabel's," she say, and we pack up all of our things, close up the classroom, and head to Jazzy's car.

We is sitting in she light-blue hatchback around the block from school, waiting for it to warm up. Winter. First it was very whimsical and fun, but now it feeling cold and dark and make me feel too much feelings. Jazzy put on BLK LVRS while we waiting for the car to heat up and the speakers is bumpin' a good vibe, but my spirit feeling tight and sad listening to QWN. I start to hum along, thinking of the heat of Trinidad and trying to lift the feeling from my heart.

"I love this car. My dad fixed it up for me for my birthday. Since he got out of jail a couple years ago, he always trying to make up for all them years he was gone, although I tell him I ain't tripping. I ain't mad I'm done with that bus life though," she said, adjusting the dials on the heater.

"It's cool how you just yourself and tell your parents who you is," I say to her, thinking of my mom and the day by the water and how it feel she stopped loving me after that. I try to imagine her accepting me as I am and I'm hurting more because I literally can't imagine it.

"I do feel lucky actually, because I know kids who don't come out because they know their parents will trip. Or they've come out and got kicked out. That's why I understand Ursa's situation. It's fucked up because we are just being our true selves. I was scared, for sure, but my mom always taught me you got to be yourself or else you end up someone else you probably won't even like." She rocks back and forth to the music, while huddling into herself for warmth.

I is feeling tears well up in my eyes and I trying to breathe them back inside me, but I feel I is going to fall apart instead. I slowly begin to erupt and then I bawling and can't stop.

"Girl, you okay? What's up? Is it about Mabel?" Then she just reach over and just holds me. I start to choke on sobs, pouring out months of pushed down ache. I is feeling Mabel and Neri and Queenie and Epi and my mama, my dad, the snow and the ocean and the stars and ice, life and death, all in my throat holding words down and pushing truth out.

It hard to speak, I'm so plug up with feelings, so I just breathing and crying on Jazzy. She snuggle me up and it make me cry more.

"It's okay, get it out, I ain't scared," she say, and I just let myself go into she arms, because I can't really do anything else.

She holds me for a long time. And after I calm down a little, she pulls out her water bottle from her backpack and some tissues and gives them to me.

"You don't gotta tell me anything, okay, girl? Just cry, okay? It's okay," she tell me, and I relax into her.

"Jazzy . . . ," I say, and I is able to breathe deeper and I is calming down in she arms. "I had a friend in Trinidad . . . she was more than just any type of friend," I say. Jazzy is really quiet and keeps holding me. Once I say those words, I say everything else.

"She went to my mother's church and she was the pastor's granddaughter. She sing real beautiful and make me feel like I belong, even though I ain't want to be there. She name is Neri and I really love she," I say, and Jazzy still here, holding me tight. Jazzy listen, and we is just here in she car. I tell she everything about me and Neri's C.H.U.R.C.H.

"'Cause I love Neri, my mama send me from Trinidad." I cry into the cold air that freeze the tears to my face, but Jazzy's arms warm me up.

"Awww, Audre, girl, it's all right to cry." She holds me tighter. "What you went through was traumatic and then being sent off. Dang, girl. And your dad don't even know, so you been bottling that up on top of it. That can't feel good."

"Jazzy, I miss Trinidad. I love it here also. I didn't want to come here initially, but my father has been good to me and I ain't know I was going to make real friends. But I still feel like I got life in Trinidad too that feel interrupted. I is feeling like I ain't know what to do and my spirit feel so heavy, it so dark and cold here and it feel like my spirit is that way too." I tell her that Neri get sent away to Tobago with her elder cousin.

"So you don't even have contact with her either? I wonder what she is going through." Jazzy sits up and then closes her eyes in thought.

"Jazzy, I just feel like I is bad luck. After all a that, I is sent up here and my first friend turn out is dying. And, to be honest, I think I is getting feelings for she too." I'm unable to shut up now, and Jazzy leans back and looks at me and starts smiling.

"Oooh, see, I knew it, girl! Awww . . . That's so sweet. And complicated too. Love always is though. I'm sure she feels for you, too, though, boo. You are adorable. Plus you got that sexy accent and you're so sweet."

I surprised hearing her describe me in those ways.

"But, Jazzy, I is telling you, there must be something wrong with me. Ever since I young, I never feel quite good inside, and now I is messing up everything that come by me."

"Are you blaming yourself for Mabel's bizarre disease? That ish is just effed up and nobody knows why bad stuff happens, especially to someone so dope and chill as Mabel. But it don't make it yo' fault, girl," she say, looking at me deeply to see if I is trusting what she was saying. "Matter fact, you be the main one being there for Mabel and making her feel good during this sad situation. Making her all of them Technicolor juices, watching cartoons with her, and just helping her feel less lonely. That's what she probably needs more than any of those crazy treatments she's getting in that hospital." Jazzy grabs my hand, holding it firm. "We all scared and don't know how to handle it, but you are a real one, Audre, and you just love her." Her hands are on my face now, wiping away my tears with her soft fingers. "You are a good person, okay? Even if your mama can't see it." Her words feel nice to hear, but I still struggling in my being. But I glad I tell she about Neri, Mabel, and how I is feeling.

"Okay," I say, "I better get to Mabel's, even for a little bit today." I look down at my fingernails, chipped and bitten, with my favorite yellow polish peeking out of the tips of my new gloves that transform into mittens.

"Can I take you someplace first, though? It's a place that makes me feel good when I'm feeling a lot."

I say yes and then we drive off just as new snow begins falling.

Jazzy take us to a quiet place in the woods of a park I've never seen before not too far from school, Minnehaha Falls. We walk by ourselves, silently, for a while until I see a waterfall frozen in time. It look stuck mid-fall, cascades of crystal. I gasp quietly at its prettiness.

"Come on, we can get closer." And she leads the way, and I explore behind her, examining bits of tree and leaves that poke through the snow. I hold them and feel their life and power.

"*AHHHHHH*," Jazzy screams when we're close to the falls, her chest to the sky, her mouth open wide, and the waterfall, the icy goddess we worshipping sing it back at she, echoing back from she cold and silver chest and throat.

"I like to come down here, when I ain't feeling right, and just explore. Sometimes I scream until something feel different."

We explore the cave that the frozen waterfall has made of itself. We sit down and take in the quietness. I take deep breaths, and I feel still within this cave, within myself.

MABEL

"I THINK IT'S STUPID, and I'm mad that they would even contact us," I hear my dad say. I got up to go to the bathroom in the middle of the night and could hear their upset voices through the walls.

"I think it just makes it feel more real or something for you, and you don't want to deal with that. We are seeing the same thing, 'Quan, and I know it has me messed up," she says, and I walk closer to their door so I can hear better. "I feel all of the hope in the world, and I also feel exhausted trying to be optimistic when some days I just wanna bury myself in a hole, remembering how it felt to have her living and swimming inside of me." I wonder if she has her hands on her stomach, remembering me inside her. "I don't even remember life or who I was before her. I honestly pray every night, I will wake up and this will be a dream, 'Quan. Or that I could switch places with her."

"Coco, could you stop saying that?" I can see my dad, fists balled up, but with no opponent he can see to hit. "I don't want anybody sick. If they are telling her to think of her dying wish then she is going to think she is dying, and we need her to be hopeful."

"You know she is not a little kid anymore, right? You don't think she understands what she is feeling in her own body? You think she doesn't know that this thing most likely will be how she dies? I feel like the longer you take to accept this, the longer I gotta sit here and be emotional and sad by myself. I think it's selfish as hell of you," Mom says with a snap in her tongue.

They go back and forth like this and soon I feel more tired than ever. I walk away from their door and back to my room. I lie in my bed and feel numbness like I'm in a tunnel and somewhere at the end of it, a limitless feeling. I look at Whitney looking down on me and wonder about where she is and where I'm most likely going to go soon. I wonder how she feels about being in heaven. That is where I assume she is, I guess, because she was a Christian and sang about Jesus a lot. I hope if that is where she wanted to be that is where she is. That she's with her daughter and that she can sing and it is as pretty and divine as Trinidad and Black Eden and that she can have any kind of lover she wants and that she is free.

I don't know where I think I'm going to go after I'm no longer me and alive, even though now I think about it all of the time. I would like to watch over my family and be there for them still, especially Sahir. I'd like to be there in the way Audre talks about her ancestors. In the way that I sometimes feel Whitney watches over me as I get sicker. Afua believes that we travel to other stars and lifetimes, that our souls will unfold into new dreams and lessons. Some days, I just don't want to feel sick anymore, wherever I end up. I just want to feel free in my body and away from doctors and machines and drugs. I want my body to stop moving into irreversible oblivion. I want my body to feel alive and beautiful like in that rainstorm with Jada or with Audre in Black Eden.

I also hope my friends and my family miss me. I want to have meant something to people and not just be someone folks is sad about for a little bit, because I died young or whatever. I hope Sahir wears my Biggie T-shirts and thinks of me when he eats chicken dumpling soup. I want Audre to think of me when she is eating raspberries and hears Whitney.

I think of Afua and all that he has done from a room smaller than mine and with people beating him and keeping him away from his family. I wish that he could get back his life and get to feel rain and nature and love and all of the things that I'll miss about life.

I slink out of my bed and walk to my parents' room and knock on their door.

"Mom and Dad, please let those people know I have a wish. I want for Afua Mahmoud to be free," I say, as soon as they open up their bedroom door. "If they want to know what I want for my life wish, it's that my friend can have life. I don't want anything else besides that. Contact them, and let them know that is what I want: for Afua to be released from death row and returned back to life in this world with his family and friends." I already know I ain't gonna back down.

PISCES SEASON

nobody knows how to swim that deep
you got to be born there
gills fastened to your ribs
in the watery placenta of Neptune

you only dream when you are awake
everything so ancient it is happening in the future
to survive on this earth we escape into ourselves
hide in plain sight, finding solace in vice and lovers

no light, no air, no need
all this is a dream anyway
mysteries only the ancestors
know how to swim to the bottom of

bioluminescence is deep see melanin
flashing wisdom in your own skin sparks of cosmos in
the depth of your watery dark
when an ancestor is coming back to the earth
old ladies dream of fish swimming through lakes
of remember and forget
then they catch the babies like fisherwomen
on the starlit sea of Sankofa

AUDRE

LAST NIGHT I SLEPT OVER AT MABEL'S, and we had a dreamo treatment. She has been so weak and tired since she last radiation. She has lost some weight, so she is feeling cold all of the time, but she still has energy and is able to eat somewhat. Ms. Coco and I made her a bath with herbs and oils to warm her up and help her sweat. Then Mabel and me both got into our pajamas and just laid in her bed talking about astrology and life and playing BLK LVRS. Her room is dark and quiet with moonlight flowing in on us and I feeling mellow with her.

"Audre?"

"Yes, Mabel?"

"You know I wouldn't be hurt if you ever didn't want to lime with me. If you went to a party or something dope. I know there are cool things that you could be doing with the homies, that is tighter than watching *Waiting to Exhale* with me and André 3000."

"I where I want to be. I get to hang out with people at school anyway. I like chilling here," I say. I like when she say "lime," in she Yankee accent.

Mabel get quiet and she nod.

"Could you tell me a story about Trinidad, if you feel like it? I always feel like I'm there when you talk about home," she say, and this make me wish I could take her to see Trinidad one day. I would love for she and Neri to meet. They is the two best friends I ever have in life that make me feel like I special and belong. I don't always feel like I can talk about home without being very sad. Even though I am feeling more a part of Minneapolis and life here, I still miss my life in Trini. I feel to tell Mabel something I never could tell she before. I inhale real deep and then exhale. I want she to know my truth.

"Okay, I is going to tell you a story, it ain't a happy one, but it is a real one. Remember when I come up everyone thought I was into church?" I say. Mabel start to giggle a little bit.

"I almost forgot that, because I know you now. But now I do remember your dad told my dad that you were all about your church and Jesus and then when you got here, you was like nah," she say, her soft breath feeling nice in my ear.

"Well, it was because I was very involved in the church, mainly because my mother and stepfather forced me to go. But then I started going to their church, and I meet a friend, Neri. And . . . she became a very special friend to me." I glance over at Mabel and she is looking at me and her eyes are like they always are. Gentle, sweet.

"After a while, we used to go by the water and lime after church, just talking and swimming. Then things started to get different between us, we started to feel feelings that was deeper than just friends . . . we fell in love." I say this for the first time and it is true. "I ain't know I could feel anything like that for anyone and it was the best feeling." I take another breath and say the last part. The part that is the hardest.

"My mother caught us together one day, and it was very bad. My mother get so vex, she get violent. She decide she ain't want to deal with me no more . . . So she send me to live in the States with my father." I is feeling my tears dripping down my face and I can't say nothing else. Then next thing, I is bawling. Mabel wraps me in her arms. I look and she is crying too.

"Wow, girl . . . I'm so sorry. You ain't deserve that. I don't even know what to say, Audre. I'm sad and mad that you went through that." And I know she mean it.

"I always wondered about your mother, but I figure she just wasn't around much and you was mainly with Queenie. I guess it was more complicated than that."

"Mabel, I'm sorry I ain't tell you before. I couldn't really say nothing before because it still hurts." I heaving in my chest, crying still.

"I'm glad you told me, Audre. You are always there for me and I want to be there for you too. Do you know what happened to Neri?" she asks me.

"She get sent away like me. To Tobago, but I ain't heard a thing yet about she. Queenie been trying for me to find out something, but she ain't finding out nothing," I say.

"How Queenie feel about you and Neri?" she asks me.

"Queenie say it was okay and she always know I was this way. She and Episode both try and get my mom to change she mind, but she ain't want to hear a thing. I was so sad to leave. If you ain't become my friend, I think I would've die, yes." After I say that, I realize what I said was something stchupid, since Mabel actually is maybe gonna die.

"I mean, I sorry, I ain't know why I say it like that," I quickly say. And Mabel nods and then starts to smile.

"It's okay, I know you ain't mean it no kind of way. And low-key, I think if you ain't become my friend, being sick like this would have been the worst. I feel so sad about what happened to you and that you got sent away from a place you love so much. And then I feel bad and selfish, for being happy you came here and became my friend. I could only imagine how bad Neri misses you, 'cause if I lost you as a friend, I don't know what I would do."

I feel torn too. Mabel snuggle up to me with she head on my shoulder and holding my hand. I still have tabanca in my heart from leaving Trinidad and losing Neri. But I feel that in the hurricane that my life went through, maybe Spirit was leading me to meet Mabel and connect with she too. I feel even since we was eleven and I came here to visit, something was special about her and when I was sent here this time I still feel she was special. Like when she brought me back to Black Eden and let me eat raspberries and be weird. Next thing I hear is a loud snore. Mabel is passed out and sounds like a congested frog croaking. It strange but I love the sound of she snoring. I close my eyes and sleep catch me too.

AUDRE

"SO I TELL HER, this is the wish she wants to give for her life and that I think it's actually a beautiful request. Instead of Disney World or meeting Taylor Swift—no shade to these other sick babies—she wants to leave a revolutionary legacy and change this brother's life," say Ms. Coco with her phone pinched between her shoulder and ear, while she swirls around the kitchen making tea and scrambling eggs. I overhear her talking to her sister Niiki on the phone, while I make a smoothie for Mabel on the other side of the kitchen, before I go to school. I ain't trying to listen, but Ms. Coco ain't making it easy.

"Then, this Life Wish fool gonna ask me, and girl, ooooh, this still got me hot! She gon' ask if we put Mabel up to this? Niiki, that's when I cold snapped on them! Like why would I coerce my sick daughter in this way, the fuck? They was the ones who called us about this wish shit. And now that Mabel has this wish, they showing their politics instead of trying to see what they could do. Afua already been in jail since he was Mabel's age, thirty-something years. Ain't he served his time? He still says he didn't do it, so why not let him free? Hmm-hmmm. Yup"—Ms. Coco listening—"Oh, what happened next? Girl, I hung up on her," she says, cutting up fruit and putting it on a plate. I is cleaning up and still not trying to listen, yet I is hearing everything. My phone buzzes and I look down and see that Jazzy text that she is outside. I finish up the smoothie, and put it in the fridge for Mabel later.

"Do you know what Life Wish is?" I ask Jazzy, after plopping in her ride and swinging my bag to the back seat. She is burning incense and it smell sweet. She has her hair in a box braid bob with she baby hairs in beautiful swirls on her forehead and by her ears. She rolls off into the early morning fog toward our school.

"Good morning to you, too, boo. Nah, did you Google it?" Her eyes are trained on the road and she's hunched over her wheel like Auntie Pearl do.

"Oh, I sorry, good morning. Yes, I did; they supposed to give young people who is sick and dying something they want. When I was leaving today, Ms. Coco was talking to she sister about how they asked Mabel what she wanted and when they found out that she wanted to free Afua, they ain't want to give it to she," I say.

"Hold up, wait, what?!" Jazzy pulls over. We is still a couple of blocks from school. She turns her body around and looks at me, and I can see she is really vex, same like I is, about this whole thing.

"Afua, who is in prison, who write she the letter and wrote that book she love and reads all the time?"

"Yeah, girl, remember we all reading that book now? That's my new favorite book."

"Well, she asked Life Wish to let he free as she wish, and they won't because of politics. Ms. Coco say she get so vex, she hang up on the stchupid woman who work there. Girl, I is so vex too when I hear this. Why won't they even just try? She is dying and this is all she want: for she friend to live. These adults is just being stchupid and useless," I say, and it really hit me when I say it out loud. That she wants to save he life.

"Mabel is so dope for doing that! Damn, as usual, she ain't even thinking about herself. I woulda been basic and ask for VIP tix to see the Minnesota Lynx and chill with them for a day. But not Mabel! She out here asking to save this man's life. Sometimes I just can't stand how unfair this whole dying thing is, ughhh!!" Jazzy is looking down at her lap. She starts shaking her head and then starts yelling and beating her steering wheel. "This ain't fair!"

I find myself start crying and screaming too with she. And we is sobbing and yelling. And then we just crying. We cry for we friend, and the tears come from deep, unstoppable and cleansing. We look at each other, and we is just crying and watching at each other. I know I is looking wild, but I feeling wild too. Jazzy face is all snot up and wet, she lipstick smear and she mascara make she look like a jumbie.

And I ain't know why, but it look funny and I start giggling, then try to stop it, but then it rumble out my body and I bus' up laughing even harder. I never see she out of place in she face. And it feel good so I can't stop. Jazzy start laughing too and yelping and screaming in laughter, then I laugh even harder 'cause now she sounding like a jumbie too. After a while, the car is fogged up and warm and my stomach is hurt from laughing and crying. Then we start exhaling loud with long sighs, like when you're really laughing and you need to slowly pump the brakes down on it.

"This our girl's last wish on this planet. She just want to free a brethren who deserve to not live like he a slave 'cause of this Babylon system," I say, and I holding on to my pouch underneath my sweater and I feel a tingle in my body, like flickers in my skin, like a current is in the car with us. "What if we plan a walkout at school?" I say. The idea pop out my mouth before I know what I'm talking about. I was remembering vaguely Mabel talking about another school walkout before.

"Ooooooh, girl! YASSSSSSSSSS! Now, THAT'S an idea! Let's do a walkout and get some attention for our girl and her wish. Show them there are no backsies on wishes, bitches! We finna get Mabel her wish reparations!" she says, and she start grinning real big and her excitement give me hope.

"You think it could work? Like we could do it tomorrow?" I ask.

"Honey, you know I got this, and Imma holler at Ursa. And Prism will be down, and the other student groups would love to help Mabel and Afua . . . Oooh, girl, we gon' be in them hallways, like, 'Mabel forever! Free Afua!' And get people from band, just playing some jams with horns and drums, and we all loud as hell, clanging cymbals in the streets, like CRASH! CRASH! Wake up! CRASH! Get up out your house and get our girl her wish!" She pulls out she phone and start typing. "Lemme start texting homies and figuring it out. We should also talk to Ms. Sharkey and Mr. Trinh, because they could help us too and they really love Mabel. Audre, this is a really good idea. I think we at least have to try our best to get Mabel her wish and get Afua free."

"I feel that this is right, in my blood I feel it," I say.

"Aud," she say, "I think about when we get older and doing our thing and figuring out life and get to be grown and move out or whatever, that Mabel—if she don't live—won't get to do that. This why this gotta work, so she feel like she will always live on . . . And no matter what, we gotta always be cool and connected to her and each other. Even if you is in Trinidad and I'm in South Africa, Ursa in New York, and Mabel is in heaven or in Black Eden. We will always be fam."

ARIES SEASON

spring Ram
child of the new leaves,
beginnings and daybreaks.
curled horns, fury and fire
heat spiciness unveiled
passion overwhelming energy to become
the newness of all thing

i am the first green
bud within the seeming never-ending frost,
seeking sun is the desire to erupt.
a break into life, a possibility
for lushness and becoming.
the pop off, the sho nuff, the hotheaded uncle
black knight. skin filled of fight

the honey with the thick thighs
in a red dress
prepared to bring you to goddess
through the fire making of rubbed thighs
smiles and sacred lust
i am the hot block
the corner of action

of possibility
of tricksters
of fools

MABEL

"**CORNELIUS**, *I'd gladly buy that fight from you. I would love to bus' someone stchupid ass today as a cool down from dance," I say, stepping from behind a couple of bystanders who there to catch a fight between the Davida and Goliath of Laventille. It is evening, after my African and modern class. I is walking up into the small red brick and steel houses, green hills and dirt road by we house, and I humming, "Sun is shinin'," my sandals getting coated and scraped by earth and rocks. I feeling free and irie after dancing for hours, but when I overhear commotion and I realize what going on, I jump in right away.*

Cornelius, a friend since I young, is the Davida, a skinny and red child who live downstairs from my auntie Norma's rum shop. He four-teen like I am and always been an easy target because he small and does move like we girls and hang with us. He sometimes even would wear pieces of we girls' clothes and is often prettier. And although Cornelius is small, he mouth big and he use it to curse and maco people who mess with he even if he get he ass cut. The Goliath in the mix is Earl, a mean, funny-face bully who live down the hill from we and think he a gangster. Earl fantasize he some kind of ladies' man because he lie to everyone about pum-pum he getting from girls in Laventille, which he, in truth, ain't the recipient of. He even fix he stchupid mouth to throw my name into the lie and that's why I find myself impulsively volunteering to cuff down he tail in Cornelius's place.

"Elizabeth, I don't fight girls, so mind yuh business, nuh," he say, looking from me to Cornelius, he original victim.

I slice my body between Earl and Cornelius and square myself in he gaze so he see I is serious. "But what if I does fight boys, Earl? What if I will pay money to stand in Cornelius's place, so I can beat one specific, stchupid, dotish, arrogant, lying boy ass?" I ask.

Cornelius with more sense than most boys shamelessly slink away once I offer to defend he in battle. Earl look me down and size me up. I is lanky and muscular with no tut-tuts to speak of in my leotard and jeans and my little Afro. I go to the barber to make me look like Miriam Makeba. Earl peel he face into a hearty laugh at the idea of me as he opponent.

"Yuh letting Elizabeth fight for you? This picky-head bitch is too ugly to do anything but fight," he say, leaning into the space of dust Cornelius disappear from, while spitting "Elizabeth" into the air, the name that never feel like it belong to me and which no one, even me own granny, don't call me.

"I might need to whoop your ass, because ain't no one teach you how to stay in yuh place as a woman," he continues.

"Fuck yuh mudda, Earl," I say, upping the ante and listening for the crowd to gasp and egg we on at the fighting words, my mouth a reckless weapon. "I is waiting for you to put me in my place."

"All right, nuh. You leave me no choice, Eliza—" And before he finish insult me again with my birth name, I cuff he, springing on him like a panther, tired of he postponing the festivities. I whirlwinding and

punching, kicking and scratching. When he grasp for my body, I swing
my arm under he chin and twist he around to the ground, pretending I
is Bruce Lee.

"Get-t-t-t-t yuh ass off me before I whoop yuh, you crazy mudda
cunt!" he says, choking words through the passageway I is blocking with
my armpit on he throat.

"Whoop me, nuh? I see you was about to beat up Cornelius, like he
yuh rag doll. So whoop me, nuh!" I show he a mudda cunt.

"Uhh-uh-h-h. I-I-I-I don't. Fight-t-t-t. Girls! Stop . . . squeezing . . .
my . . . neck . . . It's . . . too . . . tight-t-t-t . . ."

I is wrapped around he neck, like I is a boa constrictor, and I is cuff-
ing any part of he I can grab with my next arm.

"Tight as your pantie up your ass in a second if I hear again you
telling people you and I fuck. I ain't want no part of the frowsy sadness
between your legs," I whisper into Earl's ear, as he struggles against my
power like a trapped bug, choking and spitting against the air. Just then
I hear Daphne's voice crack my triumph with duty.

"Queenie! Queenie! Bring your ragamuffin ass here! It's Bamba
Rose, she wander off again. Come let we find she!"

My big sister is coming down the hill from by where we live, already
swiftly headed in the direction of town. I, without hesitation, release my
grip, giving Earl one last shove as I walk past he. "And, unless yuh name
is Sister Mary Rose, I is Queenie to you, yuh understand? Go play with
yuh self." I throw the words behind me, cut through the crowd, and fly
behind my sister to look for our beloved great-granny.

Walking through the tracks and alleys of Laventille trying to keep up
with Daphne, whose long legs and steady stride carrying she towards the
main road, where we have found Granny in the past.

"*I thought when you turn fourteen you would be done fighting, Queenie,*" *Daphne say, glancing back at me.*

"*You ain't even know what happened.*"

"*How is it I live my whole life and I figure how to avoid fights, but you is in one every week?*"

"*Because people does have a problem with me . . . and this time, I was protecting Cornelius.*"

"*No boys likes a girl who is always fighting in the street.*"

"*Good. I ain't want to deal with they foolishness.*"

"*You say that now . . . ,*" *she says, like she know better.*

We walk up the road into the hills where Granny's sister used to live, before she died giving birth to her eighth child, thirty years before I was born. The house still belong to our cousins. When we ask if Bamba Rose come through there like she sometimes do, none of them see she. We head down the hill until we pass by our auntie Norma's bar. We ask she if she see we granny.

"*Yes. Headed to the panyard. She pass by here for a shot of rum,*" *she say. We thank her and keep searching.*

"*Since when she does drink rum?*" *I ask Daphne, as we walk toward the panyard and the sky becomes dusk around the hills of our home.*

"*Since today, I guess,*" *she says.*

"*I ain't know what is going on with she,*" *I lament, hoping for some commiseration.*

"*Let we just find her first, Queenie,*" *she says with her usual non-distractible determination. Her pace, quick and steady, her hair pressed and curled neatly under her ears. Walking in silence behind my sister seems to be my permanent existence in this life.*

Our Bamba Rose is becoming a new woman as of lately, and it make she pick up and leave from time to time. From since we young, she would always be home. Watching we kids, she read she books, clean and cook around the house, and garden a lot. But she always right by we home. But since last year Granny wants to be in the street, telling nobody where she going. And we is the ones who must always find she. It is slowly becoming twilight, as we approach the yard, and we is already feeling the steel rhythms on the breeze. I sway a little feeling the pulse of softened metals in the melodies. In the yard there is a circle of drummers from all over Laventille, sweating and focused on the rhythms.

Folks is there liming and enjoying the atmosphere. I can't imagine where my granny would be within all of this. But then all of a sudden, we do see she. She have every piece of gold she owns gathered from her jewelry box and adorning her. And she is wining she waist like an expert, and she looking happy, smiling into the evening air, with a Carib beer in she hand. Daphne and I both pause by the entrance of the yard, watching our granny be a self we never see. I feel it almost wrong we seeing she, but also it make me smile. Was this wining always in Bamba? Daphne look confused too.

"Uh, um, Queenie, we should get she, okay?" she say, like she is convincing she self.

"Okay, Daphne. But we should probably let this tune finish, nuh?" I say, and she nods.

When the song done we come close to Granny and she smiles at us with recognition.

"Y'all is late! Yuh waste some real good bacchanal," she say, sipping the last sip of her beer, her smooth and soft skin shining with sweat from the night heat.

"You ready to come home?" says Daphne, lacing her arm with our great-granny's and guiding her to the door. "Come with we nuh, Granny," I say, while I lace my arm on her other side. When we walk out the yard, back home, a silver moon hangs fat, almost full on the horizon

of Port of Spain. The mellow evening casts a blue on Granny's dark skin, and all three of our feets slide forward in unison like ballerinas, moving at Granny's pace.

When we reach the house, Daphne goes in to work on she schoolwork, and I sit with Granny in the yard, we both ain't ready to go inside yet.

"When I little-little, I would have a particular dream over and over," she say, her eyes is looking ahead into the past as she talks. "I is walking in the bush in Saint Vincent, by where I is born. I ain't seeing nothing, it all dark but I feeling that is where I is. And everything is fuzzy and real shadowy, so I is barely seeing it, but like I say, I is feeling it," she say. "I look above me and a set of glasses fall from the sky onto my face and then I is seeing everything around me and it beautiful shiny and sharp. That is when I start seeing things in my dreams, getting messages. Mmm-hmmm . . ." She close she eyes as a breeze drifts past us.

"My grandmother from Senegal, I ever tell you? She prettier than night, tall and strong. My father born Saint Vincent, Black Carib," she say. "They is who teach me how to deliver babies and release souls from wombs, heal people from they deathbed. They know how to cure every-thing from all the bushes that grow around where we live. You will know these things too." She has the certainty only old people speak with.

I is in she quiet. Listening to she thinking and she breathe and the birds and bugs awake to the evening.

"My whole life I always wanted to know who I really is," she say.

"You ain't know who you is?"

"I think I is still figuring it out, yes. Even this old. I live my whole life doing for other people; I only now seeing who I is. Life is hard for we women, because we strong and the world ain't wan' to love us for it. From since I young, I see it," she say. A flock of corbeaux birds is flying around in the distance, carving the sky with their wings.

"You know we brought we seeds and we Gods with us from Africa when we came? When they steal we, they work we people so hard." She take a breath and grab my hand. "But we always fighting and killing and burning people who trying to control we souls. I ain't want you to fight. You is free, Queenie," she say. She look in the distance and start pointing beyond the sea.

"We people come from the star tribe, you understand?" she say and I ain't know what she mean, but I listening. She hands are shaping her story with the words, each finger have at least one gold ring on it and her wrists swing in gold bangles in the purple night.

"We had to hide what we know and what we believe. We had to be free on the inside of we, where the white people couldn't see it," she say, and she eyes is piercing mine to listen to each of she words.

"We read the sky and hear how the plants sing healings." She grab a leaf from the bush on the side of we house and chew it up in she mouth. "This leaf is to remember your mother's dreams." She finish chew and then swallow. She still got every teeth in she head.

"Bamba Rose. I think you look real, real good with all of your gold on, so."

"I always like gold. This all the gold people leave me over the years once they gon' to glory without me. I never feel I could wear it. But today I decide I wan' sparkle every day of my life, now."

"You is free, Great-grand. Yuh old, you is free," I say, and she giggle at me.

"You is free too. 'Cause I is ol', I feel like people finally let me be." She pause as if she is in thoughts far away from us and this time. "But you, Queenie. Don't wait to be free." And she smile at me, and I nod and hug she. We sit on top of Laventille and we both free. The runaway and the fighter.

AUDRE

A COZY AND WARM FLUSH OF INCENSE and Alice Coltrane hits
me as soon as I get in the door. I take off my boots and coat, I
tired and ready for a nap. All that energy was beautiful, but now I
feeling like I gon' conk out. I went to tell Mabel the news, but Ms.
Coco said she was still sound asleep, so I came home.

My dad is on his laptop at the dining-room table when I get
home. And soon as he sees me walk in the door, he is smiling at
me and lowers the music down. "How did everything go today
with your peaceful riot?" he asks. "It was peaceful, right?"

"Yes, Dad, it was. I was really, really nervous, and it was like
nothing I ever experience before. We was taking over and making
noise where usually you can't, like it was J'Ouvert morning." I
carry my backpack in and give my dad a kiss on the forehead and
then keep telling him what happened. "So many kids leaving they
classroom and was in the halls with us, boy! Then we all meet up
in the cafeteria and it was bacchanal there too, Dad, but a peaceful
one. But then Jazzy pull everyone together, just so"—I lift my fist
up in the air like she did—"and she hand up over she head like she

a Black Panther and it is the sixties. And then she ask that we all boom love to Mabel and then she tell everyone who Afua is and what Life Wish do." I walk into the dining room. "Dad, I can't believe we did it. I was so afraid, but we was able to get people together and we was a force," I say, dropping onto our couch across from the dining-room table where he is sitting.

"I'm so proud of y'all, baby! I can't believe my daughter is a young revolutionary. You know your first protest was in utero? I remember me and your mama while she was pregnant with you went to a protest against police brutality. Maybe you got some of that radicalism sprinkled on you from back then," he said with a nostalgic smile to a past that I ain't feeling any connection to. No matter how I try to imagine my mom and him in love and together, I can't.

"I couldn't be any more proud of you," he says, beaming joy, and I feel he truly has pride in me as his daughter, which is a feeling I have never really felt from my mother.

"It was for Mabel," I say, and pull the throw blanket over me, feeling a chill as usual, yet also a new warm feeling that I have had since I come from Minnesota. I think it come from having a dad who just loves me no matter what.

"The way you have committed to supporting Mabel and have been so hardworking at school, in a new city—shoot, a new country—girl. I hope you see how off the hook a little sista you are." He is looking me in the eye to see if I know he means what he is saying. I nod and looking away already feeling too much feeling, especially after the protest.

"Thank you, Dad. I'm grateful to you too and how nice you have been to me," I say. "At first, I struggled with adjusting to being here, but I do feel like it has been better than I thought it was going to be. And getting to know you has been good." I sit up to feel more sturdy. I feel a question I been curious about travel up from my heart and it sitting at my throat now and I force myself to be brave. "Dad, can I ask you a question, please?"

"Yes, of course, girl." He closes his laptop and turns to me.

I pause for a second, almost afraid to ask, but then I just let it out. "What was it like when you and Mom were together?" I say the words, and they live there between us. Then he nods and smiles a little smile and then chuckles to himself. He leans back and I can see he is thinking.

"Well, it was an interesting time in my life. Makeba and I were young, but we also had an instant connection, and it felt magical," he says, and he is looking at me and beyond me into a place where his memories live. "I fell in love with your mama, her intensity and confidence. Even her accent was my favorite sound. I would save her messages on my answering machine for weeks. And of course she is a very beautiful person too, timeless and natural." Hearing he describe my mother from another time was like hearing about someone different altogether. I curl up in myself and I listening real close. "And I like to think she fell in love with me too. Even though I was an awkward dude, always seeking something, some knowledge or understanding," he says, and he places his hands on the prayer beads around his neck. "Did I ever tell you I was in a punk band, Audre?" he asks, and I start giggling and shaking my head no.

"Oh, wow, yuh serious? You ain't ever tell me that!" I leaning in wanting he to keep talking.

"When I first moved up here from Chicago, I was in a all-Black punk band called Nanny Neptune. Oh Lord, let me show you some pictures. Girl, let me tell you, I been so many cats in this lifetime." He goes and gets a photo album from his bedroom and then sits down next to me on the couch and opens it up. "Anyone look familiar?"

And there he was. My dad's face, for sure, but he looked like a baby, with none of the facial hair he has now and skinnier, but still his kind eyes. I can't help but see some of me in his face. He head was shaved, except in the back he had a ducktail of dreads. He had a yellow T-shirt with Nelson Mandela on it, black jeans that were real tight-tight. He even had eyeliner on. I turn the pages and see black-and-white pictures of him with two other Black dudes and one Black woman, and they all punked out and looking real, real cool.

"I played the bass and sang some songs. Sehet, the drummer, was who introduced me and your mother. They both studied communications at the U of M, and she invited your mom to come to a show of ours in this little bar on the West Bank," he says, slowly paging through the photos with his hands that look like mine. "And I still remember seeing her for the first time, after almost twenty years. Your mom has always stood out. She had come to our gig early to hang out, and Sehet introduced us. And when she said hello, and told me her name was Makeba, and the lilt to her voice was so pretty and strong. That was it, I was straight up in love," he says with a shrug. "I still remember how she was dressed to the nines—a blue dress, her hair was laid in this cute little short do. I remember looking at myself, and feeling so bummy. It was my style back then, but still, she made me feel underdressed to my own gig, that's how fly she was." He starts to giggle, covering his face with his hand, embarrassed. "She took a seat at the bar and watched us do our thing. The whole show I thought about her. Our band's music was hella political, and our shows were loud and rowdy, mainly a way for us to exhaust some of our frustration at life. I mean, I would feel so free on the stage and be screaming and yelling," he says. "Audre, you ain't going to believe but I would jump out into the audience and roll around on the ground with my bass, it was wild, yo," he says and we both are cracking up imagining his antics.

"Go head, laugh at me—people thought I was cool then, girl. So anyway, we had one sorta love song that I had written for the band, and I decided in my youthful boldness to dedicate it to 'Makeba, the goddess from Trinidad.'"

"Oh no, Dad, yuh serious?" I say, and we is both almost crying from laughing.

"Yo, I was a major nerd. Like, here I was—this young sensitive brother—trying to impress a sophisticated foreign woman, have pity on me, okay? It's the best I had."

I turn a page and see him and my mom snuggled up and she is smiling so big and looking at him, and he is grinning and looking at her. They looked like they loved each other, even though they looked as different as different could be.

"After the show, I asked if I could take her out some time and she gave me her number. I called her the next day, and we were on the phone for like five hours together. She was so smart and intense, and I wanted to know everything about her and she would ask me about my life too." I am looking up at him and seeing the young man still in his face. "She agreed to let me take her for Ethiopian food by campus and then we walked by the river. After that it was a wrap. We were different, but we also really loved each other. And two years later, we got pregnant with you in your mom's junior year," he says, adjusting his glasses while rubbing his face, and I could tell from his voice that this time is harder for him to talk about. My courage still with me I ask another bold question.

"Dad. Am I why y'all broke up?" It was a thing I had always wondered, and I think in some ways had just assumed was true. He looks over at me and starts shaking his head no.

"We broke up because we were young and very different people. You were a magical force that we got to create together, girl. I'm glad you chose us as your parents, although at times I wish I knew how to be a better father to you, especially when you were in Trinidad," he says and I hear the regret in his voice.

"Do you think Mom loves me?" I blurt out. I ain't never get to speak to him about real stuff and now I was desperate to get information about me. Information I feel like I have always needed to know.

"What, Audre? Of course she does, baby."

"I feel like my whole life she ain't like me," I tell him, all of my honest feelings coming out with tears. He gets me some tissues.

"These are some heavy questions, honey. I'm glad you asking them, to be honest. Obviously, you have had a unique upbringing and set of parents, and of course you gonna have questions."

"I can take whatever the real truth is okay, Dad?" I tell him.

"I'm going to answer all of them the best I can, but I also want you to know that I will always love and respect your mother. We made a miracle together, and she taught me a lot about who I am," he says, taking in a deep breath. "I know your mom loves you, more than life itself. Okay? You don't have to worry about her loving you."

I still don't believe him, or rather, I think he doesn't know who she is now and how much she is ashamed of me. "But I don't feel it," I say. "I really don't feel that she love me, Dad." And the tears is dripping down my eyes around my nose, as is trails of snot that I am soaking up in the tissue my father brought for me.

"I'm sorry, baby, I wish you didn't feel that way," he says, and he puts his arm around me and dabbing at his own eyes with his tissue.

"I know your mom is struggling with how to love you as a young woman who fell in love with another girl in a way that she doesn't understand." As he says it, I freeze and then start to tremble. I is trying to understand. He knew all along?

"Wait, Dad, you know about everything? Mom told you?"

He looks me in the eye and nods. "Yes, she did and she was confused and upset by it. I told her that I have no problem with you loving whomever, Audre. She asked me if I wanted you to live with me for a while, and I told her absolutely." He takes a deep breath. "To be honest, I wanted to make sure you were okay as well as know you before you were grown."

There is a silence. I don't know how to feel. Betrayed? Grateful? I just feel my body get more and more floaty and light, feeling all of this information washing over me. About my parents and me back in time and my dad knowing about Neri.

"I just assumed you didn't know since you never brought it up." I look up at him briefly and then look back down at my fidgeting fingers, wondering what he is thinking.

"Audre, I guess I was trying to find the right time. I wanted you to feel like you could share who you were with me in the way that it made sense for you. I grew up with parents who treated me like their property, and I always wanted you to feel like you was your own person, even if I ain't understand it. When you came, I could see you were so depressed and not wanting to talk about anything, I tried to just give you your space and time."

I nod, understanding better.

"Dad, I'm glad that you still love me." I lay my head on his shoulder.

"Of course I love you, girl! You can love whoever you want, just as long as you loved in return." He put his arm around me and snuggled me in. "There is nothing you can do to lose my love. I mean for real, girl. Your dad got your back and will ride or die! Like even if you kidnapped a whole pound of puppies, I would help you evade the law and raise them in the woods," he said, and I look at him giggling through my tears, because he is such a nerd. But he is my dad. For real.

"Audre, I think what many parents struggle with, mine included, is that they may not know how to love us in the way that we need. I think that being a parent can bring up a lot of your own fears and traumas and a lot of parents don't know how to not pass that own to their own kids," he says. "Let me tell you a story about when I was young in Chicago."

Dad tells me how when he got into punk music at fourteen, teaching himself bass and wearing all black clothes and makeup, his dad did not know how to handle it. His dad called him terrible names, like "faggot" and "pussy." He even fought with his own son. "I was always a more sensitive cat, and he would always come at me," my dad tells me. And so he left Chicago at seventeen. "It wasn't until after he died when I realized that was his stuff and not mine. He grew up in the south and experienced a lot of racism and abuse too and that's all he knew, but I didn't have to be like him. It wasn't that he didn't love me, it was that he didn't really love himself." My dad stares at his hands as he speaks, his eyes glistening with tears.

"In my experience, your mom has always struggled with the blues and being hard on herself. Some people are like that and it isn't a thing they can control always. Even before you were born, Audre, she would get depressed and nothing would make it better. I thought being her man, my love could make it better, which was a young and arrogant thought. When we found out you were coming, we were both so happy. She was going to stay in school and graduate right after you were born. And she was such a happy pregnant woman, I foolishly thought her depression was cured." He leans back and smiles. "Queenie even came up for a month to cook and help us get ready for you, and she cooked up all the curry your mom and I could have ever dreamed of, excited for her grandchild. She helped us make that little funky one bedroom apartment into a beautiful home for our little family. It was a really special time."

I imagine all of them, getting ready for me back in the day.

"After you were born, her blues came back and they didn't leave. I was trying my best to work so that I could pay the bills, be a new father and still play music. And to be honest, I wasn't being the nicest guy at all. She was too sad and overwhelmed by motherhood to go to class and dropped out. I felt confused by what your mom was going through and I would say insensitive things and sometimes stay out with my homies to avoid our drama," he tells me. "When things got pretty bad with her depression, she and Queenie talked about her moving back with you for a little while, to help her get her spirit together, and I could use the time to get myself together too," he says. "But then when she got there, she realized that she didn't want to leave Trinidad. And she also realized that she didn't want to be with me anymore. And that was that," he says with cool clarity. It was quiet between us after that last sentence. I had never heard these particular stories.

"How did you feel, Dad?"

"Goodness . . . ," he says with a long exhale as he leans back. "To be honest, I was hurt about it at first. We argued and argued. Five months after you all got there, I came down to Trinidad to see you and try to get her to come back to Minneapolis. But when I went to Trinidad, I got to understand what she was missing. I had never left the US before and hadn't known what it was like to be in a place where you didn't feel the oppression of America, where you had Black people in power and there was a pride in being from some place. I missed you and wanted to bring you back, but I would be by myself raising you in some free-floating life. But in Trinidad you had family everywhere: a grandma who adored you; all kinds of aunties, uncles, and cousins. You had fallen in love with the beach and the food, and you even had a Trini accent developing in your little baby talk," he says, and I feel the young man in him, crying and divided within himself. "And, Audre, I couldn't bring myself to take you from all of that, even though being away from you was so, so heartbreaking. So we decided you would live in Trinidad primarily and I would visit there and you would visit me and we would correspond. We tried our best over the years to co-parent you in two different countries."

He pauses and shrugs a bit. "But I will say, having you here these past couple of months has been the best time in my life since your mom and you left."

I sit there and let all of what he said settle into me. I feel like he gave me a piece of me to myself. "Dad. Thank you for telling me all of this. I'm grateful you are my dad."

"Awww, chile, you love to see me cry? And I'm even more grateful that you're my daughter, Audre. Did I ever tell you where you name is from?"

"A poet, Audre Lorde," I say, which is what my mom told me years ago.

"Yes, but there was a quote I found of hers, when your mom was pregnant, that made me want to name you after her. 'If I didn't define myself for myself, I would be crunched up into other people's fantasies for me and eaten alive.'" He recites it smoothly from memory.

"I knew I wanted you to be a kid that always felt free to be yourself, since I never did. Anyway, thought you should know that too," he says. I lean my head on his shoulder and think of my name. My phone buzzes in my pocket and I pull it out and see a text from Jazzy. It simply says:

Girl, this shit done blowed up for Mabel. We did it! It's on the news, girl! #Mabelforeverfreeafua

TAURUS SEASON

the Black girls crave dirt to chew
taking commune from the soil
sucking and chewing the minerals out the land
like marrow out of bone
absorbing somebody daddy tears
digesting somebody mama rage
they make delicacy from the leftovers

they lay down on the earth
and its night
they lay hands on they own throat
singin' rock steady to the stars
and it was church on clay and patience and
they welcomed the stillness

they was birthed from the mother of sweetness
of honey and cinnamon and rose and rivers
of sugarcane juice to drink

the goddess crowned of horns
don't test her
raven skin women of Hathor
pleasure conjurers shaved heads and pretty smiles.
they collect the wisdom in the heartache

and accumulate secondhand books
to waterfall they lives and they make queendom
from the forgotten spaces we was banished to
and laugh when the sun rise on they dynasty.

MABEL

THE SPRING AIR HAS BEEN PARTICULARLY WARM and all of the mountains of snow that had inhabited the city are slowly melting away from sidewalks, backyards, and tall trees. As we drive north, there is a chill, but you can still feel the warmth at the edges of life ready to take over. I'm next to Audre in the back seat, with Ursa in the front passenger seat, and Jazzy driving. We are heading to Lake Superior to hang out at a cabin, owned by a family friend, that our family used to come to every summer, but haven't for a couple of years. Audre has never been to Lake Superior, and I can't wait for her to see it. I remember when I was a kid, I used to think it was the ocean, and as usual I wonder what she will think of the freshwater sea, how it will compare to the sea in her heart.

This is the first time we've all been together since the #Mabelforeverfreeafua protest, and I still don't know how to thank them, though I've been trying. Turns out that the protest didn't even need to go viral or make CNN. Turns out that Afua and me had a bodyguard, and she wasn't a basic Kevin Costner white boy. My mom got the whole story. A woman—a Black woman—on the board of Life Wish, who's also the CEO of some new tech company, heard about the protest. Turns out she went to law school with the woman who just got elected attorney general of New York—another Black woman. And now it looks like I'm going to get my wish. Kinda. We'll see.

When Mom explained all this, I remembered the dream—of teenage Queenie helping out the other kid. Of Bamba Rose's words: "Life is hard for women, because we strong and the world ain't wan' to love us for it. From since I young, I see it." So we look out for each other—old, young, whatever.

"So tell me about myself, Mabel. Astrologically speaking, that is boo." Jazzy interrupts my thoughts from the front seat, her face focused on the road ahead, while Ursa is next to her bumping her head to some trap music. I have an astrology book on my lap and several blankets wrapped around my thinning and always-cold body.

"Well, I will do my best, 'cause I'm still learning." I'm searching with my finger to find her birthdate. "Hmmm . . . So, Jazzy, your Sun is in Taurus, which you know already. Your Sun is, like, how you reflect out into the world and how people know you, and Taureans are very bold and beautiful," I say.

"Preach!" says Jazzy.

"And confident in themselves . . . They are also an earth sign, so that makes them grounded and reliable. And Taurus is ruled by Venus, so that is also why you are very loving and dress cute all of the time," I say, as my finger continues down the page to see the diagonal arrow symbol next to her Moon placing. "Umm . . . let me see. Moon in Sagittarius and Mercury in Gemini seems to make a lot of sense too, because you are very fun and adventurous as well as love to study a lot of stuff," I say, and keep looking at my book and after months of studying astrology, I'm feeling strangely natural at understanding how to explain what the symbols and stuff mean.

Jazzy giggles. "I don't know what none of the astrology stuff means, but what you saying is on point. You got skills, Mabel." She drives us past tall pine trees on either side of the road and encourages me to continue.

"Well, also your Venus is in Aquarius so in matters of love, you are very . . . hmmm. How do I describe this . . ." I think for a second. "You need a sense of freedom and also for things to be deep. You love the world, and a love relationship for you has to be intriguing on more than just physical ways, since Aquarians fall in love with energy and intelligence," I say, looking through my notes on Aquarius in my astrology notebook.

Jazzy sneaks a quick look over at Ursa in the passenger seat, while Ursa gazes back at her with a look of love. She places her hand on Jazzy's thigh.

I've been sick and away from them most of the year, and seeing them together is really sweet. Ursa has never actually been with someone before, and Jazzy is making her smile in ways that I ain't ever seen. I look over at Audre rocking a turquoise and blue headwrap and looking out the window through her thick glasses.

"Audre, how are you doing?" My question seems to whisk her away from deep in thought, and she turns to me smiling.

"Oh, yes, I good. I just enjoying listening to you all and watching at all of the trees and ting pass by, it real pretty. How are you feeling, Mabel? You need tea or anything?"

I tell her that would be good. I used to cringe and feel stupid when Audre would first do things for me, but she helped me get over that and I'm grateful, because she has truly made the last several months not as bad.

She adjusts my blankets to snuggle me in better. She digs into my bag with all my medicine and special food and pulls out a thermos of an herbal tea blend her and my mama came up with. One of my parents' conditions of this trip is that all of the homies would promise to take care of me and call and text my parents about how I'm doing periodically. Audre, of course is my dreamo nurse, so she is the most natural of all of the homies at this. It took a lot of persuading for me to want to go. I feel like my body is unpredictable, and it's hard to be sick, but now I'm glad I came.

I was eager to show Audre the view of the lake, so we left everything in the car, and I hustled the homies to the big sliding glass doors that looked out at Lake Superior. Ursa opened the doors and helped me onto the patio with Audre at my back.

"So wait, now. This is supposed to be a lake? I can't believe it so big and wide," Audre says, as we look off the balcony and at the horizon of Lake Superior that is blue with craters of snow at the edge of it. We meet eyes and I offer her a wing of my blanket. She snuggles in next to me.

"I could look at this lake all day," says Jazzy, with her chin hooked on Ursa's shoulder and arms around her waist.

After a few minutes of quiet on the patio, we head back into the house and take in the space we will be at for the next two days. This place is more like a really nice bougie house in the woods than a cabin. The place is cozy, painted in earth tones and filled with soft and sturdy furniture, colorful artwork and board games galore and DVDs and old-school VHS tapes. And there's a Jacuzzi on the patio too.

Ursa walks into the kitchen with me and sets a bag of groceries on the counter. She looks at me for a second and then puts her arm around me. I lean into her. It feels good to be here with her.

"You my day one forever, Agnes Marie," she says and gives me a tight squeeze. She releases me, leans back, and we look at each other in the eyes. "You my day one, Lil' Puma," I say and we hug it out again. I feel my skinny self against her much stronger body. It has been hard to be so sick and see my friends be so healthy and strong. Especially Ursa, I think, since we was homies growing up. "I know things have been different with me, and I haven't really known how to talk about it," I say and my face starts to tingle with tears. Ursa looks at me. Her face is so pretty. I've always thought she had the prettiest skin, and her eyes got that feeling of family. We say so much just looking at each other. Her eyes is crying too.

"Mabel, I wish I knew how to be there for you. I tried and I just felt like I didn't have anything to give you. What could I say?"

I understand. I didn't know what it would feel like to be around her either. My body is not the same, and it can't do things it used to do. I've missed playing ball with her and kicking it in Powderhorn Park or Black Eden, doing skits and dropping bars.

"I was being weird too. It's hard to know what to do, I guess. We all new to this terminal-illness life, I guess. But I ain't gonna lie, I think I'm killing the game . . ." I start to giggle and Ursa, taking a second to get it, starts to laugh too. She puts her arm back around me and I feel less heavy. My body missed talking shit and laughing with my homie.

After dinner, I sit on the patio alone bundled up with sweaters, scarves, and blankets. The cool air feels refreshing on my face. The sky on the water transforms before my eyes, giving colors to the sunset. Nothing else seemed more perfect to me. I swear there are pinks that I've never seen before, and I want them painted on my memory. Wild blues and several kinds of purples. Then the sun swallowed up the layers of gold it gave to the world, slid into hiding, and the sky started to quietly bling stars. I start to think of each star like they are an ancestor, wondering about what life and death felt like for them. Were they scared? Do they feel me wherever they are? I wonder who I will be when I'm gone. Or if I will be anything at all. I think of Afua too and wonder has he ever seen a sky like this and it hurts me that he might never.

"Hot tub party, baby, baby! You got five minutes to get ready!" yells Jazzy, opening the screen door quickly, and closing it before I can protest.

We all soak in the hot, bubbly cauldron in cobbled-together swim-wear—sports bras, tank tops, boxers, and panties, our massive towels thrown to the side of the hot tub. It was like this crazy, magical moment. Hot chlorine water bubbling, while the cool air hovered around us. The sky is filling with thick clouds that are floating above us now. Jazzy bends over the side of the tub and grabs something out of her pants pocket.

"Look at what I found in my dad's weed stash," she says,

dangling a little bag with gummy animals inside. "He had a whole bunch, I know he ain't gonna miss four little runaway magic bears! Y'all wanna eat one? No pressure, but I kinda was thinking it might be fun."

"Oooh, look at who's being a bad girl. I have always appreciated this side of you," says Ursa.

"Well, I go back goody-goody tomorrow, so enjoy it while you can, boo. It's a special occasion with our girl, Mabel, so I had to come through dripping. And Daddy smoke like a chimney. This is his contribution to the struggle," Jazzy says.

"What is it supposed to feel like?" I ask. I know my mama smokes with my auntie Niiki sometimes and they come out of her bedroom, giggling and inspired to cook gourmet foods. But I've never tried.

"Do the edibles make you feel irie, like when you does smoke it?" Audre asks.

"I've read that it is supposed to give you a body high a good and mellow feeling," says Jazzy.

"I've smoked once and I didn't really feel anything. But I love candy . . ." Ursa grabs an orange gummy, and Jazzy grabs a blue gummy. My mom and dad have been giving me medicine with CBD in it that helps with my pain and anxiety, and this doesn't seem that much different. I think about it for a second and then decide, YOLO over FOMO for once. I take a pink one out of the bag, and me and Audre share it and also a purple one.

"I could get used to this bougie life. Real quick," says Ursa with her head leaned back, looking at the stars peeking through the suddenly cloudy sky.

"Steupse. This winter ting does last forever," Audre says.

"Dang! Is that snow? It's the middle of April and snowing?" Jazzy asks the universe.

"Why you sounding surprised? You from Minnesota, girl." I close my eyes and feel the jets bubble down my body. I feel lighter, like I could float out of the water.

"But I'm like sixty-eight percent sub-Saharan African according to my DNA, fam, so my blood ain't used to this life," she says, lighting an elegantly rolled joint.

"Why is it always pretty, somehow?" Audre takes a hit, and we watch the sky fall slowly onto our heat. I use my hands to play in the bubbles. In a moment I get the joint and puff it. I cough the fuck out my lungs, and everybody start kiki-ing. I pass it to Ursa, and I start laughing too. After my lungs relax, I let my body jiggle in the hot water. I lean back and look at the sky and let the snow drop on me. It feels like a dreamo session. I look around at Ursa, Jazzy, and Audre, and they are so beautiful. I like feeling like I belong to them, like we are a crew. I'm happy I have friends who are good to me and have accepted me, even when I'm being sad and in my feels. I'll miss them, wherever I go.

We are all calm and quietly watching the lake and the falling snow.

"Anybody else feel the bubbles on their coochie and kind of like it?" Jazzy make a silly face and laughs like a hyena. I bust out because I totally did feel it on my coochie too.

"Y'all think that ting is working? I feel . . . different," says Audre, smiling with her eyes closed.

"What if, in the first hot tubs, people were paid to eat lentils and chickpeas and just sat in hot tubs, farting all day?" asks Ursa and then her and Jazzy bust out laughing really hard. I start laughing at their laughing. Audre's head is leaned back, looking at the sky and catching snowflakes on her tongue, in her own world. I nudge her, and she looks at me and starts to giggle. She swims over to me. She leans her head on me as we laugh at Ursa and Jazzy taking the snow from the sides of the tub to throw at each other. We talk shit and laugh and play and splash in the hot tub for a while longer before we wrap up and go inside to put on our pajamas.

"Who wanna twerk off to my bae's song?" Jazzy says, as she brings out fresh Rice Krispie treats and puts on Janelle Monáe. Me and Ursa are sitting on the couch enthralled by the electric fireplace, and I'm still feeling high. Jazzy rolls up on Ursa and starts to pop her booty. She has on Winnie-the-Pooh PJs and Ursa's in a fuzzy turquoise owl onesie with her hijab off and house slippers that look like the stolen feet of a cartoon grizzly bear. Ursa gets up and starts dancing with Jazzy, grooving all cute and sweet like. I feel like I've been laughing since we got here, but I ain't wanna stop.

Then Audre comes out the bathroom, her face shiny with coconut oil. She's wearing a fuzzy long-sleeved lavender nightie and head scarf, looking cute like a sexy island granny. Jazzy grabs Audre into the dancing and challenges her to a twerk-off. Audre grabs the edge of her nighty and then starts moving her hips in circles while expertly shaking her booty. Then she puts her hands on her knees and starts to bend down and then pop her booty up and down, real smooth to all of our amazement. Like her island self. Watching her move like that, all free and comfortable in her own skin, makes me a little bit warmer than even the Jacuzzi left me feeling.

She is beautiful and I love her. I mean like really, really love Audre. With all of me. I knew it for sure in that moment, and I could almost cry at how happy she makes me, just by her being her. She comes up to me bundled on the couch and extends her hand to help me up. I get up wobbly but with no hesitation. I start doing my little two-step and she takes me by the waist and starts to wind on me. As we dance close, I let myself fade into her. We dance and somehow I'm not feeling weak or sick at all. Maybe it is the power of Audre.

After the dance party, Ursa and Jazzy say good night and head to the room they share. Audre and I stay in the living room, watching the fire and snuggling under blankets. I don't know what it is about a fire or a body of water, but I can just look at them forever. I mean just stare and think and feel. Audre's head is on my shoulder and my head is leaned on hers. My favorite thing to do is snuggle with her. I literally feel better when our bodies are near each other.

"Audre came through with the dirty wine from out of nowhere. Jazzy started salivating," I say.

"I's a Trini. What yuh expect? I was born wining. I the one that is surprise at you! I ain't know you had all them moves, nuh. Yuh tink I wasn't watching at you?" she said, looking up at me and smiling.

"What? You didn't have faith that I could twerk that ass on you, Audre?" I say, pretending to be smooth.

"Yes, yuh bamsee was shaking up, that's for sure. You was looking like you was feeling it."

"Why do I feel like you are coming for my dance moves, low-key Audre?"

"But wait, nuh, it you the one saying you is twerking. I ain't know that was a twerk. I just saying you look like you was feeling it." We laugh harder and the gap in her teeth is so pretty. I think I ponder that a couple of times an hour—how pretty her lips and mouth are. She snuggles in closer, and we watch the fire in an expectant, but kind of awkward silence. Expecting what I'm not sure.

"How are you feeling, sweetie?" she asks, and I feel my heart want to open up. I feel brave when I'm with her. I think I've been asked "How are you feeling?" a jillion times since I was diagnosed. And 99.9999 percent of the time, I respond, "I'm fine." Whether I feel sad or like I wanna barf or I can't sleep or can't stop thinking dark thoughts, I just say, "I'm fine." The way Audre asks this time makes me feel like I want to tell her how I feel, for real.

"Audre, I'm really afraid. I hate how it feels to be in my body and feel it change up on me, all the time." In saying this to her, I feel less afraid. She reaches for my hand underneath the blankets, and I get more strength to tell her more. "Audre, I wonder about what it will be like to die, to be honest. I wonder what if I could be this ancestor and be there for people? Be in heaven with my grandparents and maybe even see Whitney and Prince? Or some other lifetime or star or multiverse like Afua talks about?" She listens to me and winces a little at my words. She leans up and looks at me directly in my eyes and I feel her all over me.

"Mabel, I hope you is here forever and ever. I pray about it and I ain't giving up. But if you must go, can I ask you something?"

"What, Audre?"

"If you could visit me sometimes? I'm going to miss you so much. Could you figure out a way to show up in a dream and chill with me?" Her eyes fill up, and mine are filling up too.

"This might be weird to say, Audre, but I would be checking for you a lot, a lot, if I become an ancestor. I'll have your back and show up in your dreams and shit," I say, and start laughing through my tears. For a moment, I'm not afraid to die. Like I would be okay if I would still be able to be a part of her life, even if I was leaving mine. I'm going on to be something else, even if I don't know what that is, at least I will always be a part of this family. I will always be Mabel, in some form, in some universe.

"Yuh betta show up in my dreams them, or I'll be real vex, yuh understand?" I don't know if it's the weed or the lateness of the evening, but Audre's accent is more splashy and reckless and she is killing me softly and I think if I have to die, let it be softly. In her arms, in her smell, in her gap.

"Audre, can I ask you a weird question?" I say to her, and she perks up and looks at me. And I look at her for a while and it's kind of awkward.

"I would like to kiss you one day if you're into it," I blurt out.

"Mabel." She pinches her eyes closed and then opens them. She smiles. "Gyal, you know that is a statement, not a question, right?" She smiles and slowly brings her lips to mine. They are so soft, and I'm so hungry for them, I gasp for air, seeking her with my own lips. We embrace each other in a new way, but with a desire I've had since I saw her eat raspberries in Black Eden. We kiss for a while and at first I wonder if I'm good but she seemed into it so I just let myself enjoy kissing Audre.

"You want to do more than kissing, Mabel?"

"I do. Are you into that?" I ask her.

"Can I help you take your clothes off?"

I smile and nod yes.

She lays me down on the couch, climbs on top of me, and unbuttons me and she moves so slow, I close my eyes and take it in. I wanna remember every second of it. With her help, I unlayer her. We are under the blankets and wrapped up in each other. She kisses every part of me, from the top of my du-rag, my ear-lobes, eyelids, collarbones, and my breasts and thighs, she kisses me like she has wanted my body too. I feel full and alive with every kiss. I need all of her touches. I moan for pleasure instead of pain, I somehow can accept feeling good, even in my sickness. She is so soft. She straddles above me and allows me to touch her. I slide my hands along her waist. Her thighs. Her thick thighs. I just wanna worship her body forever. I kiss her thighs and kiss and lick and suck on her nipples. It's beautiful and I'm shaking before I calm down. We are keeping each other warm. I feel healed in other ways I didn't know could exist. The fire is rippling quietly in the room. The snow is falling on a big beautiful lake outside. And I melt right there. I die, right there, the sweetest disappearing into her. All night and into the early morning.

MABEL

IT'S A WARM SPRING DAY and I'm under the lilac bush in Black Eden and it smells like spring, soft and sweet and like fresh earth. My dad has made me a little spot in his garden with sleeping bags and comforters and pillows where I usually would do dreamo sessions with Audre. He is doing spring things. Breaking dirt with pitchforks and shovels, thinning out predictable perennials that return every year, lilies, mint, hostas, and more. They are either to be composted or replanted in some other garden. He thoughtfully digs out each plant and places them in a pile to be sorted into their destinies. André 3000 is prowling around the plants and stumbles upon me in the process. She sniffs my comforter right where my feet are and then hits it with her paw. She then walks up my body and smells my face, very gentle and curious. After approving, she snuggles up next to my neck.

When we got back to Minneapolis, Mom and Dad were waiting to tell me about Life Wish. An envelope with details on the plan for me and Afua arrived right after we left for the lake.

"We didn't want to interfere with you and your homies' trip," my mom explains as we read the contents of the envelope together. It explained our meeting with Afua. We would get to spend a couple hours with our families in Coney Island in New York. We would be provided with a furnished apartment in Brooklyn and transportation while we are there and a food budget. Reading it was unreal. It wasn't what I wanted or what he deserved but I was grateful and moved deeply inside, anyway.

"Can Audre come?" I asked.

"Yes, baby."

"Without a doubt."

I have probably read the letter seven times a day, processing that I was going to Coney Island to meet Afua. Where *The Warriors* was made, Coney Island! It seems like a weird place to meet, but the fact that we meeting at all is straight-up weird. I close my eyes and feel good to be wrapped and swaddled up in my dad's garden; the breeze is cool and sweet on my face and I feel protected by his green majesty that he has created for his family and his community—and maybe his own peace of mind, as a Black man who has been through a lot. Black Eden is our church, our temple, and our place to feel safe. I open my eyes. André 3000 has vanished again, and I see my dad looking at me, smiling with sweat on his brow and tears streaming down his face.

"Hey, Dad, is everything, okay?"

"Yes, honey. I was just remembering something from when you was a baby, something about your face when you was sleeping reminded me of it." He leans his shovel on a nearby tree and walks over to my garden bed and sits next to me by the lilacs. He rubs my du-ragged and shaved head.

"What was it?"

"How when you was a baby, I would put you in a laundry basket, because you hated your car seat. I would fill it with blankets and toys and I would walk you to the basketball court to show you off to my homies." I close my eyes and turn to his voice, envisioning my baby self.

"All of these sweaty-ass brothers would stop they game and coo-coo with you and ask if they could feed you and sang you songs when you would get baby frustrated and cry. My perfect baby girl." He smiles through his tears, and pulls his handkerchief out and dries his forehead and cheeks and I snuggle my body toward his direction, taking in this story of my baby life.

"Me and your mama learned how to wrap babies up with fabric from Mrs. Roma, a Ghanaian woman who lived in our old apartment building who used to watch you too. After we learned how to do that, you refused to be carried any other way," he says laughing and with more tears gliding down his face.

"Dad?"

"Yes, Mabel?"

"Would you lay down and smell the lilacs with me? It's kinda dope."

He pauses and then nods as he lies on the earth close to me, a little awkward at first, but then I feel him get more comfortable. We lie there just quiet and breathing with the earth beneath us and under a canopy of greenery I helped make with him. An improvised dreamo treatment, one to help my father and his feelings about life.

"I don't think I've ever actually just laid my ass out in this garden."

"It's nice, hunh?"

"Yes, just peaceful. I need to do this more often."

We lie there and are still for a while. I'm connected to him in a way that, I guess, I always felt. Just something in us feels the same, even though we are different and don't always understand each other. One thing I have always felt from my dad is his love.

"Mabel?"

"Yes, Dad?"

"I think this is my new favorite spot in the garden."

"It's bomb, right? I love it, too. Dad? I don't know how you are going to take this," as I say this I feel him tense up and take a deep breath. I look over at him and his eyes are filled with tears, just like mine. I look at my father's eyes, which look like mine. I take a moment and continue on.

"But, Dad, if you ever miss me, wherever my spirit goes, if you come to this spot in Black Eden, I'll try to be with you."

His face crumples as he brings the fabric to his face to capture the wetness of tears pouring out. I grab my handkerchief from my hoodie pocket, wipe my face, and then kiss him on his bald and shiny forehead, like me, Mom, and Sahir do.

"Okay, Mabel, I will, baby, I will," he says through sobs cracking his voice slightly.

"And something else too, Dad."

"Yes, honey?"

I take a deep breath and say what for some reason I really needed to tell him.

"I'm in love with Audre. We are both in love."

He looks at me and nods. I can't tell what he feels right away.

"Baby, I know."

"Really? How do you know?"

"When you first got sick, that girl would be over here taking care of you in ways I could never know you needed. I see her love for you and I'm happy. You deserve it, baby." He kisses me on my forehead.

"And when she would be around your eyes would light up, like mine do when I see your mama. That's when I knew. Terrell never lit your eyes up —unless he came through with some cookies or a shake or something for you to eat. Poor Terrell," he says, laughing.

"Dad, I really like cookies." I laugh too.

"I know, baby. Thank you for telling me about you and Audre. I know I ain't as cool and down as your mama, but I love you more than the universe can hold, Mabel. Love is sweet and I'm glad you got someone who you love and loves you back," he says and starts singing.

"It's so gooood, loving somebody, when somebody loves you back," he croons out into the trees of Black Eden.

"Dad, you can low-key sing good you know?"

"For real, sweetpea? Your mama would say that too. I used to sang in church choir, back in the day you know."

"I mean you ain't quite at Luther status yet, but you can hit some notes," I say.

"Dang, baby girl, you had me thinking I sounded like a young Teddy," he says.

"Dad, I said you got low-key skills. I love your voice. Keep singing."

"Okay. Hmmm. How about some Stevie?"

I nod, and he starts singing.

He sings the song "As" into the spring air, and I doze off on a raft of his shy but earnest baritone.

AUDRE

I IS IN MY ROOM, folding up my clothes, when my dad knocks on my door.

"Come in," I say.

"Hey, honey." He walks in with a package.

"Something just came in the mail for you from Trinidad." He hands it to me. It is from Queenie, sent express. She ain't say she was sending anything, but I'm happy with the surprise treat. He leaves me alone in my room to enjoy my special delivery. I swear I can smell she in the paper, and I always grateful to get a shell or a rock from home or something sweet she make for me—or maybe a little thing from Epi and Sarya. When I open the package, I see she send pone that she make, some fever-grass tea, tamarind balls, and then I see a note from Queenie attached to a letter . . . from Neri.

Audre,

I finally receive something. I sent it right away. I didn't want to tell you, because I know you wouldn't have sleep or

eat until you receive it. And of course, I had to make sure to
send you a little taste from home, or else you would feel I ain't
love you. Love you, baby. I hope the news is good. I pray it is.

Love, Queenie

My breath feel like it scared to come out my body, I is so
shook. My stomach is mashing and dipping, my hands and underarms are sweating, and I shaking trying to open the letter. I been
wanting to hear about Neri so long that I accepted I probably
would never hear from her. I look at she handwriting and feel a
gush of feeling drench me as I open up the letter.

Audre,

> *I praying that you get this letter. I trust Queenie will get*
> *it to you somehow. How are you, my Audre? Is your father*
> *and America being good to you? I hope that you are happy*
> *and free. I miss you so much, it terrible. "Audre" is my favorite*
> *sound. I feel like whenever I is walking in the bush or by the*
> *water, I hear your voice or a wind that say your name. Audre,*
> *I feel like it been many moon and many years since I see you.*
>
> *I safe now, but where I was sent was terrible, and I almost*
> *don't want to tell you what I been through because I don't*
> *want you to be sad for me. The blessing is that I'm safe now*
> *and have met people who is like us and have save me. For a*
> *while, I feel like I wasn't gonna survive the tabanca that live*
> *in my spirit from since our last day by the sea. Every day, I*
> *wake up, and think of us by the water and our love and also*
> *that moment when your mom snatched you from me. I ain't*
> *never feel more powerless than when I couldn't save you.*

*My grandfather bring me on the ferry to Tobago early
one morning. Between the rocking of the boat and he silence
toward me, I feeling sick and cracked in my own body and
yet also somehow I feeling numb, like all of the feelings in my
body run away and hide from me.*

*When we reach to Tobago, an older cousin of his, Tantie
Lynn, who live there pick us up and bring us to she house in
the hills. She a old woman, who tall and strong, and had on a
navy dress with hard black shoes. She greet me good evening
without barely looking at me. When we reach she home, I ain't
know what they talking about but I know they settling on a
plan for me. My grandfather hand me over and said bye, and
she son go to drop he back to the ferry and that was it. Like I
not he blood, like I a problem he finally get rid of. I ain't hear
from him since. And I swear this woman he leave me with,
Tantie Lynn, take pleasure in punishment. After he leave, she
tell me that she will correct my sickness and run the demon of
perversion out of me and that, thanks to she, one day, I will
get married and have children and be a good Christian wife
and mother.*

*This is the part I hate remembering, but I feel I must tell
you. Early the next morning, Tantie Lynn wake me up and
tell me to kneel down and pray. Prayers I know my whole life,
but they is feeling like unfamiliar curses in this context. She
hands is strong and gripping my shoulders and she is holding
me, all the while praying to get this demon out of me. And I
thinking, How could they call loving you anything demonic?
Whose God is this? She shake me and pouring water on my
head and forcing me to pray away my sinning and save my*

soul. And then, the rest of the day, me cleaning she house with she and working on she land and cooking for she and she son, who live there too but barely acknowledge me. Then again at night we reciting scriptures until it time to sleep. It go on for weeks and some months like this.

Audre, this part I is not proud of, but I steal from Tantie Lynn purse late one night and break out. I dress up in my school uniform and walk miles in the middle of the night, all the way to the ferry. I was on the first ferry back to Trinidad that morning. Once I reach Port of Spain, I take a minibus to Saint Augustine, where my cousin Brenda go to school. I ain't have a plan, except I hope she will let me stay with she, until I could find a job and a place for myself. I hanging out in the library, I walking around the campus, and trying to figure out how I can find she. I eat a doubles a day and saving my money. I washing myself in the bathrooms. I find places to tuck up and sleep on campus. For three days I do this. I walking all day until it reach night. I asking around and no one knows my cousin Brenda. On the fourth day, I head to town to try and find something to eat and figure out a plan.

When I reach town, I see a spot selling doubles with a big line. When I get into the line, I see a girl keep looking back at me, like she know me. She skin dark and she got a long dark ponytail down she back. She got a sweet smile. I don't know she, so I ignore she. Then she tap she friend to look at me and he smile too, and I ignoring the two of them. Then they both come to me and say they see me at that party last week at Heaven's Gate and that she name is Ingrid and that he is Dragon. I say that wasn't me and if that place is a church, *and they start laughing and telling me, no, it's a gay dance club in town. I shock that there is a place for people who is gay and even more shock that they think they see me there.*

And, Audre, all of this emotion well up in me and overflow out and I start to cry like I crazy. Right there, in front of these strangers. Ingrid take me to sit down under a tree from everyone and send Dragon to get we doubles and Stag beer. For the next two hours, I tell them everything about you, what happened to us, Tobago, and how I came to Saint Augustine to find my cousin, who I ain't been able to find. At that point I ain't care what they think, I just needed to tell my story. I ain't care that I look like some crazy schoolgirl. Dragon tell me he was kick out of his house too when he was young and that I was going to be fine. Ingrid tell me she accept she love women when she reach university. Ingrid say that she and Dragon live in a place called the Rose Maroon house, not far from the doubles stand with some other queer kids, and I could stay with them until I figure my stuff out.

Besides Ingrid and Dragon, there are two other kids who live here. Dragon's boyfriend, Mark, and Teresa, who is the oldest in the house and was rejected by her family when they found pictures of her dressed as a woman. She used to repress who she really was for her family, pretending to be a man, like they see her to be, but she say she always knew she was a woman. After the pictures were found, they told her if she ever dressed like a woman they would kill her. She left that night and stayed with friends until she found this house. All five of us is like family, the first family I really ever feel I have.

*Right now, I is working for the landladies of the house
who live upstairs, Ms. Roslyn, who is a professor, and Ms.
Hosana, who is a seamstress, helping them with sewing and
different odds and ends, while I try to figure out what I will
do next. They are in their sixties and is like us too. They say
I can stay here as long as I need. These people saved my life,
Audre. They help me feel like I deserve to live and be myself
and I ain't have to be ashamed for how I love.*

*Audre, I remember the first day you come to church. I see
you right away. Something about you stood out to me. It seem
like you belonged to another place or time. This may sound
silly but you feel like you was some lone and awkward angel
from the eighties. You had them back-in-time glasses and a
fluffy dress. And I wanted to know more about you. You seem
nervous to be there, so I decide to welcome you to the church
and introduce myself. The whole week I thought about you
and when I saw you the next Sunday, I blurt out and ask if
we could sit with each other. I tell myself so that I could help
you be more comfortable and follow the service. The next
week when you bring me the yellow flowers, my whole heart
bouncing and thing and after that you had me wrap up in
your realm.*

*I know we young still, but what we had was the divine, I
is convinced. After your mom find we, I praying to get a sign
of what I should do. I had feel like I had destroy both our lives,
because I love you and you loved me. I realize that it was we
C.H.U.R.C.H. that helped me know what it feel like to know
love. I hope you get this letter and I hope that you is safe and*

that I will hear from you. As always, I love you forever and
hope that I will get to see you and hold you in my arms again.
If you ever can figure out a way to Trinidad, you could live
with us.

Your rebel always,
Neri

I read the letter over and over and over again. I can't believe that these papers in my hand was once in Neri's hand in Trinidad. I feel the carving of her handwriting in the paper, the texture of her in the script. I don't know how to handle all of this news, and all I can do is soak in the downpour of feelings drowning me all at once. I'm thinking of all that Neri went through and how I wish I could have been there for her. I give thanks to all of the ancestors, the universe, and Goddess for bringing she to safety and to people who care for she. I feel so far away from her after being in Minneapolis and my life here, yet I feel so close to her, like we was just in our C.H.U.R.C.H. yesterday. I grab one of the bags of tamarind ball and take one and place the sticky, tangy, and sugary ball rolled by my grandmother's hands in my mouth and lie in my bed, on top of my laundry, and curl up on myself. I ain't know what else to do. As I chew and dissolve the tamarind in my mouth, I search with tongue and teeth for the seeds within, that are smooth and hard and from a tree at home. I look out my window at the tree whose branches now hold small leaves, little promises of lushness. I lie there and play with the seeds in my mouth until I fall asleep.

AUDRE

SEEING MABEL WITH THE SKY AND SEA as her backdrop is one of the most sweetest things I ever get to see. I feel like I longed to bring she and the ocean together forever and it finally happen. We are arm in arm with a bunch of white carnations in our hands. We are sneaking little kisses and singing Whitney songs. We are saying prayers for the safe journey of Mr. Afua, who is on he way from a Pennsylvania prison to meet Mabel and all of his and her loved ones at Coney Island, he favorite place to be since he little and a place that Mabel has always wanted to go, because of a movie called *The Warriors*. He is set to reach here in the late afternoon or early evening.

Me and she is barefoot, walking in the sand, walking in rhythm with each other. It is a warm June day and Mabel moves slowly, her attention lingering in every step she takes, our feet leaving traces of us behind us. I have a yellow dress, my skin trying to feel every piece of sun I can. Mabel is in a pair of colorful African pants we get for her yesterday in Brooklyn, her BLK LVRS T-shirt, and a green zip-up hoodie. It's summer in New York, but she still feel a cold chill in her skin, even when it warm. The sand under our feet is turning darker and wetter the closer we get to the edge of the water. Every experience we share, I is praying for it to last forever. Every single thing of this journey with Mabel, I drink up and sip slow, coding it into my heart: The commotion of city and subways and cars and people and then an amusement park on the edge of the sea. Coney Island with my friend, my love, and my co-conjurer.

"Audre, look at the waves. You finna put your toes in the water with me, right?" The joy in her smile catch my heart in a way that I needed and I smile back at she. I bend down to roll up she pants to she knees.

"Look, nuh, you think we come all the way here and we ain't going to dip we self in some kind of way, gyal? This will always be my real church," I say, grabbing her by the waist and snuggling up in her arms. We are acting so silly and foolish and it feel good. Despite the sickness, she skin is sparkling and shining with coconut oil. I think of Neri in Trinidad and in my heart I invite her to be with us and the water.

Come Here U Rebel, Come Here.

The meaning I give to the letters of C.H.U.R.C.H. when I is in Trinidad with Neri feel real in this moment with Mabel. Somehow, I, the rebel, ended back at the ocean, my eternal mother of eternal love, with my special Mabel. I thank the ancestors and Creation for this moment.

"I love you, Audre. You are my favorite. My favorite feeling, my favorite smell, my favorite sound," she say.

"Mabel, you are everything. Absolutely everything. I love you so much." I pull her to me and kiss her, long and soft.

"Audre, I will always love you."

We continue our walk.

As we come closer to the water, I anticipate the wet lick of the first wave on our feet; in fact, I is yearning for it. Mabel stops me when we almost to the edge and just stands and looks at the beyond in front of us. Then she closes her eyes and lifts her head to the sun, and I see the rays is kissing she up. I lift my head and close my eyes so I can bask in it too. That is when our feet is submerged in a flash of coolness and we still holding each other tight. We open our eyes and laughing from the feeling, and we throw the flowers we brought as offering to the grasp of the waves that licked at our ankles and calves. We kiss a long kiss. We get splash good again and laugh away from each other's lips. Mabel ease back a little from the water, but I walk in a little deeper and bring my dress up higher around my thighs. I let the salt water encircle my legs in a soak that feel like I been needing since another lifetime. It is weird to be at the ocean and not be in Trinidad. But I here with Mabel and I feel my Blue Tantie Goddess welcome us.

"Mommy, what is the Middle Passage?" Sahir asks as he snuggles into Ms. Coco.

"The Middle Passage is when our African ancestors were packed into ships and brought to the Caribbean, South America, and the States. It was horrible and scary for them," she said, leaning on Mr. Sequan, with Sahir laying his head in her lap looking at the water.

We are all laid out in a haven of blankets, pillows, and love with Mabel. Mabel's family, my dad, and me. We started off the day looking at the sea, taking in the palette of love and ancestors' bones. There was a ceremony at Coney Island happening for the ancestors of the Middle Passage. Ms. Coco had learned that every year in June, Black people from all over New York and beyond come to honor and pray for our ancestors from Africa who were at the bottom of the Atlantic Ocean, and it happened to be the day we are meeting Afua. Our parents thought it would be nice to experience the pilgrimage and enjoy lunch on the water. Further down the beach from us are so many sojourners—women, men, children, elders in all kind of different cinnamon, mahogany, obsidian, cocoa, and tan—walking to the edge of the water, dressed in all white, beholding and in ceremony with the oceanic burial ground. All of them here, like that remind me of Trinidad in a kind of way.

"Mom, why were they taken away?" Sahir asked, while his mama stroked his head.

"Hmmm . . . We still trying to figure that out every day, honey." She kissed him on the forehead. "It was the scariest nightmare and it was real life. When they got here, it was still a nightmare. But somehow there was always magic within us somewhere, and we was talking to God and living and being limitless."

Port of Spain is a big city, but New York City could swallow it whole and belch it out. It seem to go on forever. I try to imagine Queenie and my mom living here for so many years away from our sweet island home. I look at Mabel, who is asleep after our walk to the water. She has been very weak and needing to take more rests. Mr. Sequan had made a little beach bed with blankets and pillows for Mabel to snuggle up in. Sahir and I snuggle up in it with she too. On the drive to the ocean, we had picked up some doubles, roti, and pholourie for the beach at a shop near the house we staying in Brooklyn. Mabel took a little nibble off mine, since she has heard me talk about how much I love it. When she was done with her little tastes, she drank veggie broth and green juice that her mom brought her in her thermos.

Mabel looks so happy. Content, amongst all of us, who love her. We watch the water and realize that this journey is a big journey for us all. A homecoming for Afua and Mabel.

The van Afua was driven in from Pennsylvania is parked at a service entrance of the Coney Island amusement park. Police cars and yellow tape block off the entrance to the carnival. Several police accompany him from where he lives in the prison in Pennsylvania. They all get out and look around and then one of them helps Afua out of the van. When Mabel first see Afua, she start to cry. Afua is tall and strong, and real soft and big. When he stood there before us, it was like seeing a long-lost great-great-grandfather in flesh in front your face. With handcuffs on his wrists and a buffer of uniformed men and guns.

His eyes are deep and pure. They search everything around him, the faces, the amusement rides, the sky. He looks young, but also grown and wise and timeless. And overwhelmed. He is smiling with tears dripping down his face at the sight of us. His mother, whose name is Ms. Rose, walks up to him, gray dreads wrapped in a bun, her arms circle 'round he neck and he leans his head on she shoulder. A couple of guards organize his other family members into a receiving line. We hang back while his family connects with him. After a little bit, he is introduced to Ms. Coco and Mr. Sequan, and they hug him. And then they bring Mabel forward and she hugs him too.

They all talk to Afua, smiling and crying. I hang back to give them space, but I want also to see Mabel as she meet she friend for the first time. I hear Afua ask Mabel, "Is that Audre?" and Mabel nods and he smiles in my direction. "Nice to meet you, my Aquarian family," he says, and I bring my hands into his large one.

"It is very wonderful to meet you, Mr. Afua." Now my dad and I are shoulder to shoulder amid the families.

"Mabel, thank you for giving me a chance to see my bright and beautiful sun outside of those walls before either of us leave this earth." Ms. Rose is holding Mabel hand and looking at her with glistening eyes. "I call Afua my 'sun' because he always shine bright, no matter what, even in prison all of these years. You have no idea what this is doing to my heart to see him breathing free air. I will never forget this, ever, ever, EVER!" She hugs and kisses all who came with Mabel. Then Afua's family, his aunts, uncles, brothers, nieces, nephews, and cousins follow her lead, with more hugging and kissing. All of the families is crying and holding one another, like one big family reunion. The moment is so sweet, I feel like I am levitating off joy I ain't know I would ever feel.

Afua has six hours to spend before he has to get back in the van. We all give them some space so they could talk and thing, through the amusement park. They is walking side by side, Mabel in she hoodie, moving slow, Afua in he handcuffs, navy work pants and a light-blue shirt that say D.O.C. in big letters in the back. Mabel and her long-lost friend is talking and leaning slightly toward each other, amidst a carnival, with several armed guards never more than ten feet away. All of us family and friends trail behind. The crowds of regular people part for us, not sure what to make of it all.

"Audre, don't be disgusted by your old man, but Imma 'bout to get me a foot-long with all of the fixins. It's a Coney Island thing that I just gotta do," my father tell me, looking like he sheepish young self and acting as if I the parent he need to get approval from.

"Live ya life, Dad. But if that hot dog start a fight with all the roti in yuh belly, yuh look for dat, eh," I say, and he nods and smiles at my warning.

Coney Island have a feeling like it been here since the beginning of time. I look at the stars start to twinkle above us slowly in a sky that is the strangest blue. Like a blue I ain't ever see before if I is real. It look like it mix with lavender and periwinkle and amethyst. I staring at it for a second, and I feeling something in me yearn to fly into it. The sparkling lights of the rides and food stands are dazzling against the plum alchemy of the sky becoming. With rickety boardwalks, dried and smoothed by salt and sand and people. The air feel hot like a kiss, and the ocean breeze find its way to my scalp and cheeks and it remind me to slow down and take all of this in. The sky and the way my body feels. The way my heels feel in my sandals and the sensation of the African fabric I have wrapped around my shoulders and the blue above me ripening into blackness.

GEMINI SEASON

we was sister teaching brother
how to read by oil lamp and moonlight

ancestors deprived of power
over our own minds and bodies
multitasking in plain sight

singing blueprints to freedom
while cutting cane and harvesting fields
we dream her in the library in the future
mercury mind silver tongue
with books under her arm from each section
her mind can't drink enough

it fly low on every possibility
wants to know all of the knowledges
stolen from her ancestors she ain't forgot
she lay on her stomach and read till her back hurt.

she runs the distance of her yard seven times
the distance from past to future she lay down
and read some more and remembers the ways
that spirit flies

through the night of mind
shape-shifting seamless through duality
and she one with her thoughts
she whole and two parts

MABEL

"YO, THIS IS WILD. SURREAL." Afua speaks slowly and softly. His voice has a gravel to it, and traces of a New York accent. We are walking among armed guards and our families. The amusement park was unblinking in its lights and spectacle.

"Mabel, I'm kind of shook right now that I'm in Brooklyn. On Coney Island. I keep on feeling like Imma wake up . . ." I look at his eyes whizzing around and looking at everything around us, he closes his eyes for a second. Coney Island which is even overwhelming to me, so I can't imagine how he feels. "Thank you with all my heart. I still can't believe it at all."

"I feel the same way, Mr. Afua," I say awkwardly, because I feel like I know him, but I really don't. "This place is lit. I've never been to New York or Brooklyn ever. We was on the beach today too." I notice how his body seems comfortable walking with handcuffs and guards around him. I'm distracted and a bit disturbed by the guns, radios, and handcuffs sparkling from each of the hips of the men escorting us. I do my best to not let their presence take away from this unbelievable moment of the two of us being alive and outside under the sky.

"You liked the beach?"

"I loved it."

"There is still something about this place, even after all of these years. It's changed so much, yet looks exactly the same as when I was a kid. Like the Cyclone? Looks like it did in 1987 and how it probably looked from forever."

I look up at Afua, and I wonder how all of this moment feels. I wish that he didn't have to have those handcuffs on and that he was free. But this is all we got, and I'm grateful even for this.

We spend most of our day talking while armed guards follow us. My parents spent time with us too, getting to know Afua, but mainly our families and friends are nearby also enjoying the park and giving us space.

We were given unlimited vouchers for concessions, but there wasn't much I could eat, so I sipped on a fruit-and-protein smoothie, while Afua ate a foot-long with everything, waffle fries, a strawberry milkshake, and cotton candy. I don't know why I was surprised at his food choices. He savored them with appreciation.

"There was this elder who lived in my building growing up who said he could never eat cotton candy," he said, taking a bite of the pink sugar puff floating in front of his face, "because he grew up picking cotton and he hated it that much."

"I'm grateful that we get to be here with our families, but I wish that I could have got you free," I say.

"Mabel. Don't worry about me. How are you feeling?"

"I'm feeling . . . peace. I feel like life is mine, in some kind of way," I say. I notice Audre with Uncle Sunny, a little bit of ways behind us. Audre and me catch glances and smile. He chuckles and his shoulders shake and he nods.

"I know, I feel that too. Just for this moment, I feel a bit of freedom. How am I on death row and in Coney Island at the same time?" He laughs some more, looks up at the sky, and shakes his head.

"Sometimes, I wonder if I weren't dying, who I would be. As small as it is, this little life is mine, and I love it," I say.

"We are what life makes us; even if it's a tragedy, sometimes you can still blossom something fruitful from it."

I look over at Afua and he is staring slowly at everything around him and walking slow. Then he pauses and takes a deep breath.

"This is a perfect moment."

"It is the most perfect moment that ever was."

The time felt like no time at all, even though it is six hours. The evening is warm and easing from twilight into a navy sky. I'm feeling lost as to what to do with these last moments with him. A gray-haired older white man in a gray suit approaches us. Earlier he had introduced himself as a warden at the prison where Afua was locked up. Mr. Belfield. He was a direct but kind man.

He warns us that we've only got thirty minutes left for Afua's visit, but if we'd like, Life Wish has arranged for us to ride the Cyclone.

"You'll have the whole ride to yourself for one loop. Apparently one of Life Wish's board members wanted to make sure you two had this opportunity. She said no visit to Coney Island is complete without riding the Cyclone." He says this with a tender smile, but I can tell he's a little confused about the arrangement.

"I love roller coasters. I'm in," I say, without a second thought.

Afua looks between me and the warden, hesitant. His eyes settle, then he nods.

"Yes, thank you. I wonder if it is still as rickety," he says.

"I'm sure it is," says the warden, and we are guided by the armed security alongside our familial entourage to the Cyclone.

I hear it before I see it. A series of loud metal clicks pause and then you hear a whoosh and a loud flutter of screams. The roller coaster is made of steel and wood painted beach white, like it was found washed up from the ocean. Like a shell, belonging to another time. Audre slides by security, gets close to me, and squeezes me tenderly.

"You couldn't pay me to ride on this blasted, shaky thing."

"You would definitely pee your pants," I tell her, and she kisses me on the cheek.

Afua is helped into the car by security and then handcuffed to the ride.

I slide in the red leather interior beside him in the very front seat. I slip around on the leather as I settle in.

"Enjoy the ride, baby. We'll be right here," my mama says. She and my dad both are smiling at me with Sahir beside them. I look over at Afua, and he is looking ahead and a bit nervous.

"I can't believe I used to ride this shit as a kid. I'm feeling afraid. I don't know if my little jailbird heart can take it."

"Don't worry. How many people have taken this ride before? We got this." I feel bold in that truth.

"You're right. Let's see what this ride got." He grabs the bar in front of us, smiles at me and then faces ahead. We hear a big click, and the cars begin to move. After what seems like forever, our car edges to the highest beam-and-plank summit on the ride. We both gasp at the sight ahead of us. All we see is the limitless black sky and all we hear is the roar ahead before we descend into an unknown thrill.

AUDRE

AT THE END OF THE CYCLONE, the caterpillar of cars returned to its starting place, but their car released nothing more than two butterflies into the stars.

They freed themselves. Mabel and Afua are gone, only the handcuffs remain dangling from the lap bar. No one could explain it, but somehow I understood. The sky reclaimed them somewhere between the ocean and its blackness.

I knew the sky was speaking Spirit. I felt it the moment we reached the water that day and Mabel was as sparkly as the diamond reflections on ocean water. There was a zook that let me know Spirit was moving with us. I felt something limitless in my heart, when we was arm and arm and we give them white flowers to the goddess of protection and the mother of all waters. She, the one who cleanse our sorrow and hold our dreams. I felt it again when the sky was merging with ocean as they were devoured into twilight and then night.

I feel Mabel. She is with me always. I feel she, a sweet electricity that has belonged to every heart that has known this ancient and sacred kind of loving. The kind of love you eat like a rasp-berry from each fingertip or like a mango, ripe and unleashed in love and sharing. A love that carries lifetimes of sweetness and care.

Mabel. Loving on you is prayer, like the prayers of bees is honey. We loved on each other like we always been. My fingers caressed your naps in this life. It placed oils. And we was infinite and knew how to love. On the scalp. Along the cornrow and on each other. These coilings was anointed like a real love. We was a cosmic conversation, before I even met you in this life.

ACKNOWLEDGMENTS

The journey of writing this book was profound and juicy, and along the way, I was blessed to realize that I was surrounded by so much love, magic, sweetness, and power. Thank you to all of the wild witches, wizards, deities, shaman, and soul sweeteners in my life, known and unknown, named and unnamed, who have shown me love, wisdom, and protection in my journey. So much love to all of my ancestors whose blood and magnificent existence protect, empower, and celebrate me. Sweet and glittery gratitude to my queer ancestors for your magic and fierceness.

Profound gratitude to the Leo Queen, Whitney Houston, for being a divinely important ancestor to this work and helping draw it out in ways that were tender and curious.

Limitless gratitude to: The divine Alexis DeVeaux, who was the Queenie to my Audre. Thank you for being another wild mommy to me and doula-ing me into an author with all of the sweetness and Libra beauty you hold. My editor, Andrew Karre, for everything. To have a Virgo editor for such a dreamy and layered book was what I needed. You are an amazing person and editor, and I was very lucky to have you on this journey. My gratitude is overwhelming. My agent, Tina DuBois, for being so encouraging and thoughtful at every turn of my journey with this book. Thank you for your fierceness and believing in me, my writing, and this book in ways that truly have empowered me as a writer. You are a jewel. Shannon Gibney, thank you so much for your belief in me and for making a life-changing introduction! You are my big sister in this work and I'm so grateful for you and your brilliance and passion.

So much love and appreciation to: My wifey for lifey, Ngowo Nuemeh, for being on this and all journeys with me. Your love and support made me strong and tender for this work. Your snuggles and cooking and patience while I did my wild and emo artist writer thing was sweetening and nourishing. I love you so much, my Leo king lover of Sweetness! MWAH!! To my baby bear Isley Nuemeh and my goddess-chile Sanyah for reminding me through example to honor my little Juji in all ways.

Gratitude to: My parents, Ingrid and Melvin, for errrrthang. Mom for your sweetness and wildness and all of my Trini-ness. Dad for your complexity and limitlessness. Thank you as always for the spaceships of your bodies and the blessings of your souls. To my grandmas, ancestral grandfathers, sisters, brothers, uncles, aunties, tanties, nieces, nephews, cousins, and dem who been in this life and journey with me and who have supported me in so many ways and been spaces of love and connection.

Special and sweet thank you to: My Trinidadian family, Kelvin, Ann Marie, Roslyn, Tantie Roma, Tantie Patsy, Gemma, Alana, Sparkle, Khalid, Amanda, and all who welcomed me with love and openness and shared stories. To Tony for driving me all over the island and having philosophical conversations with me. Denicia, Shaden, Leah, Dannii, Adisa, and Stephanie, y'all introduced me to a dimension of Trinidad that I so deeply needed and the book was better for it. Angelique Nixon, for opening your home and for introductions, vibes, earthquakes, homemade meals, and cute cats.

Special thanks to: Lisa Allen Agostini for walking the streets of Port of Spain with me and giving me your time, humor, and warmth while in Trinidad. Thank you for bringing me to connect with your group of teen writers in POS. Your insights about spirituality in Trinidad were so important to me and this book. Malaika and Richie Maitland for your time, stories, and introductions for this project. Erin Sharkey for being a Sagittarian goddess, with your support and encouragement for me and this work and just being an amazing friend and co-creator. Valerie, my Aquarian soul sister, for reading this book at various stages and loving me and witching with me in this lifetime. Mackenzie, my Libra bamboo boo! Thank you for your love and belief in my emo ass and dreamo sessions. Sharon Bridgforth, a loving mentor and whisperer of all things sweet, queer, our people, and jazz. Senah for reading the manuscript at so many different points in the process, offering encouragement and being an important nerd on my path. Bao Phi, Diane Wilson, Nneka Onwuzurike, Jessica Lopez Lyman, and my Beyond the Pure Cohort for giving feedback to early drafts of this work.

Thank you to: Zyon Gray and Wendell Jones for your astrological wisdoms and brilliance, as well as sharing your stories and experiences with me. Naimonu Jones, Chani Nicholas, Rob Breszny, Alice Sparkly Cat, Imani Cohen/The Hood Healer, Joanna Martine Woolfolk, Linda Goodman, and countless astrologers on page and online who have inspired me in the radical and ancestral magic of astrology.

Thank you to: Alexis Pauline Gumbs and Sangodare for being so warm and sweet in your support and magnificent in your magic. Tananarive Due for being one of the realest and sweetest in the game and for empowering speculative stories from magical souls. VONA and all of the staff, faculty, and writers who created a beautiful and encouraging space for my writing. My whole Speculative Fiction Crew, Aaron, Ariel, Jacqueline, Joseph, Latanya, Maya, Muriel, Nia, Rosana, Stefani, T.K.!! The limitless emo nerdery of our communal love was such a sacred well for my heart and soul. adrienne maree brown, for all that you have done to encourage and support pleasure in this world, in my spirit, and within this book. Nicole Asong Nfonoyim-Hara, Kylie Osterhaus, and Christina Beck for giving me space to write in beauty in ways that were so important. Turkey Land Cove for the time, space, and pampering while at a critical time of my writing this book. My land-dyke and friend Erika Thorne for being amazing and supportive.

Thank you to all of the teachers and students of the Minnesota Prison Writer's Workshop. I write this book to remember all of the millions of souls who will sleep behind bars under the same stars as me and away from their families and how our society must do better by you. Thank you to Mumia Abu-Jamal, asha bandele, Angela Y. Davis, Assata Shakur, Stanley Tookie Williams, Malcolm X, and countless stories and books I have read from people who have experienced and lived with and through incarceration. You shaped and transformed how I understood the prison and legal system in this country. Your accounts were transformative to me and my life journey. Thank you to Orisanmi Burton, who gave me critical insights and references for the Afua sections.

Thank you to every young person I have worked with from Powderhorn to Harlem. You were in my heart anytime I struggled with the soul of this piece. Thank you.

Thank you to the Jerome Foundation, Art Matters, Minnesota State Arts Board, The Pillsbury House, The Loft, and Intermedia Arts for generous support towards the completion of this manuscript.

Thank you to Alice Walker, Toni Morrison, Octavia Butler, Audre Lorde, Bilal, June Jordan, Dizzy Gillespie, Sade, Sun Ra, Nina Simone, The Roots, Laurie Carlos, Rosa Guy, Grace Jones, Prince, Thelonious Monk, Missy Elliott, Alice Coltrane, Dr. Sebi, Queen Afua, Kiese Laymon, Marlon James, Donte Collins, De La Soul, Janelle Monáe, Tupac Shakur, Lauryn Hill, Billie Holiday, Ntozake Shange, Erik Ehn, Haruki Murakami, Erykah Badu, Yasiin Bey, The Pharcyde, Biggie, Sokari Ekine, Saidiya Hartman, Roxane Gay, Edwidge Danticat, Talib Kweli, Queen Latifah, and countless and limitless other creators for creating art that helped inspire me to become the writer, artist, thinker, and revolutionary that I am and inspired this book in some way.

THE STARS
AND THE BLACKNESS
BETWEEN THEM:

A Playlist

"Consideration" — Rihanna

"My Love Is Your Love" — Whitney Houston

"Everything Is Everything" — Lauryn Hill

"Come Over" — The Internet

"Pop Life" — Prince

"So Afraid" — Janelle Monáe

"Pink + White" — Frank Ocean

"Concrete Jungle"— Bob Marley and the Wailers

"Lucy" — Destra Garcia

"Scenario" — A Tribe Called Quest

"Tempo" — Lizzo (feat. Missy Elliott)

"Butterflies" — Floetry

"Between Us 2" — Shafiq Husayn (feat. Bilal)

"Your House" — Steel Pulse

"Pelas Sombras" — Arthur Verocai

"Superwoman" — Stevie Wonder

"Thieves in the Night" — Black Star

"O.D.O.O." — Fela Kuti

"Beyond the Shore (Badaba)" — MMYYKK

"Alone & Unafraid" — Eliza

"Telephone" — Erykah Badu

"Umi Says" — Mos Def

"Tender Love" — Meshell Ndegeocello